A Question
Of Inheritance

ALSO BY ELIZABETH EDMONDSON

VERY ENGLISH MYSTERIES
A Man of Some Repute

OTHER WORKS
The Frozen Lake
Voyage of Innocence
The Villa in Italy
The Villa on the Riviera
Devil's Sonata
Night & Day
Fencing with Death
Finding Philippe

Elizabeth Edmondson

A Question
Of Inheritance

THOMAS & MERCER

Text copyright © 2015 by Elizabeth Edmondson

Published by Thomas & Mercer, Seattle

www.apub.com

ISBN-13: 9781503947856
ISBN-10: 1503947858

Cover design by Lisa Horton

Printed in the United States of America

For H.E.S. and Wolfie

Chapter One

Scene 1

Lord Selchester swerved to avoid a pheasant. 'There's a lot of wildlife out today. All determined to rush under the wheels of this automobile.'

'Say car, not automobile. You're English now,' Polly said.

Her sister, Babs, was having none of it. 'I'm not. I'm American and always will be.'

'You can't be Lady Barbara if you're American,' Polly said.

'Who'd want to be English? They must be a race of midgets to drive automobiles as small as this.'

'They don't have oil, so gas for cars' – Polly emphasised the word – 'costs more than in the States. Smaller vehicles, less fuel.'

Glancing in the rear-view mirror, Augustine Lambert Fitzwarin, formerly Gus Mason, now eighteenth Earl of Selchester, saw his younger daughter push her spectacles up her nose and settle back into her book.

As he steered the automobile – no, Polly was right, car – through the winding roads of the English countryside, he thought of his ancestors making this same journey across the centuries. On horseback, then in carriages. By train and then by car. Travelling from London or back from the fighting fields of France or the searing heat of Jerusalem. Back home, to Selchester. To Selchester Castle.

Ancestors he knew nothing about; ancestors he didn't even know he had until a few weeks ago.

Forty-two years of being Gus Mason, American citizen: growing up in Virginia, going to college at Notre Dame, falling in love with the ancient world, translating Homer and Vergil, serving in the war – all that made sense. That was familiar; that was who he was. Trips to England over the years, and a year as a visiting fellow of an Oxford college had got him used to English ways, but he'd never dreamed that he'd end up with an English passport, an English title and an English castle.

'It's going to be strange,' he said. 'For all of us.'

'You'll get accustomed to it,' Polly said.

'I just hope you won't resent it as time goes on. Being uprooted like this.'

Polly turned a page with a rustle. 'Deracinated.'

Barbara gave her father a glowering look. 'I didn't need to come. I could have stayed in the States.'

'Not at seventeen, you couldn't,' Polly said.

'I could have gone away to college. Not come to England, to some mouldy castle. She gazed out of the window. 'It's like we're driving through a cloud,' she said. 'England's just one big cloud. Cloud, rain and fog.'

'It's mist,' her father said.

'Fog,' said Polly with certainty. 'Like in Dickens.'

'They grew vines in England in Roman times,' Gus said.

Babs sighed. 'Please don't tell me the Romans got to England.'

'Of course they did,' Polly said. 'It's why it's called Britain, because the Roman name was Britannia.'

Gus had never been able to arouse in Babs the least spark of interest in Romans or Greeks. 'The mist and fog would have suited Vergil. Do you remember how foggy it was when we were in Mantua, where he came from?'

'I remember Mantua perfectly,' Babs said. 'I remember how I got bronchitis and nearly expired and Polly had food poisoning.'

'And Vergil did go off to Rome as soon as he could,' Polly said. 'Where it isn't damp and foggy. Cheer up, Babs, at least Odysseus never came to England. And all the Roman soldiers went home centuries ago.'

'Talking about people going home, who are those types who are living in the Castle right now?' Barbara said. 'I can't believe they're still going to be there. Why haven't they taken themselves off?'

Gus said, 'I thought I told you.'

'You did,' Polly put in. 'But Babs never listens to anything she doesn't want to hear.'

'Freya Wryton is my cousin – our cousin – and she's been living at the Castle for the last seven years, looking after it. Ever since her uncle, the last Lord Selchester, died.'

'Why don't you say "my father"? And he didn't exactly just die, did he? He was murdered.' Polly liked precision.

Yes, he had been avoiding the word. It took some getting used to, having a father for the first time in his life. Even a dead one. 'A man called Hugo Hawksworth has been staying at the Castle as well. With his sister Georgia. She's about your age, Polly. She'll be a friend for you.'

'She will not. I choose my own friends, thank you, and they won't be whiny English girls.'

'Haven't they got homes to go to?' Babs said. 'If we've got to live there, we don't want a lot of strangers in residence.'

'I don't formally take over from the trustees until everything is sorted out on the legal front.'

Letters Patent. Hassles about giving up his American citizenship in order to take up the title. And the money. He'd been left speechless when the lawyers – solicitors, he must remember to call them that – told him the size of his inheritance. And the likely tax bill. 'Freya says they'll move out after Christmas.'

'There's a housekeeper,' Polly said. 'Bet she'll be like Mrs Danvers in *Rebecca*. Sinister, resenting you being the lost heir and wanting to push you over the banisters. Bet she'll annoy the hell out of all of us.'

'Mind your language, please, Polly.'

'The English say anything, look at Shakespeare.'

'You aren't Shakespeare.'

Polly went back to her book.

Scene 2

The motorcyclist, glad to reach his destination after a long, cold ride from London, slowed down as he came to the open gates of Thorn Hall, and stopped in front of the red-and-white pole that barred his way. He took no notice of the large sign on the gatepost that said, 'HM Government, Department of Statistics, Private, Keep Out'. He knew the Victorian pile didn't house a single statistician.

Thorn Hall had been a secret establishment during the war, known locally as the 'Hush-Hush'. The removal of War Office signs and the apparent arrival of another government department didn't fool the town for a moment. They might not be able to give a name to the Service, but they all knew that what went on at the Hall was to do with Intelligence.

Just as they knew that top-secret nuclear research went on at what was known locally as the 'Atomic', a government scientific establishment, a few miles outside Selchester.

Selchester was used to secrets.

The man on duty at Thorn Hall came out of his hut and greeted the courier from London. 'Late today, Phil.' He took his pass and stamped it.

'There's nasty weather blowing up from the east,' Phil said. 'I shan't hang about.' He kicked his motorbike back into life and roared off towards the house, ignoring the speed signs and only slowing down to take the curve round the small lake.

He propped the motorbike up in front of the main entrance to the house, extracted a buff-coloured box from one of the panniers and clumped in through the front door. He went up the marble staircase to the first floor, where Mrs Tempest, secretary to Sir Bernard, head of station, had her office.

'Morning, Mrs T. Not much today. Just a couple of things for Sir Bernard and Mr Hawksworth.'

He took the envelope she handed him in return. 'Ta. Shan't be up again until after Christmas. Have a merry one.'

Then he headed for the canteen to have tea and something to eat before starting back to London.

Scene 3

In a small room two floors and a wing away from Sir Bernard's spacious quarters, Hugo Hawksworth was sitting at his desk. He pushed back his chair and rubbed his calf hard, grimacing as he did so. His leg, scarred by a bullet, cramped when he sat too long. Then he went back to the folder that lay open in front of him.

Rather to his surprise, Hugo was enjoying the job that Sir Bernard had asked him to do. Ever since Burgess and Maclean had vanished in 1951, the Service, certain they were in Moscow, had been nervous that there could be others of their kind still among them. Soviet agents rising up the ranks, taking on more sensitive and senior posts.

'Investigate,' Sir Bernard had instructed him. 'You're good at that. Go backwards and forwards in the records. Look for anomalies. Missions that failed. Agents who behaved out of character. Anything that might indicate the presence of other traitors in the Service.'

'Is there any point going back that far?' Hugo asked. 'Burgess and Maclean were up to mischief now, not back then.'

'The seeds of treachery were sown in the thirties. Mostly in Cambridge, which was a hotbed of communism, as you well know.' Sir Bernard had taken his degree at Edinburgh University. 'There'll be others of their kind still in the Service, rising up the ranks, getting promoted, having access to really sensitive material. We have to be watchful, Hugo. Take nothing and no one for granted. Good war record, impeccable background, successful missions: don't trust any of it. Let suspicion be your watchword.'

So Hugo, amused as always by Sir Bernard in commanding mode, had hidden a grin and gone off to find Mrs Clutton, the Archivist who worked as his assistant.

She, as always, had been one step ahead of him, and several files were already on his desk, flagged with her comments and notes. Her mind was a miracle of minutiae with everything indexed and cross-referenced on cards stored in narrow wooden drawers in her office. Her capacious memory linked people and places and events in a way that Hugo found extraordinary. Mrs Clutton could probably do his job better than he did, he reflected, as he opened the first of the files.

The thirties weren't so long ago, but those pre-war years seemed to belong to another age, when viewed from 1953. Hugo found it fascinating to look through the papers in those buff files. Letters, telegrams, secret messages from embassies. Photographs of places, some of them reduced to ruins during the war. Photographs of people, strangers smiling into the camera or caught unawares. Typed reports on flimsy paper, handwritten notes; all the paraphernalia meticulously preserved and filed by Mrs Clutton.

For three weeks, Hugo had been following the trail of a man whose failure to succeed in his pre-war missions was, he was now fairly certain, due to nothing more than an extraordinary degree of incompetence. Victor Emerson was unquestionably the kind of man who should never have been let loose in the field, and Hugo wondered why he ever had. On paper, he seemed all right. He was fit enough, and had passed all those tests that Hugo once had. He'd played rugby at school and for his college at Cambridge and seemed altogether an admirable recruit at the time that he joined the Service.

But everything he touched went wrong. Buses crashed while he was travelling on them to meetings that then never took place. People he was due to talk to were rushed to hospital with appendicitis or broken limbs. He'd been snowbound on the wrong side of a border in a region where snow was a rarity. He'd lost his passport, had his wallet stolen, been arrested in mistake for another man.

Hugo picked up Emerson's photograph and looked at it thoughtfully. He knew him slightly, and remembered him as being an extremely civilised person. He had a passion for art and knew a great deal about it. There must have been some streak of romanticism in him, a feeling that he was going to be a Bulldog Drummond, which accounted for him ever making his way into the Service in the first place. Hugo flipped through more of his record, although he now knew it almost off by heart.

In fact, there was no point in wondering why the man had ever joined the Service. The reason was obvious: it was the same reason that Hugo and so many others had been recruited. They came from the right background. They had the right connections. And until Burgess and Maclean defected, ripping apart these cosy assumptions, this was considered to be the best kind of screening there was. If you were 'one of us', you would not betray your country.

Yet those two had, and the chances were that others had also, and were doing so at the moment.

But not Victor Emerson. Hugo felt sure of that.

Scene 4

The telephone rang on Hugo's desk and he reached out to lift the receiver. Mrs Tempest's clear, clipped voice came down the line. Sir Bernard wanted to see Hugo. 'At once, please, Mr Hawksworth, if you wouldn't mind.'

Hugo, deep in pre-war Vienna, resented the interruption, but he wasn't going to say so to Mrs Tempest. He closed Emerson's file, got to his feet, bent over to give his calf another rub, pulled on his jacket, straightened his tie, grabbed his stick and limped off down the corridor for the five-minute walk to the other wing.

Mrs Tempest, installed at her desk in the room next to Sir Bernard's, looked up and nodded at him through her open door. He knocked once on the oak door at the end of the corridor. Sir Bernard called out his usual, 'Come', and Hugo went in.

Sir Bernard was smoking a pipe. This told Hugo that he'd been thinking. Hugo sometimes wondered if Sir Bernard liked to think of himself as a Sherlock Holmes, mulling with intellectual vigour over a one-pipe problem. He'd never look the part, though; there was nothing hawk-nosed or eagle-eyed about Sir Bernard.

Sir Bernard looked at him over the top of his glasses and came straight to the point. 'Something has come up that I need you to look into. A request from London, arrived this morning.'

'Is it urgent?' Requests from London were, in Hugo's opinion, nearly always bureaucratic, trivial and time wasting.

Something of what he was thinking must have shown in his face, because Sir Bernard gave him a sharp look and said, 'You're too inclined to go your own way, Hawksworth. I like to see initiative in my team, but when word comes down to look at something in particular, I expect you to focus on it. I don't know what else you have on your desk right now, but I want you to give this priority.'

'Of course. What is it?'

Sir Bernard tapped the file in front of him with an authoritative finger. 'It's outside the area you've been working on, as it relates to the post-war period.' Sir Bernard sucked at his pipe. He wasn't an efficient smoker and he inhaled a lungful of smoke that sent him into a paroxysm of coughing.

Hugo waited for him to recover. When Sir Bernard had got back his breath and savoir faire, and the red colour was fading from his face, he said, 'Did you ever come across a man called Zherdev in Berlin? Anywhere? Aleksandr Zherdev?' He pulled a grainy photo from the file and flicked it over to Hugo.

Sir Bernard went on. 'He's the Cultural Attaché at the Russian Embassy in London. A recent appointment. He's been thoroughly vetted by our people there and by Special Branch. They put a tail on him, investigated his past history, all that kind of thing. He's been pronounced clean, but they want a final word from us in case there's any indication he was involved in intelligence back in the thirties.'

'What exactly do you want me to do?'

'Do a trawl through the records. It shouldn't take long. They've done a thorough job on him in London, you can be sure of that. This is just to dot the i's and cross the t's. So they can sign off on him.'

That meant, Hugo knew, that Mr Zherdev would be demoted from the hot list and only checked on in a routine and superficial way once or twice a year.

'They're being fussy, if you ask me. This man was some kind of an actor before the war. He fought in the Red Army like any other patriotic Russian and then joined their foreign service. Not likely that the MGB would want him, is it?

Hugo looked down at the photo Sir Bernard had slid across the desk. He'd never heard of Aleksandr Zherdev, but he recognised the face in the photo. The last time he'd seen him had been in Berlin in 1946 and he'd known him as Gregor Orlov. A major in the MGB, the Soviet Ministry of State Security. One of Hugo's contacts, and one who, as far as Hugo knew, hadn't had dealings with any other of the Western intelligence officers who were in Berlin with the Army of Occupation.

Hugo said, 'I'll get on to it first thing in the morning.'

Sir Bernard said, 'No, I want you to start right away. Brief Mrs Clutton and she can get straight on to it. Tell her you want every scrap of information relating to Zherdev.'

Hugo was annoyed. 'I'd hoped to get away early today. The new Earl will be arriving at the Castle, and I feel I should be there.'

Sir Bernard looked up at that. 'Lord Selchester? He's coming today, is he? You've met him, of course. And that'll mean you and that sister of yours will have to move out of the Castle, I suppose.'

Sir Bernard had lodged Hugo and Georgia at the Castle in September, when Hugo came to Selchester to take up his job at Thorn Hall. Accommodation was scarce in the town, and as a trustee to the missing Lord Selchester's estate, Sir Bernard had no qualms about billeting the Hawksworths there.

'We'll move out after Christmas. I don't suppose you've heard of anything in the accommodation line?' Hugo said.

'People in the town know that if anything becomes available, we always have people working at the Hall who need a place to live. You'll find something; don't worry about it. In one of the outlying villages, if not in Selchester.'

And wouldn't that be fun. Hugo, to whom England had always meant London, had got used to living in Selchester. At least

Selchester was a town. But digs in some rural hamlet in the depths of the countryside? No. That was a step too far, and Georgia would hate it.

Sir Bernard tapped his blotter with the base of his pen. 'I think I might come along and welcome Lord Selchester myself. Tell you what, you go along and get started on that stuff and we'll drive together to the Castle.'

Scene 5

By three o'clock in the afternoon, it was getting dark. A mist was rising from the river, and on this day of the winter solstice, the shortest day of the year, sunset was early.

Freya Wryton and Dinah Lindsey were sitting at the desk in Dinah's little bookshop in Selchester, sorting out paperwork.

'You've come back looking the picture of health, while the rest of us are beginning to take on our normal English winter, living-under-a-stone appearance,' Freya said, as the pool of light from the desk lamp illuminated Dinah's face. 'In your shoes, I'd have stayed in Egypt longer. The warm climate obviously suited you.'

'That's all very well, but I have a business to run,' Dinah said. She waved an arm at the shelves that lined the walls from floor to ceiling. The shop was tranquil and comforting, the bright colours of the book jackets contrasting with the small black panes of the bay window. 'I'm so grateful to you for helping out here while I was away.'

Freya said, 'I enjoyed it.' Which was true, although she'd be glad to get back to her writing. She opened another box file and started leafing through a stack of invoices. 'These are all in order. Everything's up to date, and the ones that need dealing with are clipped together. I've added comments if there are any queries.

Some of the bills need to be paid, but there's nothing urgent.' She looked at the clock that was attached to one of the beams. 'I can't stay much longer. I need to be back at the Castle before they arrive.'

Dinah didn't need to ask who 'they' were. 'How strange to discover that you've a cousin you knew nothing about. Although not half as nerve-wracking for you as for Sonia to discover she has a half-brother she didn't know existed.'

Freya said, 'Sonia's not taking the news awfully well. Of course, there's nothing she can do about it. Her half-brother inherits, and that's that.'

Dinah thrust the last of the bills onto a spike and sat back. 'I'll go through the rest of these later. Tell me about the new Earl. When I left, the mystery of Selchester's murder hadn't been cleared up. The Earldom was due to lapse, Sonia was going to sell the Castle to a hotel group and all our lives were going to be turned upside down. I come back from six weeks among the pyramids and, lo and behold, a new Lord Selchester has popped up out of nowhere. How did it all come about?'

Freya said, 'Some brilliant detective work by Hugo and me. And a lot of help from Hugo's Uncle Leo. You never met him; you were in London when he arrived and then you went off to Egypt. You'll get to know him soon enough, because he's coming here for Christmas.'

'It must be a bit of an upset for you at the Castle, having the new Earl come for Christmas. And I gather it's not just him. Don't look at me like that, I didn't rush out the moment I got back to catch up on the gossip. As it happens, I'd hardly unlocked the door before Jamie came running over from the Daffodil Tearooms. Loud kisses, tut-tuts about my tan, "Nothing worse than the sun for the complexion, I'll recommend a super cream," and then to the heart of the matter.'

This didn't surprise Freya; Jamie thrived on gossip. 'He must be delighted to have someone who doesn't know all about it. Although I dare say Jamie's version won't be accurate. He loves to embroider.'

'No invalid wife, no five daughters?'

Freya laughed. 'Jamie is outrageous. The new Lord Selchester is a widower. He has two daughters. One nearly grown-up, I think she's seventeen, and a younger one who's thirteen.'

'It isn't premature for them to move in? There's no question about it? Has his claim to the title been proved? After all, it isn't just the Earldom, there's the land and money and the Castle.'

Freya said, 'There's no question of the inheritance; it's now just a matter now of getting all the formalities dealt with. There's the complication of his being an American. He can't swear an oath of allegiance to the Crown if he's an American citizen, and he can't take a seat in the Lords without doing that. The lawyers are on the job and it will get sorted out soon. He's rather bemused by it all, but really behaving very well.'

'So now you'll have to move out of the Castle. It'll be a wrench for you to leave your tower. Any plans?'

Freya said, 'I'm trying not think about it until Christmas is over. Gus has kindly said I can stay on for as long as I like, but it won't do. And then there are Hugo and Georgia as well. We were rather hoping that Nightingale Cottage might come free. It would suit them perfectly, but . . .'

Dinah said, 'That's still going on, is it? But what about you? You could do with a cottage.'

'I'll find somewhere. If the worst comes to the worst, I expect that Eileen will give me a room. She won't be doing B&B much before Easter.'

'Come here. I've got a spare room. We can clear all the clutter and the books out, and you can install yourself with your typewriter. It isn't the Castle, and it isn't the Tower, but I promise I won't expect you to work in the shop. You can get on with your own writing. I assume you're still going to finish the family history?'

Freya was touched. 'That's decent of you, Dinah. I might have to take you up on it. But I need to find a place of my own. Don't forget, there's Magnus as well. Cats make you sneeze.'

The door opened and a delivery man came in with a box. 'Two more in the van,' he said breezily, as he dumped the box at Dinah's feet. He was back in a few moments, stacked the other boxes and waited for Dinah to sign the docket.

Even as the delivery man was going out of the door, Dinah was opening the top box. 'Thank goodness, the new Rosina Wyndhams. Just in time for Christmas – they'll sell like hot cakes.'

She removed several copies of the book and began to stack them on a display table. She held one up to admire the cover, which depicted a Restoration beauty in a tight-waisted, low-cut crimson gown. '*Spoils of War*. Good title. I shall tuck one away for myself; the perfect Christmas read.'

'You don't think the cover's a bit vulgar?' Freya said.

'No. And her stories may be racy, like the cover, but never vulgar.'

Which was praise as good as any glowing review, in Freya's opinion.

'I do wonder who she is. It's a pseudonym, of course. I suspect they're written by a vicar, with a remote parish in Lincolnshire.'

'A vicar? Why?'

'Because of the secrecy. It's not natural for a bestselling author to remain so reticent; there must be a reason for it.'

Freya had a reason. Apart from an innate sense of privacy, she knew that her diplomat father, a conventional man of whom she was very fond, would be horrified to find out how she supported herself. As would the rest of her family. And as for the rewards of fame, she wanted none of them.

She looked at the clock again. 'Lord, I must rush. Back to the family gathering. It's not going to be the easiest of times. Mrs Partridge is in a state over them coming, so we've great preparations going on in the kitchen, and Georgia's in a sulk. She likes being at the Castle and I think she'd started to feel settled and secure there. But she and Hugo would have to move in any case, if Sonia had inherited and sold the Castle.' She pulled on her gloves and crammed a felt hat on her head. 'I'll try and get down tomorrow and tell you about it.'

Scene 6

Hugo thought about Orlov, aka Zherdev, as he went back to his office. Should he have come out with it to Sir Bernard? No. It was a poor photo, whose subject, if he was right, was a professional, accustomed to screen his face from any watching cameras. He might be mistaken; Zherdev could be someone else and clean as a whistle.

Or he might not.

Hugo's mind went back to Berlin 1945. A ruined city, on the edge of chaos. The German civilian population was living in a state of borderline starvation with all kinds of occupying troops in Berlin who were involved in everything from organising the gangs of women clearing the rubble, to the de-Nazification of key scientists, to black market smuggling. There were rich pickings to be had in Berlin in those days.

Food, drugs – the medicinal kind; tobacco, whisky.

And art, which was how he'd met Orlov.

The Russian had arranged a meeting through an intermediary and Hugo, wary but curious, had duly turned up at the bar that Orlov had specified.

15

Orlov came swiftly to the point in excellent English. He had information to impart and had decided that Hugo was the best man to deal with it.

'Let us understand one another. We do the same job, but we are essentially enemies. Our ideals are opposed. You believe in democracy; I know that the future lies with communism. However, there are some areas where we share values. I hate the Nazis, with a hatred as vast and deep as is my love for Mother Russia. I fought them in the war, and I am still fighting them now.'

'The war is over.'

'Please do not be flippant. I know that your detestation of Nazism and all it stands for is as strong as mine. That is why I've made contact with you. I want to tell you about some bronzes.'

'Bronzes?' What had bronzes – what kind of bronzes? – to do with him? Or with an MGB major, although Hugo was beginning to wonder if the man really was what he appeared to be.

'Be patient. I am not here to waste your time. I'm talking about a collection of Italian bronzes. Unique works of art, which are exquisite and worth a fortune.'

As they both knew, when the Russian army took Berlin, they removed anything that wasn't nailed down and sent it back to the Soviet Union. This included everything from everyday objects, which admittedly were hard to find in the Soviet Union, to art treasures. There were stories of vaults in Russia filled with famous paintings, of mines stuffed with antiquities, of packing cases of priceless porcelain stored in the cellars of drab official buildings.

None of this was within Hugo's remit. He waited for Orlov to explain.

'For reasons I shall not go into, I had to acquire these bronzes. No, I am not dealing in the black market. I was obeying orders.'

Orders from some more senior officer in the MGB who collected bronzes? Hugo doubted it. Such a request would give Orlov too much power over his boss.

'These bronzes had not been looted by the Nazis. There was nothing suspect about how they came to be in Germany. They'd long been in the possession of an aristocratic family, one of the *von und zu* lot. The family came through the war comparatively unscathed, which duly brought the eye of authority on them: had they been Nazis?'

'Even so, you bought these bronzes from them?'

'No, because they no longer owned them.'

There was nothing unusual in that. Families brought to poverty would have sold their grandmothers if there'd been a market for them.

'So who did?'

'A certain British Army officer.'

Distasteful, but not criminal. A rich Army officer could do well if he had a collector's habit.

'After we had concluded our deal, I did some asking around and that's when I put two and two together. This officer was one of the team involved with de-Nazification.'

Hugo knew all about that. Those people were responsible for issuing the certificates that declared an individual to be free of connections to the Nazi Party, and so enable the person to get a job. Fighting in the German Army was acceptable; being connected with the Nazi Party, SS or Gestapo wasn't.

Orlov had lowered his voice to a low rumble. 'I won't go into details about how I came by the information, but I discovered that this officer was issuing the certificates of clearance in return for things like the bronzes. He mostly dealt in works of art, paintings, and so on. Which he would then get back to England and sell. He didn't want them for himself, which is why he was happy to sell the bronzes to me, no questions asked.'

A shiver ran down Hugo's spine. This was treachery. Letting war criminals go free was unforgivable in any circumstances, and for a British officer to be involved . . .

'Can you give me proof?'

'I can give you nothing.'

'A name, then.'

Orlov shook his head. 'No. That you have to find out for yourself.' He laughed, a deep bass laugh. 'Don't look so angry. We deal with quid pro quos, do we not? There is nothing you can give me in exchange. I've already made you a gift of this much information. It won't be difficult for you to find out who the man is. And then he will be dealt with and a stop put to the despicable scheme he is running.'

Scene 7

Freya cycled slowly back up to the Castle. The battery in her lamp was running out and the light was no more than a dim glow in the shifting mist. She hoped she wouldn't meet any vehicles coming the other way. But once she turned through the gates and was going up the drive, she came out of the mist and into the clear, frosty air of a December evening. The stars sparkled in the sky, even though the moon, nearly full, hung bright on the horizon.

She peddled into the stable yard, wheeled her bicycle under cover and went across to say hello to her horse, an ugly piebald called Last Hurrah. She fished a sugar lump out of her pocket and he took it from her palm. She hooked her arm over his neck and laid her face against him for a moment. 'I'll take you out tomorrow, I promise.'

That was another problem, what was she going to do with Last Hurrah? She didn't think the new Earl was planning to keep horses, and he wouldn't want Last Hurrah there. She'd have to keep him in livery at the stables in town. He'd hate that. Horses were supposed to be herd creatures, but Last Hurrah had never heard that rule. He tolerated Magnus, her cat, and that was about his limit.

Freya went across the courtyard. Light from the kitchen was spilling out on to the cobbles. She pushed open the door and walked along the passage and into the kitchen.

It was a haven of light and warmth. Georgia Hawksworth was sitting at the table in her gymslip, cutting strips of coloured paper to make paper chains. She looked up as Freya came in. 'I'm too old for this kind of thing really, but Mrs Partridge said we ought to make an effort to decorate the house. She says we should have a Christmas tree.'

Freya sat down at the table and reached out for the scissors. She said, 'I'll cut and you paste. Of course we're going to have a Christmas tree, Ben's seeing to it. It will go in the Great Hall. Somewhere there are boxes of candles for the tree. Do you know where they are, Mrs P?'

Mrs Partridge took a tray of scones out of the oven in the big range and tapped them with a knuckle. 'Nasty dangerous things those candles. They drip wax and like as not will set fire to the tree. They could burn the whole place down and then what will his new lordship do?'

Georgia said, 'Take himself off somewhere else, I hope.'

'Do try to be polite to him, Georgia,' Freya said. 'He's a nice man and it's hard for him to come into all this.'

Georgia gave her a scornful look. 'If I'd just inherited a title and buckets of money and a castle full of pictures and treasures and masses of land and all the rest of it, I wouldn't deserve sympathy from anyone. I hope he has some moral sense and feels bad about casting us out into the snow.'

Freya said, 'There isn't any snow. And you're staying here until Christmas is over, and by then we'll have found somewhere for you and Hugo to go.' She paused and then went on, 'Where is Hugo? He said he'd be back early.'

Georgia pressed the ends of a recalcitrant link together and said, 'He telephoned. Something came up but he promised he'd be here in time. Sir Bernard's bringing him back. I suppose he wants to suck up to the new Earl.'

Mrs Partridge said, 'That's enough of that, Georgia. Sir Bernard will be here as a trustee. That's quite right and proper. And it'll be tea in the library, so you finish up with those chains and you can help me do the trays.'

Georgia said, 'Oh, so the new Lord Selchester is so toffee-nosed he can't have tea in the kitchen? And he's bringing two horrible daughters with him. I dare say they have awful manners. Americans do.'

Freya said, 'They'll have lovely manners, much better than yours and they aren't horrible at all.' She silently rebuked herself because she hadn't been impressed at all with the eldest daughter. 'Polly's about your age. She'll be a friend for you.' She could have bitten her tongue the moment she'd said her words. Georgia cast her a venomous look. She winced. 'Okay, okay; I didn't say that.'

Georgia said, 'Fortunately, being an Earl's daughter, being Lady Whatever she is, she'll get sent off to some posh boarding school so at least we won't have her hanging round the town.'

'I'm not sure what Lord Selchester's plans for her are.'

Mrs Partridge pursed her lips. 'It's strange to hear you talk about him as Lord Selchester.'

Georgia said firmly, 'I shall always think that the only true Lord Selchester is the bundle of bones that was dug up in the Old Chapel.

This one I shall think of as a kind of imposter.' Her face brightened. 'Perhaps he'll get murdered, too. That would be fun.'

'None of that nonsense,' Mrs Partridge said. 'He's Lord Selchester and there's an end of it.'

Georgia screwed the lid on the paste pot and stood up. She spoke in mincing BBC tones. 'Lord Selchester and his daughters Lady Barbara and Lady Pauline.' Then she reverted to her usual voice. 'Ugh. Well, perhaps the ghosts will make them think twice about living here. I'll take their young ladyships to the spot where the last Earl met his grisly fate and tell them he haunts the Castle.'

Scene 8

Hugo climbed awkwardly out of Sir Bernard's Rover. He paused, listening, just catching the sound of a distant car. That was probably Lord Selchester. Sir Bernard had parked in front of the house and Hugo, finding the front door unlocked, heaved it open and stood back for Sir Bernard to go in. To the kitchen? No, Freya would have asked Mrs Partridge to serve tea in the library.

He was right. Georgia was sitting on a pouffe by the fire, giving the logs angry stabs with a poker. Her long legs were tucked up underneath her, and she had a discontented look on her face, which boded ill for her reception of the new owner of the Castle. One glance at her face warned Hugo not to say anything. If she was rude, so be it. She might not be; if he said anything, she was sure to react badly. Mrs Partridge was setting out cups on a table standing between two of the deep windows.

'Best china, Mrs P?' Hugo said.

'That's right. I'm just going now to pop the kettle on and I'll bring in the tea. Freya said she heard a car, but I suppose that was you. Good evening, Sir Bernard.'

21

Hugo said, 'There was another car coming up to the Castle. I think it's probably Selchester and his family.'

At that very moment the bell at the main door pealed. They all looked at one another. Freya said, 'Don't worry, Mrs P. I'd better go.'

Without waiting for any of the others to follow her, she went out. Georgia said, 'I'm not going to jump up and go to greet them.'

Hugo went over and picked up another log to throw on the fire. 'Just as well. Did you know you've got a whacking hole in your stocking? You look thoroughly disreputable; you'll have to mend that for school tomorrow.'

Georgia said, 'I won't. We broke up today, don't you remember? I don't have to wear these horrible old school stockings until I go back to school so it doesn't matter them having a hole.'

Her eyes were defiant but her face was anxious. He grinned at her. 'Cheer up, old thing, I'm sure they won't be too bad.'

Georgia renewed her efforts with poker, 'I just wish they'd be not too bad somewhere else.'

Scene 9

Babs and Polly got out of the car, and Gus came to stand beside them as they stared, as if spellbound, at the dark bulk of the Castle looming over them, the battlements shadowy in the moonlight.

The castle seemed to grow out of the hillside: immense and threatening, wrapped in the silence of the countryside.

An owl hooted, startling them as it flew by on white wings.

'I never thought it would be anything like this,' Polly said.

Nor had Gus. 'We'll get used to it.'

'They say prisoners get used to prison,' Babs said. She shivered. 'Let's hope they have some heating.'

'It'll be log fires and draughts,' Polly said.

'It'll be fine,' Gus assured them. 'We'll soon feel quite at home.'

Babs looked at him with scorn. 'Whatever this place is, it isn't home.'

Scene 10

Voices, distant and then growing nearer, and the door opened. Freya ushered in the new Lord Selchester and his two daughters. There was a moment's silence as the people in the room surveyed the newcomers and the newcomers looked at them, at the room, and then, with a kind of alarm, at one another.

Georgia's eyes were fixed on Polly. She had round spectacles, thick dark hair tied in plaits and an expression almost as truculent as Georgia's own. Polly's sister was eyeing the men appraisingly. Her eyes lingered for a moment on Hugo and then she relaxed back into a look of deliberate boredom. Hugo, taking in her black clothes and black-rimmed eyes, remembered that she'd been spending some time in Paris. It looked like rather than spending her time visiting the galleries and acquiring chic she had fallen in with a bunch of existentialists.

Freya introduced them. 'Gus, this is Sir Bernard. He was one of my uncle's trustees. You know Hugo Hawksworth, and this is his sister, Georgia.'

The men shook hands and Georgia glowered at the Fitzwarin family.

'These are my daughters,' Lord Selchester said. 'Barbara and Pauline. Babs and Polly.'

Polly drew slightly apart from the others and stared at Georgia.

Exactly like a pair of cats eyeing one another, looking as though at any moment they'd fly at each other in a flurry of claws and yowls. Hugo shut his eyes for a moment, wishing that his sister had an easier temperament.

As if on cue, a large tabby cat stalked in through the open door. He looked around the room with an air of ownership and strolled over to the fireplace. He went up to Georgia, and the angry look left her face as she stretched out a hand to rub the fur between his ears.

Polly said, 'Hey, that's one big cat.' She went over to the fireplace, dropped on to her knees and began to stroke the cat along its back.

Georgia said, 'Magnus doesn't like strangers.'

Polly said, 'I like cats. And they usually like me.'

Georgia said, 'Cats usually go to people who hate them or who get asthma from them.'

Mrs Partridge came in with a tray. Not only the best china, but a silver teapot and jug and sugar basin instead of the Brown Betty that did service in the kitchen.

Freya said, 'This is Mrs Partridge, who runs the place and looks after us all.'

'Good evening, your lordship. And this must be Lady Barbara and Lady Pauline. Welcome to the Castle.'

Hugo could see Barbara and Polly thinking, She won't run us.

That wouldn't be a problem. Mrs Partridge had no intention of staying on at the Castle. 'Not with Miss Freya going. I only came to help out when his late lordship went missing and that was seven years ago, so enough is enough.'

'You'll miss the Castle after all this time.'

No. Mrs Partridge had a sensible outlook on life. 'Nothing goes on forever. I'm glad in a way that there's going to be a new lordship, but he'll prefer to make his own arrangements and I dare say will be wanting more staff.'

Tea was a slightly awkward affair, and when it had finished Sir Bernard took himself off, much to Hugo's relief. 'Good to meet you, Selchester, and we'll be seeing more of each other. It's a small place.

24

Hugo, I'm off first thing in the morning. I'll see you in the New Year. You aren't Duty Officer, are you?'

'No, Roger Bailey drew the short straw.'

'Good. Don't worry, Freya, I'll show myself out, I know the way. A happy Christmas to you all.'

As the door closed behind him, Barbara said, to no one in particular, 'I suppose he's your typical English gent. All stiff upper lip and that kind of thing.'

She lapsed back into her dark silence, no doubt pondering over the meaning of meaning.

Hugo and Freya exchanged a quick look and then Freya said brightly, 'Let me take you up to your rooms. Of course, it's up to you to decide where you want to be, but Mrs Partridge and I made up the beds for you somewhere where we think you'll be most comfortable.' She hesitated and went on, 'As it's dark now, perhaps you'd rather leave doing a tour of the Castle until the morning. It's quite badly lit in a lot of the passages, and rather cold.'

They trooped out of the room. Hugo thought that Georgia was going to stay put, but at the last moment she clambered up and followed them out. Polly looked her up and down. 'You're awfully tall. How old are you?'

'Thirteen.'

'So am I,' Polly said.

They came to the Great Hall, and Freya flicked the lights on. Lord Selchester looked stunned. Hugo was used to the antlered stags' heads, the shields on the wall and two suits of armour standing on guard on either side of the huge stone fireplace, with the Fitzwarin crest carved above it, but he could remember his astonishment when he'd first seen it.

'Oh, my,' Polly said. 'It's like something out of a horror movie.'

Hugo knew how she felt. He wouldn't be surprised to see Count Dracula perched on one of the arched beams high above their heads.

Barbara brought them down to earth. 'Cold, damp and unwelcoming. Primitive I call it, with those animal heads on the wall.'

Freya took them through to Grace Hall, less threatening but still stone-walled and chilly.

'It's difficult to see in this light, but that portrait there is of your father, Gus.'

He peered up at it. 'I guess I can see a resemblance.'

'Why do you have a telephone in here?' Barbara said.

'It's the nearest convenient place to where the telephone line comes into the house,' Freya said.

Barbara stared at her, aghast. 'You mean if you want to use the phone you've got to sit in this draughty place where everybody can hear your conversation? And you'd die of cold meanwhile.'

Freya said, sounding apologetic, 'Phone calls are expensive in England, so people mostly don't linger in here, just three minutes and that's it.'

'Three minutes?'

Polly said, 'In America, Barbara stays on the phone for hours.'

Her father said, 'In England, she won't.'

Scene 11

They ate that evening in the dining room. It was a strangely formal affair, with everybody on their best behaviour. Barbara said little and mostly gazed down into her plate. Georgia and Polly, whom Freya had taken care to seat apart, occasionally cast covert glances at one another.

Freya felt disoriented. It was so extraordinary that she should be sitting here with this stranger who was her cousin at the head of the table. If she closed her eyes, it could almost have been her uncle there. Gus's voice was so like his father's. Mind you, the late Lord

Selchester would not have been talking about epic poetry, Roman farming or the Rubicon.

Freya's mind strayed back to 1947, to that fateful evening which was the last time she or anyone else had seen her uncle alive.

Bad weather had prevented many of the invited guests from being at the Castle, and that had put Selchester into a bad temper. Her cousin Sonia, Selchester's daughter, had been upstairs, struck down with a ferocious migraine, which was why Freya had been summoned by her uncle to act as hostess. Of course, it wasn't just the missing guests that had annoyed Lord Selchester. He'd been angry at his son's engagement, and he and Tom had such a furious argument that Tom had stormed out halfway through dinner. Freya had left with him.

As she looked at the soft light of the candles reflected in the silver epergne that Mrs Partridge had insisted on placing in the centre of the table, tears pricked Freya's eyes. Such sad memories. She and Tom had only just got away before the blizzard drew in and the Castle was cut off for nearly ten days. It had been assumed that Lord Selchester had, for some unknown reason, gone out into the snow and had been caught in the ferocious weather. He had been missing for almost seven years before his body was discovered under the flagstones in the Old Chapel, and it turned out that he had never in fact left his ancestral castle. He had been murdered that very night.

Freya found herself give a slight shiver and Hugo looked at her enquiringly.

'A ghost walked over my grave,' she said, forcing her voice into lightness.

In a quiet voice, Hugo said, 'You're thinking of your uncle. And Tom.'

Freya was no longer surprised by Hugo's perceptiveness, by his almost uncanny ability to read her mind and her moods. And so she merely nodded and asked Gus what kind of a crossing they'd had from New York.

He gave her a searching look, said they'd had a day of rough seas but nothing too bad, and then Barbara, breaking the uneasy politeness of the dinner so far, gestured towards a portrait that hung at the far end of the dining room.

Freya always wondered why her uncle kept that picture here, rather than with the other portraits in the Long Gallery. The other paintings that adorned the walls of the dining room were mostly naval battles, with surging seas and improbable-looking ships firing little cotton wool balls at one another.

Freya said, 'That's Hermione, the last Lord Selchester's wife.'

'So she'd be kind of our step-grandmother?' Barbara said. 'She looks beautiful in that picture. Was she beautiful?'

Freya said, 'Is beautiful. She's still very much alive. She lives in Canada. Yes, Aunt Hermione was very lovely.'

Gus said, 'Is that by Sargent?'

'Yes. I always liked it, and it's a good portrait of her, but my uncle never cared for it much. There's a matching one of him, in Grace Hall.'

'She went away from England before the war,' Polly said. 'They were separated and never lived together after that. They couldn't get divorced, of course, because they were Catholic. Is she going to marry someone else now? It said in the newspapers that she is. Somebody called Walter Berkshire. He's her constant companion. I read about her when I went to the library and looked up about the murder.'

Gus said, 'Really, Polly, you can't believe what you read in the newspapers.'

'Not all of it, no. But there's usually some truth in the stories.'

Hugo murmured in Freya's ear, 'We're going to have trouble with this one.'

Freya whispered back, 'Not our problem. Remember, it's exeunt severally for us as soon as Christmas is over.' And then, to Polly, 'So you've been doing some research into the Fitzwarin family.'

'I like to have the facts,' Polly said with some severity, and then applied herself to the apricot tart Mrs Partridge had set in front of her. After a mouthful, she said, 'I suppose there have been a lot of murders in this castle.'

Not quite so insouciant as she wanted to seem. Sensing Polly wanted reassurance, Freya said, 'Perhaps, long ago. Not these days.'

'I hope not. I don't want anyone to murder Pops. But they caught the murderer, didn't they? So even if he didn't like Earls, he won't come back to do it again.'

Hugo broke the awkward silence by asking Gus if he played billiards.

'We don't play it in the States, I'm more used to pool. But I played billiards a few times while I was in Oxford. I suppose there is a billiard room here? I'd be happy to give you a game.'

Freya felt grateful to Hugo. It would make things easier over Christmas, if Hugo and Gus got on well together. It would be an odd Christmas this year. Not like in the days before the war. Then the Castle had been filled with Fitzwarins and friends, all generations from babies to great-grandmothers. Music and games and wonderful food. It was one of the few times in the year when she remembered her uncle unbending a little. He wasn't one to dress up as Father Christmas, he wouldn't go as far as that, but he liked to be generous at Christmas, to his family and to his tenants. One Christmas, he'd given Freya her first pony. She must remember the good things about him, his kindness to her. The fact that he had turned out to have a private life quite different from his public persona couldn't take that away.

'Penny for them,' Hugo whispered in her ear. 'You still have a melancholy look.'

Freya flashed him a smile. 'Just remembering Christmases here before the war.'

Gus overheard the words, and he gave Freya a sympathetic look. 'This was really your childhood home, so the lawyers told me.

With your father being abroad so much with his diplomatic work and you spending your holidays here . . . These last years must have been a very difficult time for you.'

Freya said, 'It all seems a long time ago. It was a different world then. The war changed everything for us here in England.'

Barbara said, 'What did you do in the war, Cousin Freya?'

What Freya did in the war was something that she never told about to anyone, but she said glibly and without thinking as she always did, 'Oh, office work, typing, that kind of thing.'

Barbara's mouth curled in contempt. 'No uniform, no real war work?'

Georgia sprang to her defence. 'Lots of people did all kinds of important things in the war and they didn't wear uniform. My mother did lots and she was never in any of the armed forces. She drove an ambulance.'

Any moment now, somebody was going to ask Georgia where her mother was, and Freya decided to prevent this happening by saying decisively that they would take coffee in the library. 'Georgia, why don't you give Mrs Partridge a hand clearing the table and then you can help with the coffee.'

Georgia rose slowly to her feet, not looking as though she was very keen on the idea. Rather to Freya's surprise, Polly said, 'I'll help, too.'

'That's right, Polly, you give a hand with the washing up as well,' Gus said. 'That was a most delicious meal, Mrs Partridge. You are some cook.'

Mrs Partridge nodded her head in recognition of what was her due, and then said, 'We'll have to see about getting ration books for all of you.'

Barbara, who was going out of the door, stopped and looked round, her mouth in an O of surprise. 'Rationing! You can't be serious. What's rationed?'

Georgia was very happy to tell her. 'Meat and bacon and butter and sugar.'

Freya said, 'It isn't as bad as Georgia makes it sound, because everything is gradually coming off rationing. And living in the country with so much provided on the estate you won't go short of anything here. But Mrs Partridge is right, you'll all need ration books.'

Polly said, 'I read about rationing and austerity. But you do have lights. I thought everybody in England sat about in the dark, because there isn't enough coal or enough power to keep the electricity on.'

Hugo said, sounding amused, 'It's been difficult, but things are better now.'

Gus said genially, 'I, too, am pleased to see electricity in the Castle. I had wondered whether we would have to cope with candles, oil lamps and flares on the wall.'

Freya said, 'My uncle was always very up to date. And when the Castle was requisitioned during the war, the Army did a lot of work on the plumbing and wiring and so on. Although there are still parts where it needs modernising.'

Polly said, 'Pops is keen on electricity. He loves messing about with wires and things.'

Gus stood by to let Freya leave the room in front of him. 'I kind of got interested in it because of going on some archaeological expeditions. I'm no archaeologist myself, the written word is my thing, but I like to keep up with what's going on in the field. Some of these sites you need to know how to use a generator and rig up lighting.'

'There are dungeons here you could excavate,' Georgia said. 'Bet you'd find all sorts of interesting things.' She gave Polly a sideways look. 'Skeletons, I shouldn't be surprised.'

Chapter Two

Scene 1

Lady Sonia was spending the midnight hours at the Blue Venetian, a newly fashionable London nightclub. Rupert Dauntsey, coming on after a dinner party, had stopped off in the hope of finding her. She waved at him to come over and join her table.

'All by yourself, Sonia? That doesn't seem like you.'

She gestured towards the tiny dance floor, where couples, picked out in pools of blue from the spotlights, were dancing. 'I'm with the Hunsonbys, but they're on the floor. Sit down, it's an age since I've seen you.'

Rupert said, 'No, let's dance.' He liked dancing with Sonia, who was light on her feet. He pulled her chair back for her, and they went on to the floor, moving into a swift quickstep.

Sonia was wearing one of her Paris frocks and was looking at her best. Hers was a Plantagenet beauty, marred only by a frequent look of discontent, which made her perfect Elizabeth Arden mouth droop at the corners.

'Are you in London for Christmas?' he asked, as he swung her expertly round.

'I planned to be, but now I've decided to go down to Selchester.'

'What, as a guest of the new Earl? That, Sonia, my love, will make you look ridiculous. Half of London knows how you hate him, since you've said so at every opportunity.'

Sonia waved an airy hand. 'Oh, that. I don't exactly hate him. He isn't really the kind of man you can hate. What I hate is his being the Earl and inheriting everything instead of me. Am I supposed to be delighted at that? I don't think so.'

'Has he invited you?'

Sonia considered that for a moment. 'Not exactly. He didn't say, "Sonia, come and share a family Christmas at the Castle." It's more that he issued one of those vague invitations, the way that people do. You know. He said that the Castle had been my home and I must feel myself free to come at any time. Any time is going to be this Christmas, that's all.'

The music ended, and they drifted back to the table. The Hunsonbys stayed on the floor for another dance, and Rupert lit a cigarette for Sonia. She sat back in her chair, a long elegant cigarette holder poised between two fingers, eyes half closed.

He laughed. 'You look decadent.'

'Oh good. I need to feel decadent before I can face the horrors of a family Christmas. I mean, only think of the company. Gus and his daughters. Freya and that man Hugo Hawksworth probably, although God knows why. You'd have thought he and his ghastly young sister would have had the grace to buzz off at Christmas.'

'I take it you're not a fan of this Hugo? Impervious to your fatal beauty – surely not?'

'Hugo's an attractive man, dark and saturnine, but not my sort. Not that he ever showed any interest in me. He runs around with that Valerie Whatsit creature. He's a fool, he'd much better ditch her and turn his attentions towards Freya.'

'Matchmaking?'

'No, I couldn't be bothered. But I know Valerie slightly, and Hugo's wasted on a woman like that.'

'So it'll be the family and your cousin Freya and this Hugo. What about your Veryan relations?'

'Thank God they won't be staying at the Castle. Aunt Priscilla always has her brood at Veryan House at Christmas. Plus Oliver; I'm taking him with me. Although not for the whole of Christmas. He'll come back to town on Christmas Eve.'

Rupert said, 'Oliver? Who's Oliver?'

'You know, Oliver Seynton. The art man.' Sonia took a deep draw of her cigarette and let out smoke in elegant little circles. 'I've said I'm bringing Oliver to advise Gus, but actually I want him to look at some paintings that are tucked away in the attic, which weren't ever included in the inventory. They're no use to Gus, they'd just be a burden to him. He'll have to sell no end of paintings and things, or hand them over to the nation, because of all those dreadful death duties. So, out of the kindness of my heart, I thought I might put him in the way of avoiding some of that unjustifiable tax by taking away those pictures.'

'A spot of theft?'

'I have as much right to them as Gus. No questions, no lies. Oliver will dispose of them quietly and discreetly for me.'

'Doesn't Oliver work for Morville's? I can't see them involved in anything like that.'

'Sharpen your wits, darling. Oliver, like any man of any sense, is always glad of a little extra. His work for Morville's is completely above board and respectable. That was the Oliver who came and did the inventory. Now I'm taking him down to Selchester in his other persona. He has quite a reputation for doing private deals for people who have assets they want to dispose of without attracting any attention.'

Rupert didn't like the sound of this. 'Do you know why your father bought these paintings? And why he kept them in an attic?'

'Heavens, don't ask me. I suppose he was planning to have some kind of new gallery. I personally would have taken all those dreadful family portraits down and used the present gallery, but you know how tradition minded he was. He said one day these would be worth ten times what he'd paid for them. Thank goodness they were tucked away. Out of sight, out of mind and therefore out of reach of the tax man.'

Rupert looked at Sonia with something like despair. Did she really not understand? 'Sonia, when people sell paintings, there's a little thing called provenance.'

'That won't bother Oliver. He knows if paintings are genuine or not, and as long as he's sure they are, the kind of collectors that he sells to aren't that fussy.' She gave him a sidelong glance. 'Anyhow, didn't you have something to do with those paintings? I seem to remember Selchester saying you put him in the way of acquiring them. You'd never have dared do that if you weren't sure they were pukka.'

'Wrong, my darling; I've never been a picture dealer.'

'Of course not, that would be quite beneath you. Anyhow, if need be, and if any of his clients ask awkward questions, Oliver will just have to a do a bit of research. That's what he has to do at Morville's in any case.'

Rupert was thinking swiftly. It was a damn nuisance this lost heir popping up from nowhere. Sonia didn't care, but if the new Lord Selchester came across the pictures or Sonia didn't convince him they were hers, it could spell trouble. Oliver Seynton might prove useful, but could he be trusted?

'Tell you what, Sonia, why don't I come to Selchester with you?'

Sonia eyes widened in surprise. 'You always go to the Westerhams for Christmas.'

'It's time for a change.'

Sonia said, 'It's all very well my accepting Gus's open invitation, and Oliver will be there for professional reasons, but I don't know that I can just invite you out of the blue. You don't know Gus.'

Rupert said, 'I knew his father. I'll be a welcome guest. I know what, tell him we're engaged. I did once ask you to marry me.'

'Yes, you did. After Tom died, when I was going to inherit the Castle and all that lovely money and land and so on. Oh, happy days! Then time passed and I don't remember you mentioning it again.'

'A man has his pride. You didn't exactly leap to accept my offer.'

'I don't want to marry you, that's why.'

'Your half-brother doesn't have to know that. If I come with you as what he no doubt would call your fiancé, he'll welcome me with open arms. How can he do otherwise? Besides, Americans have such perfect manners, he won't turn me away from his ancestral doors.'

Sonia hummed a few bars of the *Wedding March*. 'It's not such a bad idea. It's going to be a bore, a family Christmas. More fun if you're there. And you'll charm them, as you do everyone. They'll adore you.'

'If it's such a bore, don't go. Come to the Westerhams with me.'

Sonia's face took on a closed look. 'No. It isn't just those paintings. There are various other things of mine there that I want.'

Deliberately casual, Rupert said, 'Did Selchester's notebook ever turn up?'

Sonia was suddenly alert. 'Notebook? What are you talking about?'

Rupert said, 'Selchester had a notebook. He called it his little black book, you know, like the one Thurloe had to keep him safe when Charles was restored.'

Sonia stared at him. She said sharply, 'What on earth are you talking about? Charles? Restored? He's dead.'

It was easy to forget just how ill-educated Sonia was. 'Of course he's dead. King Charles II, my love, he died a long time ago. Thurloe was in charge of intelligence during Oliver Cromwell's time. You know about Oliver Cromwell? Puritan England?'

'Of course I do. That Charles; I know about him. He hid up an oak tree. Dark days for the Selchesters; they kept having to bundle Jesuits into the attics. Then he came to the throne anyhow and enjoyed all those jolly wenches, Nell Gwyn and so on. The Merry Monarch.'

'Yes. Well, Thurloe knew where the bodies were buried.'

'Which bodies? Are we back to my father and the flagstones?'

'No, we're still in the seventeenth century. Thurloe knew which members of Cromwell's circle were really in cahoots with Charles when he was in exile. And, more to the point, he knew which of Charles's circle were secretly working for Cromwell. He wrote everything down in his little black book. Which meant that when Charles was restored to the throne there was no danger of Thurloe being prosecuted or held to account in any way for having served Cromwell so faithfully. As a result, he died peacefully in his bed.'

Sonia shrugged. 'If you're saying that Selchester had a black book, I never heard of it.' She was lying. Rupert was sure she knew about the black notebook. 'I'd quite like to get my hands on it,' he said.

'Afraid he wrote notes about you, Rupert? Wicked deeds that you'd rather no one knew about?'

Rupert said, 'What wicked deeds? I've nothing to hide.'

That brought a peal of genuine laughter. 'Oh, Rupert, you have plenty to hide.'

Rupert sat back, savouring his own cigarette. 'Everybody has a few things in their life that they would rather didn't come to the public eye.'

'And, as a rising young politician with a promotion on the horizon, you don't want anyone rocking the boat.'

'What promotion?'

'You don't need to pretend with me. You saw the Chief Whip yesterday. Hamilton's got to go; such a messy divorce; it simply won't do. I hear that you're going to be the one who gets the tap on the shoulder. That is, as long as you can flourish a blameless reputation. There have been a few too many scandals in the party, aren't I right? Now you all have to be whiter than white.'

Rupert was confident that he had covered all his tracks well enough for it to be unlikely he'd to run into that kind of trouble. The few people who might be a threat to him could be headed off. Which was exactly why he wanted to get hold of that notebook of Selchester's. For if ever there was a man who knew things about people that could be useful, it was Selchester. And Rupert, having been his personal private secretary at one time, had a fair idea of just how much Selchester wrote down in the notebook he kept so closely guarded.

'Speak to your half-brother. I'm sure you can wangle me an invitation.' He stubbed out his cigarette, grinding the end into the ashtray, and stood up. 'Another turn about the floor?'

As Sonia slid into his arms, she said, 'I shan't ask Gus to invite you, I'll simply ring up the Castle tomorrow and say you're coming.'

Scene 2

Freya was on the telephone in Grace Hall when Hugo came down the next morning. She was having an animated conversation, the curly cord twisted round her fingers and a look of exasperation on her face. She mouthed at Hugo as he went past, 'Sonia.' He lifted his eyebrows in sympathy and went on his way towards the dining room.

Sonia was in full flood. 'I wish the ghastly man would drop dead. Because, unless it turns out that he's had a secret marriage and has a son that nobody knows about – like father, like son, how ironic that would be – I'm his heir. If he pops his clogs I inherit as Selchester always intended I should.'

Freya wasn't going to let that pass. 'That's nonsense. Tom was the next heir. When your father died he had no idea that you were going to inherit.'

'Of course I'd much rather that Tom hadn't been killed but I did take a great deal of satisfaction in thinking that I could sell the Castle and get rid of everything that Selchester was so keen on.'

Freya had not yet got to the bottom of the bitterness that Sonia felt towards her father; a bitterness so intense that Freya had always wondered what had been in the pills beside his bed the night he died, that Sonia had ordered her to go and collect. 'Nonetheless, Sonia, he is not going to die. He looks perfectly fit and healthy.'

Sonia interrupted, 'I didn't say he was going to catch the plague or anything like that. Accidents do happen. What are the daughters like? American rednecks? I'm sure they're quite ghastly.'

Freya took a deep breath. She wasn't going to lose her temper with Sonia although she felt like lashing out at her. 'They're perfectly civilised. Although the older one has obviously been reading rather too much Sartre.'

Sonia said, 'Sartre? You mean she fancies herself an existentialist? Oh, spare me. Anyhow, I shall see for myself, because I'm coming to the Castle for Christmas.'

She dropped this bombshell without any warning and Freya was left speechless for a moment. 'Are you sure that's wise?' she finally managed to say.

'I'm not going to stab Gus in the back or poison him if that's what you mean. He invited me to come visit, as he put it, at the

Castle whenever I liked. I don't suppose he meant over Christmas, but I intend to take him at his word. There are things in the Castle that are mine and I want to take them away. Oh, and I'm bringing Rupert with me.'

'Rupert? Rupert who?'

'Sharpen your wits, darling. Rupert Dauntsey. We're engaged.'

Another bombshell.

'You must know him. He was father's Personal Private Secretary for a while before he moved on to higher things. He's an MP now. Too, too Establishment, but he's deliciously rich.'

Freya shut her eyes for a moment. Would it be better to have Sonia on her own or with Rupert? She vaguely remembered a rather charming, suave man, who'd made no particular impression on her.

Sonia said, 'I'll come down on the twenty-third. I'll bring Oliver with me, as well. He wants to talk to the new Earl.'

'Oliver?'

'Don't you remember anything, Freya? He works for the auctioneers, for Morville's. He did the inventory for me at a point when I thought it was going to be necessary. He knows all about pictures and that kind of thing. Gus now has to deal with all the horrendous death duties, not me. So he needs to talk to Oliver, and Oliver wants to talk to him. And there are some paintings of mine in one of the attics, which I want him to look at.'

Paintings? In an attic? 'Didn't he see them when he came in the autumn to do the inventory?'

'No, he didn't need to; they were never going on any inventory. And, please remember, at that time I expected to inherit everything in the Castle, from top to bottom. That was before you went and dug out the lost heir.'

Freya said, 'You haven't invited Oliver for Christmas, have you?'

'Don't be silly, darling. He'll want to be back in London the next day. It'll just be me and my fiancé for Christmas at the Castle.'

Fiancé? There had been a distinct note of irony when Sonia said it, and it wasn't a word she'd normally use. What was she up to?

'Tell Mrs P she'll have to do something about beds. Is one of those ghastly girls sleeping in my room?'

'I'm sure we can arrange something to suit everybody,' Freya said tactfully. Barbara was, in fact, in Sonia's room. That would have to be sorted out.

'Let me know if there's anything you want me to bring down from London, darling. Until tomorrow.'

Freya put the receiver back and stood looking at the instrument. That would add to the gaiety of Christmas: a hostile Sonia, a strange Rupert and, at least for twenty-four hours, Oliver. Her mind turned to thoughts of presents and with a glare at the telephone she went to the kitchen to break the news to Mrs Partridge.

Chapter Three

Scene 1

Georgia was sitting at the table in the dining room, eating her way through a pile of toast and marmalade. They usually ate in the kitchen, but Mrs Partridge wasn't having that now the new Earl was in residence.

Across the table, Polly was eating her toast slowly and carefully. She looked up as Freya came in. 'I've not had marmalade before. It's interesting.'

Georgia said, 'Don't they have marmalade in America?'

'I usually have waffles and maple syrup for breakfast.'

Freya could see from the gleam in Georgia's eye that she rather liked this idea, but she wasn't going to admit it. 'Like in *What Katy Did*,' she said and went on with her toast.

'Where are the others?' Freya asked as she helped herself to the eggs and bacon that Mrs Partridge had left in a big silver dish.

Gus came in. 'Good morning, Freya. Thank you, I had my breakfast early.'

'Then as soon as the rest of us have finished, would you like to take a tour of your castle?'

Like a guide at some stately home, she thought as she led the way out. 'On your left . . . On your right . . . Please be careful on the staircase . . . This marble fireplace . . .' And a half-crown tip at the end of the tour. An amusing fancy, but there wasn't much of that kind of stately home about Selchester Castle. Oh, it had grandeur, but it had been built as a power base, in the days when might was right and when neither king nor neighbours could be trusted. The fine carpets, the paintings, the ornate plasterwork were all there, but they were later adornments, added when the halberds and cannonballs were no longer necessary to defend family, castle and land.

She didn't linger in the Great Hall, less sombre in the morning light. 'The older part dates back to the thirteenth century, although obviously over time various inhabitants have done work to the Castle.'

Georgia had decided to tag along on the tour and now she said, 'Are you going to show them the Old Chapel?' She went on in a clear, high voice, 'That's where they found Lord Selchester. Hugo was there, almost the moment they dug him up.'

Freya turned sharply on her. 'Pipe down, Georgia. And you hardly need a tour of the Castle; surely you've got other things to do.'

Fortunately, Gus was rather amused. 'Just like Polly, girls that age don't seem to have much sensitivity about things that upset us. I think probably we should see this Old Chapel.'

Freya made an effort to keep up her tour guide voice, neutral and without the sadness she still felt whenever she went into the Old Chapel. Despite everything that they'd found out about her uncle's death – and life – she still didn't care to think about all the years she'd lived in the Castle with the late Lord Selchester's body lying in its unorthodox and unknown grave under the flagstones.

The Old Chapel was a circular chamber, which dated back to much the same time as the Great Hall. There was a marble altar, but otherwise it was bare and plain with pillars, and arches that met in a point at the ceiling. As they went in, Gus stood for a moment, bowed his head and crossed himself.

Georgia said with interest, 'Are you Catholic too? That's what my Uncle Leo did when he came in here. But he's a priest.'

Freya said, 'All the Selchesters are Catholic, Georgia.'

'No need to sound peeved, I only asked. After all, you're a Selchester, and you aren't RC.'

'It looks like it's a long time since this was used,' Gus said.

'There's another chapel, a Victorian one, very ornate, and quite different from this.'

Polly edged closer to Georgia. 'Was he buried or was he just lying here?'

Georgia said, 'Of course not, English people aren't so stupid that he wouldn't have been noticed. He was buried under the flagstones. There was nothing left of him but bones and a signet ring when they found him.'

Interested despite herself, Barbara said, 'How long had he been there?'

'Nearly seven years.' Georgia spoke with ghoulish enthusiasm. 'He wasn't murdered in here, though, was he, Freya?'

'No, he wasn't,' Freya said. 'We don't need to talk about that now.'

She saw a look come over Georgia's face that spoke of mischief and wondered what she was plotting.

Polly asked Georgia, her voice low, 'Do you know which flagstone it was?'

Georgia, talking out of the side of her mouth in a way she'd copied from a gangster film, said, 'I'll show you later.'

Scene 2

Since Sir Bernard was going to be away and couldn't nag him about Orlov, Hugo called the Hall to say he was taking an extra day off.

Mr Dorsett, head of personnel, was unsurprised. 'Good time to take some leave. And I note that you have an appointment with the physiotherapist tomorrow. So you won't be in until after Christmas. I'll put it in the book.'

Hugo wanted to speak to Victor Emerson, but he didn't want to ring him from the Hall, even though phone calls from the Castle were just as likely to have a listener. Selchester hadn't yet been put on to the direct dialling system, and the operator at the telephone exchange was capable of listening to every word of an interesting conversation.

It would depend who was on duty. Irene always listened in, and she remembered what she heard. And, despite all the Post Office regulations, frequently passed on juicy titbits of information.

He waited until the others had left Grace Hall and picked up the receiver. A bored voice said, 'Number, please.'

Good. June had no interest in anything except her nails, her next perm and what her favourite film stars were up to.

He gave Emerson's phone number and waited to be put through.

It wasn't a private number, but the number of a firm. He spoke to first one person then another, and finally Emerson came on the line. 'Mr Hawksworth? Could that be Hugo Hawksworth?'

Hugo said, 'Good morning, Emerson. Yes, it's Hugo.'

'Good God, voice from the past. Last time I heard of you, you were doing great things in Bucharest. I suppose I can't ask if you're still with the Service. But I dare say you are, otherwise how did you get hold of me? I've been out of it for a while now, as you no doubt know.'

'It's no secret that you work for Guildern Associates. We have your number on file.'

Emerson gave a sound halfway between a grunt and groan. 'On file. Yes I suppose I will for ever be on file. What can I do for you? Let me guess. You're digging around in the past, looking at my far from impeccable record in the Service, am I right?'

Hugo laughed. 'I have to say your career was an unusual one, but that's not why I'm ringing. Tell me, exactly what does Guildern Associates do?'

'We cover it up with fancy prose in our literature but basically we trace lost works of art.'

'Lost?' How did you lose a work of art?

'Lost as in stolen, or looted or destroyed. And we also do some work on provenances if asked. Detective work, of a kind. I take it you haven't lost a painting, or you'd know about Guilderns. So what can I do for you?'

'It's a long shot, but you're the only person I know in the art world. Cast your mind back to Berlin nineteen forty-five, forty-six.'

Emerson was silent for so long that Hugo began to think he'd been cut off. 'Hello? Are you there?'

'I am.'

'Why the long pause?'

'I was pondering on the nature of coincidence. Berlin after the war has been in the forefront of my mind. I imagine for quite different reasons. What about it?'

'A Russian bought some priceless bronzes from a German aristocrat via an intermediary—'

Emerson didn't let him finish. 'You're talking about the Archangelo bronzes, which a man named Orlov acquired in dubious circumstances. I hear your jaw drop. How do I know about them? Because I'd had some dealings with friend Gregor, on quite unrelated business, and when he was instructed to get hold of some bronzes he asked my advice. He'd been offered them; were they likely to be genuine, were they special?'

'To which you replied?'

'Yes and yes. How did you get hold of the story? My contacts with Orlov were *sub rosa*. No, nothing sinister about it, don't prick up your ears and smell treachery. I just found Berlin such a leaky bucket that I kept myself to myself, as it were. It didn't make any difference; everything I had anything to do with was a disaster. Like those people who repeatedly get struck by lightning. Inexplicable but true.'

A sixth sense told Hugo there was more to this story than Orlov and the bronzes. 'You didn't leave it at that?'

'I never saw Orlov again. Nor did I hear any more about the Archangelo bronzes, which vanished from sight. But I'd heard rumours about artworks changing hands and looted paintings leaving the country under cover of darkness, so I did a spot of investigation.'

'Did you find out who was doing it?'

'I knew who was doing it in the sense that I knew who was physically getting the paintings out of the country and back to England. On which subject, my lips are sealed. But as to who was arranging the consignments, who owned the pictures, I drew a blank.'

'Looted paintings, you say?'

'The bronzes weren't looted. A lot of paintings were. Many of them taken from France during the Occupation. Which is another reason why Berlin has been on my mind. Quite a few of our clients come to us to trace paintings which disappeared in the war. A case in point – no names, no pack drill – is a young man, who is half French on his mother's side. She was not only French, but also Jewish and she was in France with her sister's family when war broke out. He was in England with his father at the time. The whole family over there were arrested and never seen again. However, among their possessions was a fine Picasso, and that, I found out, ended up in Berlin.'

Wasn't Picasso counted decadent, didn't they burn that sort of thing? Hugo didn't much like Picasso's paintings, but then he was the first to admit that he didn't know much about art of any style or period.

'There the trail went cold. I'm fairly sure it reached England, but its present whereabouts are unknown. If I'd ever been able to find out who was behind the whole sordid business, I might be able to help him. As it is, I have an unhappy client whose determination to find the painting borders on the obsessive.'

'Because it's valuable?'

'Because it was given to his aunt by Picasso himself, and she loved it.' Emerson hesitated and then said, 'I don't suppose your interest in the bronzes means you might be on to something relevant to my searches?'

'I'm not sure,' Hugo said. He didn't want to raise false hope. 'This conversation is strictly off the record. I'm ringing you from a private number. Write it down, and ring me up if you have any further information to do with Berlin. If I can help, I will.'

'Give me the number.'

'Selchester 77'

'Selchester? They dumped you at the Hall, did they? Graveyard of ambition, that place.'

Hugo wasn't going to rise to that bait. 'Not such a graveyard these days.'

'So you're living in Selchester? Give me your address, I may write rather than ring. You never know with the telephone these days.'

'At the moment I'm at Selchester Castle.'

Emerson let out a low whistle. 'Selchester Castle? Flying high, aren't you? I've had the pleasure of meeting Lady Sonia. A looker, but not the easiest of company.'

A good description of Lady Sonia. Hugo was warming to Emerson.

'Very well. I'll give you the nod if I track down that Picasso and you pass on what you can that might help me in my searches. Happy Christmas, Hugo.'

Hugo put down the receiver, pleased. Emerson seemed to have left the Service without resentment. And had found work that

suited him; that was unusual. Life in the Service didn't equip most
people for the civilian world.

Scene 3

No sooner had Emerson hung up than he received another call.
'Mr Oliver Seynton on the line for you, Mr Emerson,' his secretary said.

It was clearly a day of coincidences. 'Oliver. Good to hear
from you. I'm afraid I don't have any news for you about your
Picasso. At least nothing concrete. But it's possible that I might
have a new lead. No, I can't say anything about it at the moment.
Leave it with me, you know I'll be in touch the moment I have
something to tell you. You're away for a couple of days? Well,
nothing's going to happen as quickly as that. We'll speak after
Christmas. Goodbye.'

Scene 4

Hugo came off the phone and decided to join the tour party. Freya
frowned at him; she didn't like the humorous twist to his mouth
while he listened to her spiel.

'Go away,' she whispered to him, as the others went on ahead.
'I don't need you grinning at me, and there's nothing for you to
see.'

'Oh, but there is. You never gave me and Georgia the complete
tour; what about all those locked rooms?'

'You make it sound like Bluebeard's castle. I don't want to dis-
appoint you, there's nothing behind the closed doors except furniture shrouded in dust covers.'

She took them upstairs to see the solar and then up an oak staircase guarded by two suits of armour. They walked along dark passages lined with oak panelling and up the stone spiral staircase that led to her rooms in the New Tower.

'Not so new as that,' Gus said when she told them it had been built in the fifteenth century. He looked at Freya's desk with her typewriter and neat stacks of paper beside it, and said, 'This is where you're working on the history of the Selchester family. I should be so interested to see what you've written.'

No, you wouldn't, Freya said inwardly, and then, 'I've mostly been going through old papers, letters and household ledgers, and so forth. It's a long job.'

Polly looked up at the picture that hung on the wall opposite Freya's desk. 'Who's that? She looks just like you.'

'That's the ninth countess, your umpteen times great-grandmother. She was a redoubtable woman who held the castle against Cromwell's forces.'

And the ancestor who had inspired Freya to write her first novel.

Polly wrinkled her nose. 'I suppose that meant that her husband was a supporter of the king. A Royalist. I'd have supported Cromwell if I'd been alive then.'

Georgia instantly said, 'I wouldn't, I'd have been a Cavalier.'

Scene 5

'So much to see,' Gus said. He'd lingered by a huge canvas by one of the Carracci brothers, which he at once identified as a scene from Ovid's *Metamorphoses*. 'It's an interesting interpretation. That Bacchus there . . .'

Babs called him to order. 'You've got the rest of your life to gaze at all the pictures, Pops, and it's cold here. Have we nearly finished, Freya?'

'No, but as you say, plenty of time for you all to explore. I'll just show you the ballroom and then we'll go out to the hothouse.'

'Ballroom?' Hugo said. 'You never told me there was a ballroom.'

Freya was hunting through the keys on her ring for the one that opened the ornate door in front of them. 'It hasn't been used since before the war.' She pushed open the door.

'Like Sleeping Beauty,' Polly said, breaking the silence.

Motes of dust danced in the light that came through the windows as Freya pulled back the shutters. The wrapped chandeliers suspended eerily from their decorative roses, the chairs covered with sheets and cobwebs suspended from the ornate plaster of the cornices did indeed make the room look as though it had slept for a hundred years.

Freya knew the life it once had, of glamorous frocks and men in formal evening clothes. Those from her own memory, and, in her imagination, the silks and velvets and muslins, the gorgeous waistcoats and the tight breeches of an earlier era.

Hugo went over to one corner, his footsteps sounding on the smooth wooden floor. He stood for a moment in front of a large, shrouded piece of furniture and then lifted the dust cover.

'A piano,' Gus said, going over to join him.

'No,' Hugo said. 'It's a harpsichord.' His fingers strayed to the keys and he played a chord. The plangent sound rang through the room. 'Out of tune. They need tuning all the time.' He lifted the lid and peered inside. 'It looks as though it's in good condition, though. It's a Kirkman.'

Freya had never seen that look on Hugo's face. His habitual wry, alert, amused look had gone, replaced by the haunted expression of a man looking into some distant place. Into the past, Freya guessed.

'You know about harpsichords?' Gus said.

'I used to play,' Hugo said. He lowered the lid and flung the cover back in place.

Georgia was regarding him with disapproval. 'You never told me that.'

'I haven't touched a keyboard for years. Shall we move on, Freya?'

It was as though he'd put up a big 'Keep Off' sign, and even Georgia didn't ask any more questions. On the other side of the door, Freya paused and worked the key off the ring. As the others moved on, she handed it to Hugo. 'Gus won't mind if you come back in here. While we're still at the Castle.'

Scene 6

They piled on coats and scarves to go outside. Babs had retreated into her rather morose self, while Polly clung to her father's arm. They walked through the stable yard, where Last Hurrah looked inquisitively out from his half-door.

Polly said, 'Whose horse is that?'

Freya said, 'He's mine.' She turned to Gus. 'I hope you won't mind if I stable him here until I make other arrangements.'

Ben, who had come to the castle first as groom and then chauffeur and stayed on as general factotum during the years when Lord Selchester was missing, touched his forehead as Freya introduced him. 'Ben, this is the new Lord Selchester. Ben's been here for ever, Gus. He knows the Castle inside out.'

Ben said, 'That horse won't like going from here, Miss Freya.'

Freya said, 'I dare say he won't, Ben, but he'll get used to it.' She said to Gus, 'Ben's the one who'll miss Last Hurrah. Your father and Hermione both hunted and so back in the days when Ben first came here, there was a full stable. Now I'll just want to show you the hothouse, and then we'll go back indoors.'

Babs said, 'Hothouse?'

'It's a big glasshouse, for plants. It's more than a hundred years old. It was built by Paxton, who did the ones at Kew Gardens.'

'Can I skip the plants?' Babs said. 'I think I'd rather head back inside and burn my feet against a fire.'

'If it's a hothouse, it'll be warm,' Polly said.

'Says you. I expect it was hot for a week or so in the last century and they haven't turned the heating on since then.' She gave the exquisite iron-framed building a contemptuous look, shivered ostentatiously as she tightened her coat around her and slouched off.

Gus was full of admiration and he stood, impervious to the cold, staring up at the arched roof. 'It seems in remarkably good condition. Given what you've all been through in this country.'

'My uncle was proud of it and of its history. Various Selchester horticulturalists and their gardeners have grown rare specimens here,' Freya said, opening the door and letting out a welcome gust of warm air. 'No one was allowed in here during the war; my uncle insisted it wasn't to be used when the Castle was requisitioned. As soon as he got possession again, he made sure the structure and the glass was in good repair.' She looked around. 'It's a bit forlorn now. I remember when I was a child, Aunt Hermione grew all kinds of wonderful exotic fruits. And flowers for the house, all year round. It was a subtropical paradise in here. We children loved it. But now it's mostly used to house tender plants through the winter.'

Gus said, with real enthusiasm, 'I see no reason why we shouldn't grow more in here. How is it heated? Is it all electrical?' He bent down to look at a nearby socket. 'This all looks rather ancient.'

Ben, who'd followed them into the hothouse, said, 'Yes, my lord, all the wiring needs replacing. His lordship, his late lordship, I should say, was going to have it done, but it wasn't so easy after the war.'

Polly said, 'Pops will be at those electrics, you wait and see.'

'If you're interested in the wiring here, talk to Mr Jonquil, at the estate office,' Freya said. 'He'll have plans of all the circuits and so on.'

Gus said, 'I'd like to see those. Worn wiring is dangerous; this needs attending to before there's an accident.'

Scene 7

Freya had turned her cousins over to Mrs Partridge and taken Last Hurrah out for some exercise. So she wasn't at the Castle when her aunt, Lady Priscilla Veryan, rode into the stable yard on her big hunter. She dismounted and handed the reins to Ben, who looked appreciatively at the big bay and ran the stirrups up the leathers.

'Will you be long, my lady? I'll put him in a loose box.'

Lady Priscilla found Gus in the Great Hall. He was standing beneath the head of a huge stag, looking without enthusiasm into its mournful glassy eyes. She regarded him for a moment and then said, 'You must be Augustine.'

He swung round, surprised. 'Why, yes. I'm sorry . . .'

'No need to look at me like that. I'm your aunt, Priscilla Veryan.' She held out a hand and looked at him appraisingly. 'Yes, you have a look of my brother about you. Welcome to Selchester. I know you met my husband in London; I'm sorry I couldn't be there.'

Mrs Partridge, clutching a feather duster, emerged from the shadows. Lady Priscilla pounced. 'Ah, there you are, Mrs Partridge. We'll have tea in the library. And tell Lord Selchester's daughters to join us. Come along. My husband called you Gus, do you prefer that? I dare say Augustine wouldn't do in America.'

She made it sound as though America were some outpost of the Empire. Gus knew better than to resist this force of nature and silently followed his aunt towards the library.

She went over to the window, looked out, and said, 'We'll have snow within the next week,' and then turned her attention back to her nephew. 'So, how do you like the Castle? This must have come as a shock to you. Good thing that the Earldom isn't going to die out after all. Although you've only got the two girls, not a boy.'

Gus wondered if he should apologise for the lack of an heir, but he pulled himself together and said, 'Yes. Quite unexpected. And the Castle is extraordinary. I never in my wildest dreams imagined I'd ever live in such a place.'

Lady Priscilla eyed him appraisingly. 'Dreams, or nightmares? Is the old part of the Castle getting to you? You Americans are so modern in your outlook. Still, you'll have to get used to it. Freya doesn't mind roughing it in her tower, but nobody can pretend that the Castle is comfortable. At least you don't have a wife to complain and make matters worse. You lost your wife. In the war, was it?'

'During the war, yes, but her demise was nothing to do with the hostilities. She suffered from TB.'

Lady Priscilla pursed her lips. 'I hope your girls haven't inherited a tubercular tendency.'

'They are perfectly healthy.' He wasn't sure how to take this new relative. He was finding relatives as a whole quite difficult to get used to. It wasn't just the hovering presence of his dead father; it was all the rest of them. He'd liked Sir Archibald, Lady Priscilla's husband. But hadn't he said that they had three daughters and four sons? A large family, and more to add to his list of new cousins.

Lady Priscilla changed the subject. 'How do you get on with Sonia? She's behaving very badly. You don't want to stand any nonsense from her.'

Gus wasn't going to express his opinion of Lady Sonia to her aunt, so he just said, 'I had the pleasure of meeting Sonia when I was in London. I guess her nose has been put out of joint and I appreciate she stands to lose a considerable inheritance. But I understand she is a wealthy woman in her own right. I'm not depriving her of her livelihood.'

Lady Priscilla said, 'Sonia married an extremely rich man entirely for his money, and by good fortune was widowed soon afterwards. It would have been a disastrous marriage had he survived the war. She's certainly not short of money and, as you'll be aware, she also inherited quite a sum from your father. Although not the whole lot, which is what she had expected.'

Scene 8

Freya got back from her ride and headed for the kitchen, where she found Mrs Partridge arranging cups and a large silver teapot on a tray.

'Lady Priscilla is here.'

Freya said, 'I know. I saw Jupiter in the stables. Where is she?'

'She carried his lordship off to the library. She's asked for tea, and I'm to find their young ladyships and send them to the library.'

Freya said with a grin, 'Give me the tray. I'll take it in. I imagine Gus will be shaking in his boots by now.'

She carried the tray to the library, put it down on a table and went over to kiss her aunt. 'I see you've made Gus's acquaintance.'

'We were just talking about Sonia.'

'Are you? I haven't told you, Gus, but it seems that Sonia is coming here for Christmas. She said that you'd invited her to come to the Castle whenever she liked.'

From the fleeting expression that crossed his face, Freya knew her cousin was regretting the offer made to Sonia. But he said courteously, 'She is my half-sister. That's a close relationship, even if we're scarcely acquainted, and I'd like her to feel that she may come back to her family home whenever she wants.'

Freya said, 'When she wants is apparently Christmas, and she's bringing two other people with her.'

She poured the tea and handed a cup to Lady Priscilla, who looked annoyed.

'It's all very well for Sonia to accept an invitation but she shouldn't spring her friends on Gus like this. Who are these people she's bringing?'

'One of them is a Mr Rupert Dauntsey. Sonia says she's engaged to him.'

'Engaged? Nonsense. There's been no announcement, the family knows nothing about it.'

Freya said, 'I merely repeat what she told me. She called him her "fiancé".' Seeing the expression on her aunt's face, she added, 'It was a tease.'

Lady Priscilla said tartly, 'I hope so. Sonia is never vulgar except when she wants to be. I suppose she means she's sleeping with this man. Sonia isn't about to marry anyone. Although,' and a thoughtful look came over her face, 'I did hear that Rupert recently inherited quite a fortune from his great-uncle. An estate and a lot of money. Maybe Sonia does intend to marry him.'

Gus said, 'What's wrong with "fiancé"?'

That earned him a withering look from Lady Priscilla. 'You'll learn. Who else is she foisting on Gus?'

'Oliver Seynton. He works for Morville's, the auctioneers. Sonia brought him down here before – when she thought she was going to inherit the Castle. To do a final inventory once Selchester's death was confirmed.' She turned to Gus. 'It seems that Mr Seynton has written to you already; he wants to discuss something to do with the pictures here.'

Lady Priscilla said, 'You could do worse, Gus, they know their job at Morville's. You'll have to sell quite a lot of things, although I dare say you can offset some of the death duties by giving a few of the more valuable pictures to the nation. But Verekers will be advising you on that.'

Vereker, Vereker, Vereker and Farquhar had been the Fitzwarin solicitors for several generations. And still, in Freya's opinion, behaved as though they were advising the fifteenth Earl, back in the last century. How Gus would cope with them was anyone's guess.

'Well, I dare say I should talk to this Mr Seynton,' Gus said cautiously. 'But maybe the Christmas season isn't the best time.'

'There'll be a purpose to Sonia inviting him now, you may be sure,' Freya said. 'And he'll be going back to London on Christmas Eve.'

Lady Priscilla dismissed Oliver Seynton with a wave of her hand and brushed a crumb from her breeches. 'So, Gus, do you plan to live here? Or are you going to finish that Fellowship at Oxford and return to America? It's a mistake with an estate like this to leave it in the hands of the stewards and land agents. It's never satisfactory and not good for the tenants, but it's your decision.'

Gus said, 'It's a decision I've already taken. I reckon that since I've inherited the title, the seat in the House of Lords, the Castle and all the rest of it, I should make my home in England.'

Lady Priscilla said, 'What do your daughters think about that?'

'My younger daughter will need to go to school here, and that'll accustom her to being English. I'm not sure about my other daughter, Barbara. She's just come back from a few months in Paris and—'

Lady Priscilla looked approving. 'She's been finished, has she?'

Gus looked puzzled and Freya came to his rescue. 'She was there to improve her French.'

'How old is she, seventeen, eighteen? You'll have to be thinking of bringing her out, Gus.'

There was another look of mystification on Gus's face, and once again Freya supplied the missing information. 'My aunt means that she might do the Season, be a debutante.'

'As for the younger girl, you'll send her to St Ursula's. That's where the Selchester girls go.'

As if on cue, the door opened and Polly came in, with a world-weary Babs slouching along behind her.

Polly stopped dead and gazed at Lady Priscilla, who gazed back at her.

Freya looked from one to the other and nearly burst out laughing. Polly's plaits and her big round spectacles only slightly disguised the fact that she was extremely like her great-aunt.

Gus said, 'Come and meet your great-aunt, Lady Priscilla Veryan. This is Barbara and Pauline. Known in the family as Babs and Polly.'

Lady Priscilla looked them up and down. She said to Barbara, 'I hear you've been in Paris. It looks to me as though you've spent too much time at the Sorbonne listening to those tiresome philosophers.'

Barbara seemed not to mind this forthright greeting. Freya noticed that when you saw through the thick black eye make-up, her blue Selchester eyes were observant and even shrewd.

She shrugged, slouched even more and looked down at her feet, a bored expression on her face.

Lady Priscilla said, 'For heaven's sake, stand up straight. You'll do yourself no good with rounded shoulders like that. Do you ride?'

This question obviously surprised Barbara and for a moment she did straighten up. Then she said, uninformatively, 'Yeah, a bit.'

'Come over to Veryan House and I'll mount you. No good riding that wretched horse of Freya's, he'll have you off as soon as look at you.'

She turned her attention to Polly. 'What about you? Gus, you'd best buy the girl a pony. Let Ben find you one, he's a good judge of horseflesh.'

Polly was definite. 'No, thank you. I'm afraid of horses. I wouldn't mind a goat, though.'

Her father, Freya and Lady Priscilla all stared at her while Barbara, whose eyes had resumed their customary vacant look, gazed out of the window.

Lady Priscilla said, 'Good heavens, child, what do you want a goat for?'

Polly said simply, 'I like goats.'

'Dirty, difficult beasts. If you want a pet you'd better get yourself a dog.'

Polly said, 'No, thank you. Magnus wouldn't like it.'

Freya said, 'If you want a dog, Polly, don't worry about Magnus. Don't forget he'll be coming with me.'

Polly said, 'I like Magnus. I like cats and I don't much care for dogs.' This was said with a look at Lady Priscilla every bit as ferocious as her ladyship's.

'That's what comes of being brought up in America,' Lady Priscilla said – unfairly, in Freya's opinion.

She was interested to see that Gus was sensibly keeping out of this conversation. He was outnumbered by Selchester women. Or perhaps he had no particular views on the subject of cats, dogs, ponies and goats.

Lady Priscilla was looking at Barbara again. 'You can't go around dressed like that. Not in the country. It's completely inappropriate. It might do for Chelsea, but Selchester is not Chelsea.'

Freya heard Barbara mutter under her breath, 'More's the pity.'

'Gus,' Lady Priscilla said, 'I hear you have a cousin who brought the girls up. What was she doing letting Barbara dress like this?'

Barbara said in a deliberately drawling voice, 'Cousin Charlotte doesn't say what I wear. I'm nearly eighteen and I choose for myself.'

'That is exactly what the right kind of person looking after you will prevent. Where is this cousin of yours? Did she come over with you?'

Gus intervened. 'My cousin Charlotte doesn't care for travel.'

'You mean the girls have no one to look after them? That won't do, Gus.' She turned to Freya. 'You see to it that Barbara has some decent clothes. She can't go around looking like that. People won't like it.'

Barbara said, 'I guess they'll just have to get used to it, Great-aunt Priscilla. I'm not going to go round in tweeds and a London Fog for anyone.'

Freya wondered what a London Fog was and Barbara, seeing her incomprehension said, 'I think it's what you call a mackintosh. And those horrible wellington boots? No, thank you. If it's wet and muddy I'll stay in and read.'

Freya was impressed by the way the two girls were standing up to their great-aunt, but they looked as though they'd had enough of her.

Polly said to Gus, 'Can we go now?'

'Yes, be off with you,' Lady Priscilla said. 'I want a few more words with your father and then I'm going.'

After the door closed behind them she said to Gus, 'Nice girls, we can make something of them. Your cousin Helena, my oldest girl, is bringing out her daughter Alice next season. She can bring Barbara out as well.'

Gus said, 'I believe . . . My intention is that Barbara will go to college. Her mother was at Wellesley and—'

'If she wants to go to university she can do that after she's done the Season. Quite a few girls do that these days. It's a complete waste of time and money of course, because they just get married in the end. Meanwhile, I'll speak to Mother Joseph at St Ursula's about Polly. They'll get rid of that American accent in no time. And she needs to do something about those spectacles. A good man will find her a more becoming pair. I'll give you the name of the ophthalmologist in London that Sir Archibald goes to.'

Lady Priscilla was making for the door. 'Thank you, Gus, no need to show me out I know my well way well enough. Goodbye, Freya.'

The two cousins looked at one another. Gus sank back into a chair. 'Do I have any more relatives who are as overpowering is that?'

Freya said, 'She can be difficult, but her heart's in the right place.'

Gus said, 'Will she and her family be joining us here at the Castle for Christmas?'

Freya laughed. 'Don't worry, no. She'll have a horde of her own family at Veryan House. I expect there'll have to be some visiting but you shan't have to entertain them for all of Christmas. Which is just as well, if we have to look after Sonia and her guests.'

Gus said, 'I shall have to find a school for Polly. Would you know about this convent, St Ursula's? Did you go there?'

Freya said, 'No. Sonia did, but—'

Gus said, a twinkle in his eye, 'But? I don't have a long acquaintance with my half-sister, but I can imagine that she would have been a handful for even the most resolute of nuns.'

'She did get into a lot of trouble one way and another.'

Gus said, 'Was she expelled?'

Freya said, 'It was phrased more tactfully than that. Just that the nuns felt that perhaps it wasn't the right establishment for her. In fact, it was clear that no establishment would be suitable for Sonia and so she had a governess after that.'

'I wonder if Polly would be happy in an English boarding school. If St Ursula's is prim and proper, very English, she might feel uncomfortable there. Where did you go to school?'

'I was sent to a boarding school in the north of England. A bleak establishment and I can't say I liked it. Georgia was there, too, before she came to Selchester. She hated it.'

Gus said, 'Georgia seems a young lady with strong opinions.'

Freya decided to be direct. 'You mean the hostility she's show-ing to Polly. It'll pass. She feels unsettled, it's not been an easy time for her.'

Gus said, 'I didn't like to ask Hugo. He's her brother, but much older than she is. Are there any other brothers and sisters? What about their parents?'

'Their parents died in the war. Georgia didn't have a very good time of it. She was in London with her mother and their house was hit by a V2 bomb. She was hauled out of the rubble alive, but her mother wasn't.'

'What a terrible thing. Poor child. And so she has no one left but Hugo?'

'There's an aunt, who looked after her, only she got married and went off to America. Hugo had a job that took him abroad, but when he injured his leg last year, he took up a position at Thorn Hall here in Selchester. Georgia goes to the Girl's High School here.'

'Priscilla was talking about Babs being a debutante. I can't see it.'

Freya said, 'Priscilla thinks like that. It's not a bad way to get to know people if you're sociable, and if you like dancing and going to parties, it's quite fun.'

'Did you do this Season? And Sonia?'

Freya said, 'Neither of us did. The war came. I didn't mind, it was never what I wanted to do, but Sonia was furious. You'd have thought Hitler had started the war with the sole intention of pre-venting her from being a deb.'

'What do you want to do, Freya?'

'Don't you come all head of the family with me, Gus.' She spoke lightly, but meant to warn him off. 'I want to do what I do now, which is writing and helping out at the bookshop in town from time to time.'

'Ah, the family history. I assume you have a private income?'

If he knew how little that was after tax, he'd know it wasn't enough to keep her clothed and fed and Magnus in fish. But she wasn't about to tell him how she really made her living. The exploits and adventures of Rosina Wyndham's lively heroine, Clarissa de Witt, were best kept between herself and the page.

'I manage. Now, you'll have to have a quick lunch if you're to get to the estate office for your appointment with Mr Jonquil.'

Chapter Four

Scene 1

The train was already in, the big locomotive letting out hisses of steam as the driver hung out of his cabin to speak to the guard. Hugo's tall, lean uncle was standing at the ticket barrier talking to Mr Godley, the station-master.

Hugo was amused. Mr Godley had strong views on gentlemen in Roman collars, but he also knew that he would be treating Father Leo Hawksworth with the respect due to visitors to the Castle. Mr Godley still regretted the glory days before the war. When GWR didn't really stand for Great Western Railway, but God's Wonderful Railway. In those days, weekend after weekend, trains had brought visitors for the Castle. They would alight with their luggage and their servants, to be carried off in cars to the Castle.

As usual, Leo Hawksworth was travelling light and had a single suitcase with him. The station's only porter, Bill, eyed it gloomily, knowing his services wouldn't be needed.

Hugo got out of the car and limped round to the passenger side as his uncle came towards him. Leo adored fast cars and loved driving

Hugo's Talbot Lago, which he did at every opportunity. Hugo shook hands with his uncle, took his suitcase and put it into the boot.

Bill watched the car reverse and drive off, saying morosely to Mr Godley that it was just like a religious gent to be too mean to want a porter. Bill was a staunch member of the Union: he wanted everything to be nationalised that already wasn't; thought all churches should be pulled down; and held that those who didn't work on the railways were useless wastrels and a drain on society.

'Come the revolution there won't be no gents in peculiar collars driving away in fast cars or going to any castles.'

'Come the revolution, you'll be in one of Joe Stalin's camps.'

During the war, Mr Godley had had to put up with the indignity of having female porters, but thank goodness those days were over. Although, as he looked with a jaundiced eye on old Bill, he thought perhaps the girls had been an improvement.

Scene 2

Leo slowed down as they came to the main street. He said, 'Are we going straight to the Castle?'

Hugo said, 'Yes.'

'Has Selchester already arrived?'

'He came yesterday with his two daughters,' Hugo said. 'I gather you already met him, in Oxford.'

'Yes.'

Hugo was quick to pick up hesitation in his uncle's voice 'Don't you like him?'

Leo said, 'Indeed I do. He's a most likeable man and a fine scholar. How he'll cope with being Earl of Selchester I don't know, but he's capable and he'll learn. No, there was an incident in Oxford that slightly disturbed me, that's all. He has come into his inheritance in unusual circumstances, and perhaps there are those who haven't welcomed the reappearance of an heir.'

Hugo glanced at his uncle. 'Incident? Involving Gus?' He didn't like the sound of that.

'Yes. He wasn't harmed.'

'So what happened?'

'A car mounted the pavement and would have hit him if a passer-by hadn't pulled him back.'

'Did the driver stop?'

'No, he apparently drove off at high speed. I heard about it when I dined in college that evening. I sat next to Professor Firkin, the passer-by who rescued Lord Selchester. Firkin's no youngster, but was obviously quick on the uptake. He was still most indignant about what happened. He dislikes all cars in general and those in Oxford in particular. I think he believes that all drivers, once they get behind the wheel, are potentially going to commit some hit-and-run atrocity. However, he's an astute man and even in the flurry of saving Lord Selchester, he noticed the number plate of the car. He'd rung the police to tell them and they'd got back to him to say it was a false number plate. They think the driver must have been involved in some criminal activity, which was why he didn't stop.'

They had driven through the town, passing from the stately Victorian houses near the station, to the elegance of Georgian terraces, to the heart of the town with its higgledy-piggledly mediaeval streets in mellowed stone, and had reached the bridge. Leo took it at a rush before braking to turn into the Castle gates.

'Odd,' said Hugo. 'But it must have been an accident. Who would want to kill Gus? Sonia wouldn't mourn for him, but she's hardly driving cars at him. She'll be here for Christmas, by the way, but not arriving until tomorrow.'

'I dare say Lady Sonia hasn't taken kindly to being disinherited, although I imagine she hasn't been left penniless.'

'When they drop the H-bomb and the world ends, the one person left alive and sitting on a pile of money will be Sonia. She was very well off anyway, as you know, and she inherited money from her father.'

Leo said dryly, 'No doubt, but nothing compared to what the Castle and land are worth. Selchester was one of the lucky ones. All that time during the thirties when so many families were selling off the everything from the family silver to the houses, he got richer and richer.'

'By all accounts, he was a very shrewd man. And he left the estate in good condition and it's been well looked after since he vanished.'

'How is Georgia taking the new regime?'

'Badly. She doesn't want to move out of the Castle, although she knew we'd have to at some point. She seems to have taken the younger Selchester girl in aversion.'

Hugo couldn't altogether blame his sister. It wasn't Polly Fitzwarin she disliked, but Polly the Usurper. The blame lay with him, unable to provide a home for Georgia. And she needed stability; a pity, in a way, they'd ever ended up at the Castle. She'd been there long enough to feel at home. It was worse for Freya, of course; it really was her home she was going to have to leave.

Leo said cheerfully, 'Oh, it was inevitable that Georgia would resent the newcomer. Don't worry about it. Either they'll go on hating one another, in which case when Georgia moves out of the Castle she won't see anything of her, or they'll become close friends. Either way, there's nothing you can do about it.'

Hugo said, 'I'm sure you're right, but a little civility wouldn't come amiss.'

'What are your plans for after Christmas? Have you found anywhere to live?'

'No. There was some talk that the present occupants of Nightingale Cottage might be moving out, but I've come to think that that's wishful thinking.'

'Why?'

Hugo said, 'I've never met them; they don't really seem to play much part in town life. They aren't natives of Selchester, but then of course a lot of people aren't. They reputedly practise witchcraft.'

'Witchcraft?'

'No need to get alarmed, your help won't be needed in that line. Selchester has its share of witchy history, but I think they're in fact some breed of folklorists. They tend to stop farm labourers and ask them questions about ancient customs and rituals. I gather some of the more waggish elements amuse themselves spinning the couple strange tales.'

'How's work?' Leo was taking the climb up to the Castle slowly, mindful of the bumpy road and the sheep that were grazing on the land to either side.

Hugo watched the patterns made by the powerful headlamps, and then said, 'Interesting, at the moment. I'm burrowing into the past, into things that happened before the war. In case they reveal truths about the present.'

Leo was one of the few people outside the Service that Hugo could speak to about his work. Leo was a priest scientist, a physicist who had been engaged in highly secret war work during the war. He would have the Official Secrets Act engraved on his heart.

'The battlefield on which the Cold War is being fought and the aftermath of the Burgess and Maclean affair,' Leo said. 'Inevitable, of course, even though thankfully we aren't quite as paranoid as they seem to be on the other side of the Atlantic.'

'No, I can't see a McCarthy getting that kind of a hold over here.'

'And what about the bureaucracy, now you have a desk job?'

'I ignore it whenever I can.' That was something that had rarely troubled him when he'd been an agent working in dangerous places abroad, living on his wits, answerable to no one when on a mission. He'd relished the work, which had ended the day someone from the other side put a bullet in his leg on a dark night in Berlin.

'What you're doing now is, I suppose, a kind of detective work. You'll be good at that. You have an analytic mind plus intuition and you like solving problems. As you showed when you tracked down the late Lord Selchester's murderer.'

'That was hardly a single-handed effort. Team work; Freya and you and Georgia contributed as much as I did.'

They were driving through the archway to the Castle now, and Leo swung the car left to go towards the stables. Hugo said, 'For those first months I was at the Hall, Selchester's murder and the investigation meant that I had plenty to keep me occupied. One can hardly expect another murder.'

Leo said, 'I sincerely hope not.'

Scene 3

That night, a cold and frosty night, the silence of the Castle's ancient walls was rent by a piercing scream. This was followed by more screams; sounds of pure terror and panic. Hugo, woken from a deep sleep, reached for the gun that he no longer had. He leapt out of bed, landing awkwardly on his leg, which gave an excruciating stab of pain. He was hurtling out of the door even as he struggled into his dressing gown. Where was the noise coming from? At first he'd thought it was Georgia, but when he looked into her room, she was fast asleep. He limped along the corridor, down some stairs and then up another flight to reach the corridor where Babs and Polly had their bedrooms.

The screams were coming from Polly's room.

Hugo arrived at the same time as Freya and Gus. Leo, clad in a Jaeger dressing gown, was hard on their heels. Hugo flung the door open and went in. There was Polly, huddled in the bed, clutching a pillow, her hair wild about her. She was no longer screaming but giving out great gasping sobs.

Freya pushed past and went towards Polly, but she shrank back, holding her arms up to protect herself, shrieking. 'Don't come near me, don't come near me.'

It was Babs who saved the situation. She arrived in a long purple dressing gown, sailed into the room, took one look and told them all to stand back. She sat down on the bed and said, 'Pull yourself together. There's nothing to be afraid of and no need to cry. Stop it at once or I'll slap you.'

Polly made a gulping noise and flung herself into Babs's arms, clinging round her sister's neck, her body shivering and rigid.

Mrs Partridge had arrived, her hair in curlers and waving a broomstick – to ward off intruders, she said afterwards – and after one look at Polly, said she'd go downstairs to heat up some milk and fill a hot-water bottle.

Polly's tale was at first incoherent, but it finally came out that she'd woken 'quite suddenly, like someone had pinched me', and there, standing at the foot of her bed was the figure of a man drenched in blood. 'The room had gone all cold. It was my grandfather come back. He'd come to tell me Pops is going to die like he did. It's what happens, the head of the house comes as a death warning to his heir.'

She began to shudder again, and Babs held her more tightly. 'You had a nightmare, Polly, that's all.'

Gus said, worried, 'She's never had a nightmare before, not like this.'

'She's never stayed in a place like this before,' Babs said.

Scene 4

'I wonder what put such an idea into her head?' Freya said, when she, Leo and Hugo went down to the kitchen to have a nocturnal cup of tea. 'There are supposed to be ghosts here at the Castle. Sonia used to see them, and of course there was that maid, Hattie, who was so frightened by them. But I never heard anything like this "head of the house coming back". It's nonsense.'

'Georgia,' Leo said. 'It's the kind of thing you find in ghost stories, and so she made up a tale and told it to Polly to scare her.'

Hugo said, 'I wouldn't have thought Polly was the sort to be easily scared. She seems a most rational young lady. She has a precise mind and a passion for facts.'

'Perhaps, like Sonia, she's one of the Selchesters that does feel the place is haunted.'

'That kind of rationality can be protective. Georgia's imagination is there for all to see. Polly's may be even more vivid, and therefore alarming and best suppressed. But none of us can control our dreams,' Leo said.

'Or nightmares,' Hugo said. 'All rather Freudian for you, Leo.'

'Freud may have written all kinds of nonsense, but he had a healthy respect for the unconscious and how we fear ourselves.'

Freya, frowning, said, 'Perhaps we shouldn't have put Polly in the Blue Room. Sonia's always claimed it's haunted, although I can't remember who by. Certainly not a blood-soaked grandfather.'

Mrs Partridge came in to shoo them out of the kitchen. 'Time you were all back in bed. Lady Babs has taken Polly off into her room. There are two beds in there, much the best place for her to be. And let's have no more talk of ghosts, Miss Freya. Leave that to Lady Sonia.'

Scene 5

Georgia came flying down the main staircase, two steps at a time, leaping the final four steps in one go. She landed lightly at the bottom to find herself at her Uncle Leo's feet.

'Good morning, Georgia. No banisters to slide down?'

Georgia said, 'The banisters here are too wide, I've tried but it's not very comfortable. The back stairs are all right, but there isn't quite the sweep there is here. People who build these things don't think about that.'

Leo said, 'You're up very early.'

Georgia said airily, 'Oh, I woke up early and I was hungry, so I thought I'd come down to the kitchen and make myself some toast.'

Leo said, 'Mrs Partridge said she's going to bring my egg into the dining room.'

Georgia pulled a face. 'It's much better having breakfast in the kitchen, but of course with the new Earl and his family we have to do anything everything properly. It's not really fair on Mrs Partridge.'

Leo led the way into the dining room and said, 'I think Mrs Partridge is quite enjoying having a full house.'

'Her niece Pam is coming up to help later on today. And I'm helping, too.'

Leo inspected the dishes laid out under silver covers on the sideboard, helped himself to eggs and bacon and fed a slice of bread into the toaster. 'Are you? I'm glad to hear it.'

The toast pinged up and he handed a piece to Georgia. She sat down, spread it liberally with butter, dug a silver spoon into the marmalade and dropped a blob on to her plate.

'Did you sleep through the disturbance in the night?'

Georgia looked at him with an innocent face. 'What disturbance? I'm a very sound sleeper.'

'Polly had a nightmare. She thought she saw a ghost. She thought it was the ghost of a past Earl of Selchester come to foretell the death of the new Earl. Since the new Earl is her father, she was naturally rather upset. I think imagining a figure dripping with blood didn't help.'

Georgia attended to her toast. 'I expect the Castle is getting to her. She doesn't like it, and so I suppose she imagines all sorts of things.'

'I gather you don't feel very friendly towards Polly?'

Georgia looked at him suspiciously. 'Are you going to go all pi on me, Uncle Leo? Why should I like her? She doesn't like me, she thinks I'm a horrible English girl.'

'And you think she's a horrible American girl.'

Georgia considered. 'I don't think she's horrible. I just wish she weren't here. I wish she was still in America, which is where she ought to be.'

Mrs Partridge came in with Leo's egg. He thanked her, set it down on the table, pulled out a chair and gave the egg a neat tap with his spoon. 'I expect she finds it strange here.'

Georgia said, 'I expect she does. She doesn't understand about old things. She doesn't like the Castle, she told me so.'

'And you do like it?'

Georgia nodded vigorously and reached out for another piece of toast. 'I love it here. I like the fact that it's all cold stones and old and full of history. You can imagine all sorts of things happening here. Besides—' There was a long pause.

'Besides?'

'Besides, it's my home. Now they've come, Hugo, and I won't be able to stay here anymore.'

'You knew you were just lodging here. It was always a temporary arrangement.'

Georgia said, 'People sometimes lodge in a place for ages. I know Lady Sonia was going to sell the Castle, but it would have taken a while. We would have at least had a few more months here and then maybe we could have found somewhere else to live in Selchester.'

'I gather from Hugo that you haven't found anywhere else to live?'

Georgia said, 'No. Nor has Freya. She'll hate to leave, even more than me. She loves being in her tower. She says she might take a room in Eileen's bed and breakfast. Eileen is Mrs Partridge's sister. But living in rooms in a bed and breakfast isn't home, is it?'

Her uncle agreed. Georgia said, in a sudden rush of confidence, 'If we can't find anywhere to live, Hugo might decide that he wants to go back to London and get a job there. I've said I wouldn't go with him, but of course I'd have to, because I've nowhere else to go.'

Her uncle looked at her, consideringly. 'It's hard not having a home. Unfortunately, with the housing shortage since the war, it's the lot of many people. But, you know, being with Hugo is a kind of security in itself. You could say that where Hugo is—'

Georgia interrupted her uncle with an impatient shake of her head. 'If you're about to say where Hugo is, is home, that's not actually true. One of these days he's going to marry someone, and then what happens to home.'

Leo said, 'You'll live with Hugo, just as you do now. I'm sure anyone he marries will be glad to have you as part of the family.'

Georgia said, almost rudely, 'That shows how little you know about it. If anyone marries Hugo it'll be that Valerie, and she can't stand me. The first thing she'd do is make Hugo pack me off back to boarding school. She's always going on to Hugo about that.'

Leo said, 'I haven't met the young lady.'

'You haven't missed anything. Oh she's frightfully pretty and smart, and all over Hugo. But I sense an insincere nature. She's set her cap at Hugo and she'll get him to the altar through sheer determination and persistence. In her eyes I'm a big nuisance and

I expect she wishes I'd gone to America to live with Aunt Claire. I don't matter to her. She wanted Hugo to spend Christmas with her and her family, never mind me. And Hugo said he couldn't, because of me. But if it weren't for me that's where he'd be right now.'

Leo said, 'Don't get into the habit of self-pity, Georgia, it's not good for you. If Hugo really had wanted to spend Christmas with this Valerie, he would have done so. Don't you have a friend you could have spent Christmas with?'

'Well, yes,' Georgia said reluctantly. 'My friend Daisy said I could go there. Mr and Mrs Dillon asked me. Daisy said she'd have liked that.'

'And would you have liked that?'

'No.' Georgia had lost interest in her toast. 'I like the Dillons, but I wanted to spend Christmas here in the Castle.'

'And that's exactly what you and Hugo are doing. I can't see that Lord Selchester is going to be in any hurry to turn you out. He seems to be an extremely kind man.'

'Oh he's perfect, Polly's perfect, Babs is perfect. Well, maybe not, with all those gloomy noir thoughts.'

Leo said, 'Where do you think Polly picked up that idea of the ghost?'

Georgia shot him a glance. 'What did she say about it? Where did she say she'd heard about him? She's always reading history and stuff, I think she knows more about the Castle than even Freya does.'

'Her father asked that very question, and she said she hadn't heard it from anyone, it must just have been a bad dream.'

Georgia was silent.

Leo said, 'You told her about that ghost, didn't you, Georgia?'

Georgia said, 'Maybe. She asked if the Castle was haunted and she wanted to see where Lord Selchester died. So I showed her. And she wanted to know how he died and so I told her.'

'How much do you know about how he died?'

'I don't know exactly, because you were all mean and wouldn't tell me. But I know he was stabbed, and there was a lot of blood.'

'So you invented a story of how his ghost haunts and told it to Polly, no doubt in graphic detail, for I will say, Georgia, that you have a way with words. It acted upon her imagination and the result was that she woke screaming in the night, a very frightened person.'

Georgia said sulkily, 'It's not my fault. If she's got an overactive imagination, that's her problem.' She got up and took her plate to the tray on the sideboard. 'Don't look at me like that. In a moment you'll be praying for me, and I don't need that, thank you.'

'I wasn't aware I was looking at you in any particular way. Just think for a moment. You talk about Polly's imagination. What about your imagination? What about those science fiction stories you like reading? If you were writing one of those, how would you write about an alien arriving on a strange planet where everyone was hostile?'

That earned him another suspicious look. Then she said, grudgingly, 'You're trying to say that Polly coming here is like an alien landing on another planet.'

'I expect it is. It's another country, a foreign country for her. We may share a language, but in many ways we're very different. To Americans we must seem very poor and backward. She's come from a different world, from an American university town to an English country town. It's quite a change and the Castle would be a shock for anyone. She's never set foot in such a place and now it's her home. She's had to leave her school, her friends, her country and come to a place that is utterly strange.'

'I suppose you're saying I'm like an inhabitant of the strange planet, not welcoming her.'

He said, 'You haven't exactly been welcoming, have you?'

'I suppose not. But she's such a know-all.'

'You know quite a lot yourself. You certainly know about living in this country and in Selchester, which she doesn't.'

There was another long silence and then Georgia said, 'She didn't say that I told her about the ghost?'

Leo said, 'No. I could tell looking at her that somebody had told her. But she didn't say anything to her father or to her sister. And I don't think she will.'

Georgia said, 'At least she isn't a sneak.'

Leo said, 'Have you done all your Christmas shopping?'

'Why are you changing the subject?'

'I was wondering whether you had bought a present for your new host and his family.'

'No,' Georgia said. 'I don't have any money left.'

'I always send you ten shillings at Christmas, as you know. I have a present for you as well this year. Would you like me to give you the ten shillings now, so that you can do some Christmas shopping?'

Georgia's face lit up. 'I would like that, yes, because there's a book I'd like to get Hugo which I haven't been able to.' Then she saw Uncle Leo's face. 'You think I ought to get a present for Polly.'

'Can you think of anything she'd like?'

Georgia thought about that. 'There was a little china goat that she was looking at in the shop. I could see she liked it. Or I could get her a goose. They have a lot of geese on sale here in Selchester, on account of St Werberga and that story of the goose. She was intrigued by that story. But of course she believes in saints and miracles and things, despite the way she goes on about liking facts. I wish people could bring geese back to life, but I can't see it actually happening.'

'Mediaeval saints like Werberga do stretch one's credulity.'

Georgia said, 'All right. I suppose I have been rather beastly to her, and it isn't really her fault that she's landed up at the Castle. I just wish she liked it more. Why can't she appreciate it, instead of hating it? It wouldn't be so bad then.'

Leo finished his egg and laid down his spoon. 'We can't have other people the way we want them, Georgia.'

'No,' she muttered, 'but we can wish some of them weren't here.'

Chapter Five

Scene 1

Gus had an appointment with his land agent and the steward. Freya, feeling that he ought to show his face in the town, decided to make him jump in at the deep end and said that she would meet him in the Daffodil Tearooms at eleven o'clock.

Freya and Polly walked down into Selchester together. Polly was quite silent, although Freya tried to draw her out, asking her about the voyage and about her life in school in America.

Polly surprised her by saying, almost primly, 'I don't think I want to talk about that, thank you. Because it's all finished hasn't it? I won't ever go back there, not that I mind about the school because it wasn't particularly nice. But I did have some friends.'

'You'll make new friends. And living in Selchester won't be all bad.'

'Won't it?' She looked around. 'It's kind of quaint.'

'This is the High Street and up there is Snake Alley, which is where the Daffodil Tearooms are. I can see your father's car over there on the Green. Oh, and Babs is with him.'

'She came into town earlier,' Polly said. She called out to her father, 'Hey, Pops, we're over here.'

Gus joined them; Freya thought he had a harassed look on his face. 'Tough morning?' she asked.

He nodded. 'It's going to take me a good while to get the hang of all this. I suppose I can trust them. If they wanted to give me the run around and have their hands deep in my pockets I reckon at the moment there's not much I could do about it.'

Freya could reassure him on that point. 'You're all right with those two. I've known them all my life. My uncle trusted them and he was a good judge of character, so don't worry. There are cheats and rogues in Selchester the same as everywhere else, but those two aren't among them.'

The Earl looked relieved. 'I'm glad to hear that.'

They had reached the Daffodil Tearooms and Gus looked up at the swinging sign depicting a flourish of daffodils planted in a blue-and-white teapot.

He said, 'I guess this is the hub of the town? The place everyone comes to pick up the news and pass it on?'

Freya was amused. 'Got it in one.'

He smiled. 'We live now in Cambridge – Cambridge, Massachusetts – because I've been teaching at the university. But I grew up in a small town and I guess folk are the same whichever country they're in.'

Jamie and Richard, who ran the tearooms, were thrilled to see the little party come in. Jamie bounded over to them, emitting little squeaks of pleasure. Richard darted out from the kitchen when he heard the hubbub, wiped a floury hand on his long white chef's apron and extended it to greet Gus with less ebullient enthusiasm.

Jamie took them to a corner table, pulled the chairs back and flicked the surface of the immaculate tablecloth. 'Is Freya taking you on a tour of Selchester? I hope she's going to take you to the museum, I heard you know all about the Romans and you were picking up pieces of Roman pottery while you were out walking with Mr Jonquil.'

Gus looked startled; Freya's lips twitched.

'Go today, because it will be closed tomorrow and then not open again until after the New Year. Mrs Morrison has to have some time off, and I'm sure you'll be fascinated by Selchester's past.'

'I'll do that, if it's all right with you, Freya? Will we have time?'

'Yes. It isn't a big museum; it won't take long to see what's there. I'd just like to call in at the bookshop and then we can go on. It's quite close.'

A man in a trench coat, who'd been sitting by the door, got up. He pulled his trilby low over his eyes, laid a couple of coins on the table and left.

'Not even a thank you or a goodbye; what manners,' Jamie said. 'Now, what can I get you? I know what you'll want Freya. And, Lady Barbara, isn't it?'

Babs was slouched in her chair, a sketchbook on her knee and a pencil in her hand, seemingly oblivious to her surroundings. 'Nothing for me,' she said, without looking up.

Jamie gave a sniff of disapproval. 'What about this young lady? You must be Lady Pauline.'

Polly looked at him seriously for a little while and then her face broke into a smile, the same rather sweet smile that her father had. Her eyes danced behind the big glasses. 'Doesn't it sound silly? My name is really Polly.'

Jamie said, equally serious, 'Then you're Lady Polly. I like that. Would you like some orangeade?'

Polly said, 'What I'd really like is a milkshake but I don't think you have them over here. My cousin said you don't have the same sort of things that we do and you don't have drug stores and ice cream sodas and things?'

Jamie said, 'We don't, but Richard can rustle up a tasty milk-shake. Chocolate?'

That settled, Jamie went off and came back with a plate on which resided some of Richard's famous cakes.

Gus looked taken aback. 'At this time of the morning? I only just finished having breakfast.'

Freya whispered to him, 'You have to eat at least one, otherwise they'll be offended.'

The door bells tinkled to announce another arrival. Babs looked up, and stared, her pencil poised above her notebook. 'Isn't that Vivian Witt, the film star?'

Freya swung round. 'It is.' She waved, gesturing to Vivian to join them. The actress came over, kissed Freya and was introduced to Gus and his family. She looked Gus up and down and said, 'You're very like your father. No, thank you, Freya, I won't intrude. I'm waiting for a friend.'

Gus watched her as she sat down at a table by the wall, and said, 'She's as lovely in person as she is in her movies. Am I mistaken, or was there a chilliness about her?'

'You'll have to forgive her,' Freya said. 'I dare say she was startled to see the resemblance between you and your father. They didn't—' she hesitated. 'They didn't get on too well. But once she gets to know you, she'll be fine.'

'Does she live here?' Babs said.

'She has a cottage here as well as a flat in London.'

Polly stretched out a hand for a cake. 'I suppose she gets away from her admirers here, it must be awful being a film star and everyone recognising you.'

Jamie was back with a pot of coffee and a gleam in his eye as he began his interrogation of Gus.

'So, you're Lord Selchester, the eighteenth Earl, isn't it amazing, when we all thought there'd be no more Earls? What do you think of the Castle? How are you settling in? It's such an excitement for all of us here to have a new Earl and an American one at that. But you're so like the late Lord Selchester, we'd have known you anywhere.'

Gus took it all in good part, and also seemed to stand up to the curious stares of the people who had come into the Daffodil for their morning coffee. Freya could tell from the whispering and the glances that they all knew who he was. They were fascinated and the minute he left, they'd all be discussing him.

She said, 'You have to get used to the fact that you can't breathe here in Selchester without the entire town hearing about it.'

That caused a wry smile. 'Just the way it is back home. Only we were never anyone particular. Not what you might call the cynosure of neighbouring eyes. Here I guess a new Earl rates quite highly on the interest charts.'

'Yes, people will follow your every move until they get used to you. I wouldn't be surprised to see a welcome committee waiting for you at the museum.'

He looked alarmed. 'I hope not.'

'Only joking, but everyone in the town will know everything you've done by the time you're heading back to the Castle.'

Scene 2

Babs didn't want to go to the museum. 'I guess I'll just wander around for a while.'

Freya took the others across the road, saying, 'This is our book-shop. You'll like it, Polly. It's run by Dinah Lindsey, who's an old friend of the family.'

She pushed open the door and led the way in. Dinah, who was dusting the books on one of the shelves nearest the ceiling, looked down from her ladder at the group below. She jumped lightly down, tucked the feather duster into an umbrella stand, and held out her hand.

Introductions, and then the Earl looked round appreciatively. 'This is exactly how a bookshop should look.'

Polly sniffed the air. 'I love the smell of books.'

Dinah said to her, 'I don't know what you like reading, but feel free to browse.' She turned to Gus. 'It's a privilege to meet you. You'll find copies of some of your books on the shelves here, and Selchester School uses your translation of the *Odyssey*.'

Gus said, 'Selchester School? Is that where you go, Georgia?'

'No, I go to the Girls' High. Selchester School is a boys' public school. Only public doesn't mean what you think it does, it means it's a private school where you pay hefty fees.'

Polly tugged at her father's sleeve. 'Can I have some of my allowance, Pops?'

'Sure, honey, you want to buy some books?'

Polly said, 'Not exactly at this minute. I think I'll come back later.'

Dinah said, 'We're open until half past five today. The run up to Christmas is our busiest time.'

As if on cue, the door opened and two or three more customers came in.

As Freya, Gus and Polly left the shop, he said to Freya, 'Could we call in at the museum right now? Or do you have any particular plans?'

The museum was a two-storey redbrick building with a grand stone entrance and 'Museum' carved in curly letters above it. Freya had loved it as a child, but she hadn't been there for quite a while.

As they went in, the familiar smell of dusty old things mingled with floor polish greeted her: some things never changed.

An elderly woman with a pince-nez and a shawl draped over her shoulders was sitting at a desk inside the entrance. She greeted

Freya with a little snort of delight and came forward with a smile. Her voice was high and thin and precise. 'Well, well, Miss Wryton. We haven't seen you in here for a good long while.'

'Hello, Mrs Morrison. How are you? This is the new Lord Selchester, and he'd like to look around.'

Mrs Morrison had been acquainted with two previous Earls and wasn't the least flustered by meeting another one. She said, 'Of course, you're Mr Augustine Mason. I saw the review of your translation of the Georgics in the *Journal of Vergilian Studies*. I look forward to reading it when it's published in England.'

The Earl seemed surprised but, Freya thought, pleased. Writers always were when it turned out that they met someone who had read one of their books. A pleasure denied her, but then she wasn't a scholar poet like Gus, whose publications were eminently respectable.

Mrs Morrison was apologetic. 'I'm afraid everything is a little disorganised. Some schoolchildren were in here yesterday. It was a treat before they break up for the holidays, and we haven't really put things straight since then. Mr Hetherington came over from Yarnley to give them a talk and demonstrate some of the weapons.'

She gestured towards a wide room lined with suits of armour, swords and halberds. Rifles from the time of the Crimean War and eighteenth-century blunderbusses hung on the wall alongside a battle-axe and mace.

Gus's eyebrows rose. 'This is quite a fine collection.'

Mrs Morrison said, 'It was a gift to us, from the old squire at Thorn Hall before it was sold. Weapons were rather a hobby of his, and he gathered quite a collection. Arranged, as you can see, chronologically from the more modern ones right back to a longbow supposed to have been used at Agincourt. There's also what is thought to be a Roman sword, but that's in the Lindsey Room.'

'What's happened to the crossbow, Mrs Morrison?' Freya asked. 'I always liked that.'

'It's up in the gallery together with a modern one Mr Hetherington brought with him. He took the children out to the field behind the museum and fired the crossbow for them.'

Gus said, 'Quite a lethal weapon.' As he spoke, he turned and bent over to read a label beside a suit of armour.

A whistling sound, and then a loud bang as something struck the armour. Gus jumped back as the suit of armour toppled forward, striking the ground with a metallic clatter.

Mrs Morrison gave a faint scream and Polly, dragging at her father's arm, pointed a horrified finger towards the crossbow bolt lying on the floor.

Hugo and Gus sprang into action. Gus's concern was for Polly and he swept her up and out of the door into the next room in a flash. Just as quickly, Hugo, his leg forgotten, hurled himself towards the stairs and hauled himself up to the gallery that ran across the upper part of the exhibition room.

No one there. Propped in a corner was a crossbow. One glance told Hugo that no one could have fired it. But lying on its side, with part of it thrust through the railing, was another crossbow. Hugo dropped awkwardly on to one knee and examined it. It was a modern replica, in perfect condition.

He got to his feet and limped along to the door at one end of the gallery. Leaning over the railing, he called down to a still flustered Mrs Morrison. 'What's behind this door?'

Mrs Morrison looked up at him and said in a voice that was at first unsteady and then became firmer: 'That's one of the storerooms. Where items that aren't good enough to put on show or need work are stored.'

'Is there any other way someone could get into the gallery other than up the stairs?'

Mrs Morrison looked doubtful. 'There's a window at the back of the gallery on the other side. I suppose somebody could climb in that way. But does it look as though anyone has?'

Hugo went to see. The window wasn't locked, and he pushed the casement open and looked out. A stout drainpipe, and a magnolia espaliered against the wall. Easy enough for someone to shin up and climb through the window. Provided they didn't have a gammy leg: his calf was throbbing after his own efforts.

He came back, picked up the modern crossbow with a handkerchief round his hand and propped it in the corner beside the other one. Then he went back down the stairs.

Freya was helping Mrs Morrison reassemble the suit of armour and she said, 'Anything there?'

He said, reassuringly if untruthfully, 'I think the crossbow must accidentally have been left loaded. A careless thing to do, but it can happen.'

Mrs Morrison was shaking her head. 'Mr Hetherington is the most careful man imaginable. He left that crossbow here because he didn't have room in his car to take all the weapons that he brought in one journey. He's coming back for it later. I can't think why he would have left it loaded with a bolt.'

Gus frowned. 'It sounds an exceptionally careless thing for anybody to do.'

Polly said, 'But why did it go off now? If it had been left like that since yesterday, what made it fire the bolt? Crossbows don't fire themselves.'

Hugo said, 'The safety catch wasn't on. We heard a door up there slam; I think it must have jolted the crossbow.'

Mrs Morrison said, 'Oh, that dratted door. It has a loose catch and is always slamming shut.'

Polly was looking relieved at this explanation. 'You mean it wasn't aimed at Pops?'

'It was an accident,' Freya said, 'and luckily no one was hurt. Mrs Morrison, I think you should have a word with Mr Hetherington.'

Polly said, 'That's a second near miss.'

Hugo swung round. 'Second near miss?' He was just about to say, 'Oh, you mean the car on the pavement in Oxford', but Polly went on.

'On the boat coming over somebody slid into Pops and he nearly went over the side. He didn't, though.'

Gus smiled down at her. 'That's the kind of thing that could happen to anyone. I wasn't in any real danger. A sailor was there to haul me back.'

He thanked Mrs Morrison with grave courtesy. She was composed but had a look of concern in her eyes. He reassured her. 'No harm done, except you might have to get the suit of armour repaired. I don't suppose it's the first dent it's had in its career.' He turned to Polly, and hooked her arm in his. 'You wanted to go back to the bookshop? Let's do that right now.'

Hugo and Freya stood outside the museum as father and daughter headed back to Snake Alley. Freya said, 'Out with it. What happened, do you think?'

Hugo told her about the window. 'Someone was up there and fired the bolt.'

'No slamming door? I didn't think so.'

'Nor did Gus, but Polly didn't need to know that.'

'Was it intended to hit Gus?'

'Oh, I think so. And it isn't the first attempt on his life.'

'The liner?'

'I hadn't heard about that. But it seems that someone had a go at him in Oxford.' He told her what had happened. 'Leo told me about it.'

'Why didn't you tell me?'

'I was going to.'

89

'Now I'm thoroughly alarmed. What else are you keeping from me?'

'Freya, do you know what the exact terms of your uncle's will were? Not all the bequests, but the Castle and land and the money. What happens if Gus meets with a fatal accident? Would everything go to Babs and Polly?'

Freya said, 'Yes, and no. Selchester had set up a trust. The male heir – which everybody of course thought was Tom – had to survive for a year. If not, then the estate reverted to Sonia. That's why there was no question at first about it all going to Sonia, since Tom was dead and no one knew about Gus. Anyhow, it's irrelevant, since Selchester died years ago.'

Hugo said, 'I don't think it is irrelevant. Even though Selchester died in 1947, the death certificate wasn't issued until his body was found last September. I'm no lawyer, but I suspect that trust will run for a year from then, not from 1947. So it would still be valid.'

'You're not suggesting Sonia's trying to kill Selchester? That's ridiculous. She isn't here, she wasn't on the liner, and I doubt if she was in Oxford. She can't have had anything to do with any of that. Unless you think she's been employing hired assassins. Those near accidents that have happened to Gus are just coincidences.'

She fell silent, remembering the night her uncle had died and the tablets that Sonia had asked her to retrieve from Lord Selchester's bedside table. What had been in them? What had Sonia been up to?

Was her cousin capable of murder?

Chapter Six

Scene 1

Oliver Seynton, squashed into the back of Rupert Dauntsey's MG, was cold, uncomfortable and alarmed by Rupert's driving.

Why hadn't he resisted Sonia's invitation for him to go with her to the Castle. The closer they got to Selchester the more he felt it was a mistake to arrive just before Christmas. He wasn't staying for Christmas Day, thank goodness; the mere thought of a family Christmas at Selchester Castle filled him with horror. Even so, the new Earl had only just arrived from America and surely, whatever Sonia said, it wouldn't be the best time to talk to him.

He'd seen Sonia at a cocktail party a few days ago, and when he expressed doubts about descending on the new Lord Selchester, she brushed them aside.

'He needs to look at everything on the inventory,' Sonia had said. 'He'll want advice on what he can best sell to meet the death duties. Isn't that what you people do? What will bring in the most money without breaking up a collection? And you have to get in there before he goes to some other auction house for advice; your superiors aren't going to be too happy if he calls in Christie's or Sotheby's.'

True. 'Why now? Why the urgency?'

'There are some pictures there that belong to me and I want you to look at them and arrange for them to be sold. I don't want them swept up with the rest of his possessions.'

Oliver was confused. 'Everything is in the inventories. In the one the trustees did when your father disappeared and again when I did the inventory for you in the autumn, for valuation.'

'Not quite everything. There are some other paintings. I didn't bother you with them at the time, but now things are different.'

'Were these paintings listed separately in Lord Selchester's will?'

'Do pay attention. They aren't listed anywhere.'

'You're telling me you had pictures stashed away that you didn't tell me about and you didn't show me?'

'Yes. They're mine. My father gave them to me and I stored them in the attics. I don't have room for them in my flat in London.'

Oliver was sure Sonia was lying. 'You're planning to remove them for sale without saying anything about them to the new Earl?'

'It's none of his business.'

Now, on the way to the Castle, Oliver looked at Sonia in the rear-view mirror. She was wrapped in a mink coat and an enormous fur hat meant that little of her face was visible besides her intensely blue eyes.

Watchful Selchester eyes.

Just like her father's. Oliver had only met the late Lord Selchester once, and it had been a meeting he couldn't recall without a shudder. The cold implacability of the man's voice as he laid out in chilling detail what he knew about what Oliver had done in the war.

'I want you to pass on any useful information from the art world. Oh, not sensational sales or undiscovered masterpieces, nothing like that. No, I want to know the kind of things that people want kept hidden. Secrets. Criminal behaviour, even. Shady dealing. Names, dates, essential details. Write to me at Selchester Castle, not my London address or office.'

He didn't doubt for a moment that Oliver would do whatever he wanted. What choice did he have? Then he'd been summoned to the Castle for the weekend, an invitation he couldn't refuse – and was saved by a snowstorm and Selchester's disappearance.

He'd never told Sonia of that encounter.

Sonia snuggled more closely into the seat. 'Really, he's so rich, I shouldn't care what death duties he has to pay. But on the other hand, I have an intense hatred for all these dreadful tax people and the government that thinks it has a right to so much of our money. My father bought those paintings at a time when you could pick up things for a song, and now they're worth a great deal more.'

Oliver's conscience underwent a brief struggle. If they were good paintings, then his commission would be considerable. But did they really belong to Sonia? Or was she making a grab for them?

Sonia went on, 'If they get included in the contents of the house, then that will simply add another great lump of money to the death duties he's already got to pay. Much better if I remove them without bothering about any formalities. Father intended me to have them; that's all that matters. And don't pretend to sudden scruples, please, Oliver. You do private deals all the time.'

'Perhaps the new Earl's already found the paintings.'

'No. I told you. They're in one of the attics. And I have the only key.' Sonia produced a big old-fashioned key and brandished it over her shoulder. 'I feel sure my dear half-brother would do the same in my shoes. He'll soon realise it's his duty to hold on to as much of the property and money as he can. Besides, who knows? Something may happen to him before the nine months are up.'

What was she talking about? Was the new Earl trying to produce an heir? 'What have nine months got to do with anything?'

Sonia said, 'It's my father's will. If anything happens to Gus—'

'Gus?' Oliver said.

'The new Earl. If anything happens to him within twelve months of my father's death then, under a trust that was set up, everything comes to me.'

'Your father died seven years ago,' Oliver said.

'Not legally. Legally, he died when the death certificate was signed, after they found him under the flagstones. Such a blessing Gus didn't have a son, because while a son could inherit under the trust, daughters can't. He could rush to the altar, of course, to try for an heir, but he's been a widower for years. If he wanted to get married again, he'd have done it by now.'

There was satisfaction in her voice, which had taken on the creamy tone it always did with Sonia when she was talking about money.

Rupert, who seemed to be driving with one finger on the wheel, said, 'Thinking of taking out a hit on him, are you?'

Sonia said, 'No, of course not. I do draw the line somewhere. Although I wouldn't be broken-hearted if he met with an untimely death. Nothing painful – merely a convenient accident to take him into the next world sooner rather than later. In fact, during the next few months.'

Rupert said, 'I honour you for your scruples. What has caused this sudden and unexpected rush of morality to the head?'

Sonia said, sounding quite sharp, 'I hardly know him. I've only met him once. So I don't have animosity towards him as a person. I resent him because he's deprived me of my inheritance. Which means that ghastly anachronism of a castle and everything stays in the family instead of it being turned into a hotel, which I longed for; how much my father would have loathed that. Despite that, Gus is family. He's my half-brother. One doesn't murder one's kith and kin, Rupert, darling, however much one is tempted to.'

Rupert said, 'Afraid of what you might have to say in the confessional?'

Sonia said, 'I commit a lot of sins, but I'm not having that kind of sin on my conscience, thank you very much.' She paused, and Oliver could see a faraway look in her eyes. 'There was only one time I wanted to kill someone close to me. And there was a good reason for that. It would have been an act of justice. A man getting his just deserts.'

Rupert said, his voice languid, 'Only you didn't commit the awful deed?'

Sonia said, 'I did not. Perhaps my guardian angel was looking after me. I was too ill to do it at the time when I might have done. But he died soon after and so I don't have that on my conscience.' She took out a compact and inspected her perfect complexion. 'Of course, it's different for you. You must have killed lots of people.'

Oliver was startled, and then he realised that Sonia was talking about Rupert's time during the war.

'Yes, quite a few. It was my duty. There you are, I've broken one of the Ten Commandments over and over. Good thing I'm not a churchgoer.'

Sonia said, 'They're not my commandments. Besides, although we say "Thou shalt not kill", what it actually means is "Thou shalt not murder". Killing your enemy in war doesn't count as murder.'

Rupert said, 'I suppose not. I can't say I felt any remorse. It was a job and I did it.'

Sonia said, 'Do you think killing people in the war means that you would find it easier to kill somebody in civilian life?'

Rupert said, 'Murder?' He fell silent and seemed to be considering the question seriously. 'I suppose we're all capable of committing murder, if driven to it by circumstances. I can see myself killing a man in a fight, perhaps, or in a temper.'

That surprised Oliver. He didn't know Rupert, but he seemed to be the kind of man who was unlikely to lose his temper. He had that air of self-control and superiority peculiar to the English upper classes, which Oliver, despite having learned in the interests of business to get on with them, secretly detested.

Rupert went on, 'I wouldn't commit the kind of murder that's in detective stories, laying a trap in some subtle way so that the police won't find you. It might be interesting as an intellectual exercise, but I don't think I'd care for it. It's somehow rather unmanly, don't you think?'

Sonia shrugged. 'I wouldn't know. Anyhow let's hope the new Earl doesn't have any unfortunate accidents over Christmas while I'm at the Castle. I intend to enjoy myself and make the most of the Selchester wine cellars while I still have access to them. I have to say that much for Selchester: he did buy good champagne.'

Oliver shifted in the back, wishing that he could stretch his legs and fearing that when the car actually stopped he would be unable to climb out of the back. He could see himself having to be hauled out in a most undignified manner. In addition to being curled up in the back, he had Sonia's dressing case jammed in his stomach and Rupert's briefcase squashed under one foot. The boot of the car was small and Sonia's suitcase and Rupert's bag had taken all the space. Oliver had simply brought a small overnight bag, and that was clasped under one elbow.

'Do stop fidgeting, Oliver,' Sonia said. 'You're getting on my nerves.'

Scene 2

Mrs Partridge was in the kitchen, deep in preparations for that night's dinner. Georgia was helping; she had a large apron wrapped round her and was methodically working her way through a big pile of potatoes.

Mrs Partridge paused, and raised a wooden spoon as though commanding silence. 'I can hear a car. That'll be Lady Sonia with the two gentlemen.'

Georgia put her knife down and said, 'I don't like Lady Sonia.'

'None of that in my kitchen,' Mrs Partridge said severely. 'It's not for you to like or not like Lady Sonia. It's by her goodwill that you're here, don't forget that.'

Georgia said, 'It's not her Castle anymore. I only have to be polite to Freya, and that's no trouble because I like Freya. She doesn't look at me like I'm a black beetle, which is what Lady Sonia does.'

Mrs Partridge said, 'More like a spider with those long legs of yours. Put those potatoes down, wash your hands and go and answer the front door.'

Georgia got up from her chair. 'She'll come round the back, I expect.'

'Lady Sonia's not one for back doors.'

In this, Mrs Partridge was mistaken. Sonia had directed Rupert to take his car round to the stable yard. 'It's not like in the good old days with footmen rushing to help. It'll be quicker to use the back entrance. I hope Ben's around to take the luggage.'

Rupert drove the car into the stable yard and stopped with a flourishing squeal of brakes, nearly running into the back of Hugo's Talbot Lago. He got out of the car and waved cheerfully at Hugo. 'Nice car.' He went round to open the door for Sonia.

Hugo said, 'Yes, but not likely to be improved by a bump from your car.'

Rupert laughed. He came forward, extending a hand. 'You must be Hawksworth. I'm Rupert Dauntsey. We met a while ago. Berlin, forty-five. You were something in the hush-hush line.'

Hugo remembered Rupert now. He hadn't liked him then, and he wasn't sure that he was a man he would trust now.

Sonia stood by the MG, hands on hips, while Oliver tried to extricate himself from the back of the car. Rupert went over and extended a long arm to relieve Oliver of some of the boxes and bags encumbering him. He gave him a yank and Oliver unfolded and almost stumbled out of the car.

'Good God, I've lost the use of my limbs. Why don't you have a decent car, Dauntsey, instead of this mousetrap?'

Rupert said cheerfully, 'I never travel in the back, was it uncomfortable? Sorry, old chap.'

Georgia appeared, looking rebellious. 'Hullo, Lady Sonia.' She stared at Rupert and Oliver. 'I suppose you're Mr Dauntsey and Mr Seynton. I'll show you to your rooms, because Mrs Partridge is busy in the kitchen. You'll have to carry your own suitcases, as Ben isn't around.'

'Oliver, take my leather suitcase and don't forget my dressing case.' Sonia gave Georgia an indifferent look. 'Georgina, isn't it? I assume I'm in my usual room.'

'Georgia, actually, and yes, you are. The other two are in the North Passage.'

'Quite the little chatelaine,' Sonia said. 'Hullo, Hugo, are you still here? Tell me, is your priestly uncle with us over Christmas?'

'Yes,' Hugo said.

'Oh, Lord, that's all I need,' Sonia said. 'Come along, we can't stand here freezing.'

Hugo came to the rescue of Oliver, who was grappling with his own suitcase and Sonia's things. 'Here, let me give you a hand with that.'

Sonia swept them in and through to the main staircase. As they went up the stairs, Babs was coming down from the second floor. She paused on the landing and looked down at the little group. Oliver looked up, saw her, and, his foot on the next step exclaimed, 'Good heavens.'

Babs ignored him and said in a high clear voice that didn't sound at all like her, 'You must be Aunt Sonia.' She came down the stairs to join them. 'I'm Barbara.'

Sonia ran her eyes up and down Babs. 'Good God, what on earth are you dressed like that for? Look how you startled Oliver.' She waved a hand. 'Rupert Dauntsey and Oliver Seynton.'

Hugo watched with interest as Babs, seeing that Oliver was about to say something, fixed him with a cold look, held out her hand and said, 'Pleased to make your acquaintance.'

'Whatever happened to "How do you do?"' murmured Sonia.

Babs took no notice, shaking hands with Rupert before brushing past them and making her way down the rest of the stairs.

Sonia turned round and looked down at her. 'So that's Lady Barbara Fitzwarin. I cannot imagine what my father would have thought of her. Or rather, I can. He must be spinning in his grave.' The thought seemed to give her some satisfaction.

Just as Hugo was wondering where Gus and Polly were, they came into the hall. Gus looked up at the figures on the stairs and called out, 'Sonia, good to see you.'

Sonia leaned over the banisters and looked down. 'Good evening, Gus.' Her eyes were on Polly. 'You must be Pauline.'

'I'm called Polly, Aunt Sonia.'

'Lady Polly! Hardly dignified. And let's do without the "aunt" business, shall we? Put those cases in my room, Hugo, please. I'm dying to get out of my furs and into a bath. I suppose there is some hot water?'

Scene 3

Mrs Partridge and Freya had decided to open the South Drawing Room. Mrs Partridge was delighted to see the Castle coming back to life. 'I never was here much in here in his late lordship's day, of course, because then Mrs Hardwick was housekeeper. I used to come sometimes to help out when they had a big party on. Although not,' she added regretfully, 'on the night when his lordship was done in.'

Freya said, 'Just as well, Mrs P. Don't you remember the snow? You'd have been shut up for all those days with a murderer.'

Mrs Partridge said, 'Put it like that, perhaps it was for the best. Now mind you fold that dust sheet properly. It's murder to get them back on if they're not folded up properly.'

Freya obediently adjusted her hold on the heavy dust sheet. She looked around the room, imagining how it would have looked back in the seventeenth century, with Cromwell's troops battering the walls and the Countess and her servants manning the guns. The tapestry of the boar hunt would have been here then, and the intricate Jacobean plasterwork, but not the Gainsboroughs or the Reynolds with their elegant eighteenth-century faces.

Ben had lit a fire in the great Italian marble fireplace and, as dusk fell, Mrs Partridge went to turn on some of the lamps in the huge drawing room. Freya's mind drifted back to that night in 1947, which was the last time that a group of people had assembled here before dinner.

'I suppose we didn't really need to do this for tonight, but it's my favourite of the drawing rooms. It's odd to think this is the last time I'll be doing this.'

Mrs Partridge looked round with a keen and approving eye. 'Looks a treat. It's only right that his lordship should have things done properly.'

In 1947, the Castle was run with what was for those times an adequate staff, but a skeleton one compared to the days before the war. Freya remembered spending her school holidays here in the thirties when house parties were the order of the day. Then there had been a butler and an under butler, footmen, a hierarchy of maids, valets: the whole panoply of a great English house.

All gone. All gone, and a good thing, too. 'It's an anachronism, this place. I love it, and it's the closest thing I ever had to a home, but it's a nonsense to be living in a castle in this day and age.'

Mrs Partridge was having none of it. 'His lordship can count himself lucky to have such a fine place to live in, when you think how many people there are up and down the land who haven't got a roof over their heads worth talking of.'

'Perhaps he should throw open the Castle to homeless people.'

'Homeless people wouldn't come and live here. Not with its history and those ghosts hanging round. You have to be born to it to appreciate it.'

Gus hadn't exactly been born to it. How much did he appreciate the grandeur of the Castle? He liked the paintings, especially the ones with classical themes, and he honoured the history of it, but would he like living in it? Grandeur combined with impracticality didn't make for comfort.

She picked up a silver-framed photo, breathed on the glass and rubbed it with a duster. Her cousin Tom. Taken on passing-out day at Sandhurst. Fresh-faced, fearless, eager. He'd grown into a tough and successful soldier, whose life was war. As was his death.

Freya sighed. Mrs Partridge said, 'Either get on with polishing those photographs or find something else to do. We've no time for you to sit mooning over them and thinking of the past. It's all gone, Miss Freya. Time to move on into the future.'

Freya laughed. 'We'll certainly all be moving on soon, Mrs P.'

Mrs Partridge said, 'Yes, but we'll go out with a bang. Make sure this Christmas is one you'll remember.'

Scene 4

Freya hesitated over what to put on when she went upstairs to change out of her skirt and jersey. Were they dressing for dinner? She should have asked Gus what he wanted to do.

Polly came to her rescue. She put her head round the door. 'Georgia says, have you got a safety pin? She's broken the zip fastener on her frock and she says it's her only smart one. What are you wearing?'

'I'm not sure.'

'Mr Dauntsey's wearing what he calls a dinner jacket, because Georgia and I heard him tell Sonia he was. I asked Hugo what that meant and he says it's the English word for a tuxedo. So he's wearing one, too, and I told Pops he'd better put his on.'

Freya handed her a safety pin. That answered her question and she opened her wardrobe to take out an evening dress she'd bought when she was last in London. She bathed and changed quickly and went downstairs. No one else was yet down. Where was Hugo? He'd promised to see to the drinks and at any moment now the others would be down wanting cocktails.

At that moment, Sonia appeared, ravishing in a purple and silver confection that shrieked Paris. 'Don't tell me no one else is down. Why are we in here? Were you overcome with a fit of nostalgia, or has Gus taken a fancy to it?'

She sank on to a sofa and gracefully swung her feet up. 'Pass over that lighter, supposing it works.'

Freya handed her the heavy silver lighter. Sonia took a long cigarette holder out of her evening bag and produced a slim gold cigarette case. She waved it at Freya. 'Want one?'

'No, thanks.'

'Oh, I forgot, you don't smoke.' She tucked a cigarette in her holder, lit it and the pungent smell of the scented cigarette hung on the air for a moment.

Freya sniffed. 'Goodness, what are you smoking? It smells like a lady's boudoir.'

Sonia shrugged. 'You have such a sensitive soul, Freya dearest. Wait until you catch a whiff of Oliver's cheroots, only you won't because I shan't let him smoke them in the house. Where are the cocktails?'

'Hugo is seeing to them.'

Sonia's gaze swept round the room as though she expected to see Hugo lurking in a corner. 'Does he add invisibility to his other skills?'

'Don't be tiresome; he'll be here in a minute. He isn't the butler.'

'No, more's the pity. I hope Gus is going to employ one. Does he drink, by the way? Or is he one of these puritanical teetotal Americans?'

Freya said, 'He drinks.'

Her mind had slid away from the here and now. She'd be starting her new book in January and quite suddenly she saw her heroine Clarissa, clad in a purple velvet gown with silver lace. Coming slowly down a flight of stairs, while two figures watched her from the shadows. Candlelight. Late at night.

Sonia said sharply, 'What are you thinking about? I don't like that faraway look. How do you get on with Gus?'

Freya dragged her mind back to the present. 'I like him. He reminds me a bit of your father, but there's a side to him that's quite different. He has a sense of fun, which Selchester never did.'

Sonia gave an inelegant snort. 'Sense of fun? Father? Good heavens, no. Absolutely no sense of humour. Of course, he was so grand and had such a lofty reputation that it didn't matter. I hear you took Gus into the town and introduced him to the Daffodils.

Isn't that all rather egalitarian? A wee bit too democratic? He is the Earl after all, even if he was brought up an American.'

'He wanted to get to know some of the people in the town. It may be a good thing, his not being as aloof as Selchester was. Times have changed.'

'If he's going to live in the Castle and try to keep it all going, he'd better keep some standards.'

'You sound like Priscilla.'

Sonia said, 'I hope he's not a socialist or a communist or anything awful like that. It's no good him thinking that the Castle can become part of the town. It never has been, not in all the centuries it's been here, and it isn't going to be now.'

'He's the kind of man who finds it easy to get on with people, but I don't see him walking into town to get all the latest gossip from the Daffodils.'

Sonia moved her shoulders restlessly and rearranged her dress over her legs. 'You may like him, but I wish him at the bottom of the deep blue sea.'

'You hardly know him.'

'He could be a paragon of all the virtues, a wonderful man, but I can't forgive his appearing from nowhere and taking my inheritance.'

'If Tom had lived—'

'If Tom.' Sonia's voice was full of bitter mockery. 'If Tom. There is no "If Tom", is there? He's dead and I minded terribly, as did you. The only compensation was that Selchester died too and I thought I was going to inherit the Castle.'

'If Selchester hadn't been murdered,' Freya said, 'he might have in the end have divorced your mother and married again. And produced another son.'

'He couldn't ever have squared that with his Catholic conscience. Never mind all the other evil things he did, including the way he treated Mummy. To get divorced was a sin with a capital S.'

'You can't blame Gus. It's not as though he exactly pushed himself into the Earldom.'

'No, my sweet, that was done by you and Hugo Hawksworth and that interfering priestly uncle of his. Poking your noses in where they had no business to be, and not letting sleeping dogs lie. I'm sure Gus was perfectly happy with his life as it was; I didn't get the impression that he was overjoyed by his inheritance. It would have been much better if you'd left well alone.'

Freya didn't answer. She sat down closer to the fire, feeling the chill in the air even though the room was heated by the big cast-iron radiators tucked away out of sight.

Sonia puffed a little circle of smoke into the air. 'Father Leo gives me the jitters. Rupert tells me he's some kind of a distinguished scientist. It's a most unsuitable thing for a priest to be. And if he is a scientist why isn't he vague and absent-minded like brilliant scientists are supposed to be? I don't like it at all, a worldly and experienced priest and then studying the stars or whatever he does on top of it.'

Freya had to laugh. 'You don't like him because he stirs your conscience.'

Sonia said, 'Wrong on that one. I don't have a conscience.'

They fell silent and then Sonia said, quite abruptly, 'Have you told Gus about Selchester and what he got up to?'

Freya's head shot up. How much did Sonia know? They'd been at pains not to let word of that spread.

Sonia said, 'No need to look at me like that. I knew what Selchester was doing. All very sordid.'

'Is that why you hated your father so much?'

Sonia's face became a mask. 'That side of things wasn't so bad. He liked to manipulate people and just went too far. Which is why he got bumped off, but no, that's not why I hated him.'

'He treated your mother badly.'

'He did indeed. Even that wasn't the worst of it. Never mind. How much do Gus and his daughters know?'

'I expect Gus read or has looked up the newspaper reports of Selchester's murder. I know Polly has.'

'How I dislike precocious children.'

'I haven't said anything more to him about his father. Why should I? He didn't know him so what's the point of raking up the past. Let sleeping murders lie.'

Scene 5

Leo said Grace, and they sat down to enjoy the delicious food. Mrs Partridge had done them proud with her cooking. She was on her mettle with extra guests, and with Pam to help her in the kitchen had prepared four courses. Most of the food came from the estate, and leek soup was followed by trout from Lord Selchester's stretch of the river.

As Freya tucked into to her chicken fillets cooked in lemon and herbs, she listened to the buzz of conversation. Polly and Georgia were arguing about fishing; Leo was talking to Rupert about particles; Hugo and Oliver were discussing books; and Sonia was telling Gus the scandalous doings of a great-aunt who now lived, mercifully, in the south of France. Babs, clad in her habitual black, stared morosely down at her plate.

How like her uncle Gus was, Freya thought – feature for feature with his haughty nose and blue eyes. But his mouth was less rigid and he looked like a man who smiled a great deal more than his father had. A different kind of looks from Rupert's rugged handsomeness. And from Hugo, who was of a more wiry build than either of them: dark-eyed, watchful and amused. Oliver was dark, too, but his was a sallow colouring.

Pam came in with the trolley. 'The pie's a cherry one, made with the Castle cherries,' she announced. 'Auntie bottled them in the summer, and they're really good. Oh, and Auntie says she's sorry, my lord, but this came earlier for you and she quite forgot about it. Mr Bunbury brought it up, special; he thought it might be something important, with all those stamps and a seal and everything.' She handed Gus a parcel and began to collect plates with a cheerful clatter.

'Who's it from, Pops?' Polly asked.

Her father was turning it over in his hands. 'It was sent to our address in America and then airmailed back here. It's from Verekers, the solicitors.'

'Open it,' Polly urged.

Gus hesitated, and then said, 'I may as well.' He slid his butter knife under the seal and eased the string off. It was packed in thick layers of brown paper.

Georgia said, 'Your lawyers don't seem to know that there's a paper shortage.'

Even Babs was showing some interest now, and the table fell silent as Gus removed the outer wrapping.

One was always curious about parcels; Freya wanted to laugh at the look of eager interest on the faces around the table. Sonia had an intent look on her face, as did Rupert. Polly and Georgia looked expectant, Hugo alert, Leo was wrapped in his usual calm, and Babs was frowning to show she didn't care about such mundane articles as a parcel. Only Oliver didn't seem at all interested.

Gus drew out a flat black object.

'Is it an album, or a notebook?' Polly asked.

Layers and layers of black tissue paper came off, to finally reveal a faded photograph behind glass in a silver frame. Gus stared down at it, and then read the slip of paper that had been tucked into a corner of the frame.

He said, in a quiet voice that was full of emotion, 'It's a photograph of my mother.'

'Let me see,' Polly said, reaching out for it, but Gus was still gazing at it. 'I never saw a picture of her. There must have been photographs of her from her childhood in France, but they were all lost. In the confusion of war, I suppose.'

Babs got up and went to stand behind her father. He put up a hand to touch her face. 'She looks like you, Babs.'

He passed the photo to Freya to hand on to Polly. Freya looked down at a hauntingly beautiful face. 'Quite lovely,' she said as she gave it to Polly.

'Has it upset you, Pops?' Polly asked anxiously.

'A little, honey. I never knew her, so it's not like you looking at a photo of your mother. But one can't help but be moved.'

Pam, who had been watching fascinated, came to put a jug of thick cream down on the table. At which moment the lights flickered and went out, leaving the room illuminated only by the candles in the heavy silver candlesticks on the table.

Scene 6

Mrs Partridge's voice came from outside the door. 'Drat those lights, I can't see a thing.'

Hugo went to the door, turned the handle to open it and she came in. 'It's those old fuses, it's high time they were seen to.'

Gus got up from the table. He picked up one of the candlesticks and said, 'Where's the fuse box?'

They had had a power cut once before, and Hugo, taking another candle, said, 'It's at the far end of the kitchen passage. There's a torch in Grace Hall, we can get it as we go through.'

Rupert joined them. 'Although it won't need three of us to repair a fuse, but I can always hold the torch.'

The passage outside the kitchen was cold and dark and their footsteps echoed on the flagstones. The fuse box was located in a kind of cupboard, which had a stiff catch. They got it open and looked at the array of fuses.

Hugo said, 'I wonder which fuse has blown?'

Gus took out the fuses one by one and checked the fuse wires. 'It's this one. There's no proper wire at all, it's been cobbled together with a piece of copper. No wonder the main fuse went.' He peered at the faded lettering above the fuse. 'It's the one for the hothouse.'

'There's some fuse wire on top of the box,' Rupert said.

'Yes,' Gus said, 'I'll have to do what I can with that. It's not the right kind, but it should work for now.'

While Rupert held the torch, Hugo watched with admiration as Gus's nimble fingers repaired the fuse and put it back.

'There,' he said, brushing the dust from his fingers. He put back the main fuse and levered the stiff switch into position. A dim light came on in the corridor.

'Nice work,' Rupert said. 'Shall we get back to our cherry pie?'

Gus said, 'I'll have a look at the whole system in the morning. Can't have this happening again.'

Hugo followed him back into the dining room, thinking what a competent man Gus was. He was quite capable of changing a fuse himself, but he couldn't have done it with the speed and the dexterity that Gus had shown. The lights were on again in the dining room and Mrs Partridge was serving out slices of pie.

The party broke up early, Sonia yawning widely and declaring she was going off to bed. 'Exhausted by the drive.'

Freya didn't believe a word of it; Sonia had the constitution of an ox. But Polly and Georgia were yawning as well, and so went grumbling off to bed, followed by Babs who said she was going to have a bath. Rupert and Oliver went to the billiard room for a game and the others headed to the library for coffee and brandy.

Night settled over Selchester Castle. An owl hooted in the woods. 'Owls are birds of ill omen,' Georgia said to Polly as they parted on the stairs.

'No, they aren't,' Polly said firmly. 'And I don't believe in omens.'

Scene 7

Gus was in Grace Hall, looking up at the shadowy portrait of his father. Freya hesitated, then went over to stand beside him.

He said, more abrupt than usual, 'What was he like, Freya? Why did he marry my mother and abandon her?'

'He was a young man, who fell in love and didn't think of the consequences.'

'Fell in love, or in lust?'

He'd have to know. He was owed that. His father was more than a stranger to him, and he'd never known his mother, who had died so soon after he was born. The photograph of her had touched him deeply.

'It was a long time ago. They're both gone, can we ever know the truth about them?'

'Not what went on in their minds and hearts, no. I'd be grateful for the plain facts. I deserve that, Freya. I reckon you knew him as well as Sonia did, and you and Hugo and Leo found out about his secret marriage, and tracked me down, so that I'm here now. What made you think he might have a male heir?'

Freya took a deep breath. This was going to be difficult. She knew what kind of a man Selchester was; the way he'd treated Gus's mother was the least of it. 'Wait here a moment. I have something to give you.'

She was back in a few minutes, breathless after running up the steps to the Tower where she had her rooms.

'Read this.' She held out a letter and Gus, moving to where the light was better, read it aloud.

Oxford, May 1912

My dearest husband, for that is what you will always be to me. You have betrayed me. I leave in shame. I shall never see you again, but my heart is yours forever. May God bless you and forgive you.

Mary Louise

'Mary Louise? She was Marie Louise.'

'She liked to call herself Mary, as she had married an Englishman.'

'My father, in fact.'

'The letter worried me. I asked Aunt Priscilla if she knew anything about it, and she said my uncle had been involved with a young woman when he was an undergraduate at Oxford. Their father got to hear of it, judged it was more serious than most amours are at that age, and came down on his son like a ton of bricks. He threatened to disinherit him – oh, not the title, he couldn't deprive him of that, but he didn't have to leave him anything else.'

'But by then my father was married?'

'Yes. In a Register Office, not in a church. That's probably how he made Marie Louise believe they weren't properly married.'

'Odd, that he didn't have a church ceremony. Do you suppose he always thought he could slide out of it somehow? In which case, why marry her at all?'

'She was very beautiful; dozens of men were wild about her. She was also virtuous.'

'So the only way he could get her to bed was if she had a ring on her finger.'

'Yes.'

'How on earth did you find all this out?'

'Leo discovered that his tutor is still alive, and he knew quite a lot about it. Next time you're in Oxford, you should look him up. Your father had another close friend, who was ordained and is now a bishop. He knew even more, but wasn't keen to share his knowledge; all he wanted was to preserve your father's good name.'

'So my mother went back to France.'

'Yes, and when it was obvious she was pregnant, her father shipped her off to America, where her sister lived.'

'My aunt, who brought me up.' He fell silent, then said, 'It's not a pretty story.'

'No.'

'Did he never try to find out what had happened to her? Did he know she was pregnant?'

'I'm not sure. However, in 1918, when he was going to marry Hermione, he hired private detectives to trace her. They said she'd died, so he knew he wasn't going to make a bigamous marriage.'

'He had that much of a conscience.'

Little comfort in that. Freya wasn't going to tell him about the other sins that lay on Selchester's conscience. Not now. Not yet.

Chapter Seven

Scene 1

Mrs Partridge came into the dining room at breakfast the next day, bearing a coffee pot and the news that she'd just heard on the wireless. 'There's been heavy snow all down the east side of England. In London even. Severe disruption, they say, on roads and rail. On Christmas Eve, the worst time for people wanting to get away.'

Oliver, paused, a piece of toast halfway to his mouth. 'Disruption?'

Mrs Partridge nodded, enjoying the drama. 'They say it's coming this way, but we won't get it until after Christmas.'

Freya thought that was a pity, she rather liked the idea of a white Christmas.

Oliver said, 'I was going to catch a train back to London this afternoon. I'd better check to see what's happening.'

Hugo had finished his breakfast and he got up. 'I'll telephone the station. Mr Godley will know what the situation is with trains to London.'

He was back in a few minutes, and his face told Oliver that the news wasn't good. 'I'm afraid there's not a chance of your getting to London. It seems that they've had heavy falls of snow on top of frozen points and the lines won't be cleared at all today. Of course what with it being Christmas Day tomorrow, they're going to have no end of a job trying to get everything running again.'

Gus said, 'In that case, Oliver, you'll have to resign yourself to spending Christmas with us. You'll be a welcome guest.'

Freya, looking at the faces around the table, did not feel that this statement met with universal agreement. She liked Oliver well enough, but it didn't look as though he was too keen on the idea either.

Gus went on, 'We'll have plenty of time to go through the inventory and look at some of those paintings you want me to see; no need to do it this morning.'

Georgia bounced into the dining room. 'The Christmas tree is up in the Great Hall.'

'I know,' Hugo said. 'A big one; Ben nearly mowed me down when he staggered in with armfuls of holly.'

'Come and see,' Georgia urged.

Oliver, who looked far from merry, stayed where he was. Sonia, who'd come down late to breakfast, yawned and said, 'A Christmas tree? How too, too festive.'

'How about trying for a bit of Christmas spirit, Sonia?' Freya said.

Sonia said, 'I'll get into the Christmas mood once lunch at Veryan House is over. You may look cheerful, Rupert, but you don't know what you're in for.'

'Why? Do they have an incompetent cook? I can't believe that of Sir Archibald.'

Sonia said, 'You've not met my aunt. And with her family gathered round her, she'll be in full materfamilias mode. At her most forthright, bossy, overbearing and difficult. She'll interrogate you about your people, your education, your army career and when she's finished you'll feel like she's fed you through a mangle. Once you've been wrung dry, she'll turn on me with all sorts of questions I don't want to answer.'

Leaving Sonia and Oliver to toast and gloom, the others made for the Great Hall. Ben had lit a fire in the vast fireplace, which was blazing ferociously, but even that wasn't enough to take the ancestral chill off the hall.

'Are there any electric heaters?' Gus asked.

'No,' Freya said. 'My uncle hated them and wouldn't have them in the house.'

Hugo said, 'There's the other fireplace. Could we get a fire going in there?'

'It tends to smoke,' Freya said. 'But there's not a breath of wind, so we could give it a go.'

'I'll bring in some logs,' Hugo said. 'Ben's had enough to do. You can give me a hand, Rupert.'

Mrs Partridge, set against having wax candles on the tree, had unearthed a set of electric Christmas lights. They were in a box, and she looked at them doubtfully. 'These won't have been used for years. I don't know if they'll work or not.'

Georgia said, 'I hope not. Much more fun to have little candles all over the tree.'

Mrs Partridge said, 'Yes, and much more fun to have flames licking up over the woodwork and burning the Castle down.'

Georgia argued, 'They must always have had candles on the tree and the Castle hasn't burned down yet.'

Mrs Partridge said, 'A wing of the house of the Castle did burn down.'

Gus had taken the box of lights from Mrs Partridge and was examining the wiring. 'When did that happen?'

'During the war. When all those strange people were here doing deception and camouflage and that kind of thing. They housed a lot of them in the Victorian wing, as it was called. It had been the servants' wing, back when they had a lot of staff. The other ranks were put in there, and one day it caught fire. Burned to the ground.'

'Was anybody hurt?' Gus asked.

Mrs Partridge said, 'It happened in the daytime and so no one was in there.'

'What time of year was it?' Georgia said.

'June. Midsummer's Day. Just as well, because a lot of the men had to make do with tents before they got other accommodation sorted out.'

'In which case,' Georgia said triumphantly, 'it was nothing to do with candles on the Christmas tree.'

Mrs Partridge had to concede this point. 'They said that it might have been a cigarette that had fallen down the back of one of the sofas in the sitting room they had there. But I think it was the electrics. I heard the men used to overload the sockets with all their bits and pieces plugged in.'

Gus said, 'I didn't realise there had been another wing.'

Freya said, 'Only the foundations were left, and some rubble. My uncle had it cleared away after the war. It was at the back, between here and the hothouse. There's still another wing, in fact. Lady Mathilda's wing, on the other side. You hardly notice it from outside, because although it's nineteenth century, it was built in the Gothic style and is much smaller than the one that burned down. The officers used it in the war, and it's been left empty and locked up since then.'

Gus was still inspecting the Christmas tree lights, methodically taking out each bulb, holding it up to check it before replacing it in its socket. Satisfied, he plugged in the set. The lights flickered and came on, then went out again.

He said to Mrs Partridge, 'Are there any spare bulbs in that box?'

She handed the box over to him, and he looked into it. 'Good. Yes I'm sure we can get this going, and it will be much more practical than candles, Georgia. Apart from anything else, think of the tedium of having to blow the candles out every time we leave and then relight them. At least with an electric set it's just a question of switching them on and off.'

He replaced three bulbs and the fuse bulb and tried again. This time, the lights came on and stayed on. He unplugged them and began to drape them around the tree.

'You'll need a ladder,' Mrs Partridge said. 'I'm off back to the kitchen now, and I'll tell Ben.'

Hugo came in with a big basket of logs. 'No need to do that, Mrs Partridge. Ben's already on his way with a ladder.'

Georgia was about to switch on the lights again, but Gus said, 'Wait, Georgia. After the trouble with the fuses last night I just want to check that all the other ones are in order.'

Polly pulled a face. 'Don't fuss, Pops. All the lights work, why should there be a problem?'

Gus took no notice. 'Where's that flashlight, Hugo?'

'On top of the fuse box, I think.'

Scene 2

Gus paused at the kitchen to warn Mrs Partridge that he'd be turning all the electricity off for a few minutes. She shook her head at him. 'Shouldn't be doing that messing with those fuses, my lord. Anything needs doing ask Ben, he can change a bulb or mend a fuse. Anything more than that, you want to get the electrician in. Mr Trusby does all the estate work.'

'I thought he was the sexton,' Hugo said, remembering Mr Trusby arriving with his spade in hand when the late Lord Selchester's body had been discovered in the Old Chapel.

'He's both.'

Gus said, 'I doubt if he'd want to come out just to check things on Christmas Eve. I can do it, Mrs Partridge, don't worry. Is there a small screwdriver anywhere?'

Mrs Partridge was putting mince pies into the oven. She shut the oven door, dusted the flour from her hands and looked disapprovingly at Gus. 'There's a toolbox on the shelf in the old boot room.'

'Boot room?' Gus said.

Hugo opened the door into a small dank room with just a tiny high window. 'It's not where they kept the boots; it was where the boot boy did his cleaning work. He must have had his hands full when they had a houseful of guests. All the shoes left every night outside the guests' rooms. And he'd have had to deal with hunting boots and shooting footwear and all the rest of it.'

Gus said, 'It really was a strange world.'

'Even more strange in its glory days before the First World War.'

Gus said, 'I can't imagine coping with any more than is here already. I think one must be grateful the Victorian wing burned down. That is if it was of no particular architectural distinction?'

'Ask Freya. There's a collection of prints of prints and drawings of the Castle over the years in the library.'

Hugo found the toolbox, Gus chose a couple of screwdrivers and, joined by Rupert, who said he'd had enough of those girls arguing about tinsel, they went to the fuse box. Hugo watched as Gus turned off the current and checked every fuse. 'I only had a brief look last night, one has to make sure.'

He finished, slotted them all in place and then, removing the fuse for the hothouse, said, 'I think I'll just go and have a look at the hothouse. Something must have made the fuse blow, although the condition it was in, it could have gone any time.'

They didn't bother putting on coats but walked briskly across the courtyard and into the welcome warmth of the hothouse. The same smell of greenery and wet earth greeted them, but Gus wasn't there to admire the foliage and the plants. He walked round looking up at the lights hanging down on their wires and said, pointing at a dangling lamp, 'That's what did it, that bulb has blown.'

Hugo said, puzzled, 'Surely that fuse with the wrong wire looked as though it had been there a long time. I asked Ben this morning, and he said that nobody has needed to go near that fuse box not since Selchester . . . not since your father was still alive. Yet you'd think the bulbs wouldn't have lasted so long.'

Rupert, who was leaning against the door said, 'Unreliable things, light bulbs. They last for years or blow in a few weeks.'

There was a stepladder leaning against the wall. Gus brought it over, climbed up and removed the bulb. He gave it a rattle. 'Yes, definitely gone.' He stepped down again. 'There's no knowing, a bulb can blow and not cause any trouble or it can take out the fuses. Fuses are quite temperamental and these ones are the old-fashioned kind. So, even fixed the way it was, a light bulb could go, or several of them and it wouldn't affect the fuse. These things happen, that's all.'

'We'd better put another light bulb in before you switch the current back on.'

Gus said, 'I'll check the sockets and switches first. You have to be careful with electricity in a damp atmosphere like there is here.'

'You seem quite an expert,' Rupert remarked. 'If we ever have revolution, and you aristos are all turfed out, you'll be able to work as an electrician.'

Gus went to the corner of the hothouse to look at the array of switches and plug sockets. Hugo said, 'I'll go and get a bulb,' and set off back to the kitchen.

When he got back, Gus had finished his inspection. 'I need some fuse wire and I can get something to make sure that this is safe. I assume there is an electrical supplier of some kind in the town?'

Hugo said, 'Hodges the ironmonger carries quite a lot of electrical stuff. He'll probably have anything you need.'

They went back indoors. Rupert said he was going to go and read *The Times*, if Father Leo had finished with it, and he went off to the library. Gus replaced the hothouse fuse and said, 'Will this store you mentioned be open this afternoon?'

Hugo said, 'It should be, early closing is on Wednesdays.'

'I thought maybe they'd close early before Christmas.'

Hugo said, 'I doubt it. Business is business, and everyone lucky enough to have electric tree lights will be popping in for replacement bulbs or fuses. I think the shops will be open all day, I expect a lot of people do their shopping on Christmas Eve. In fact, if you're going down into town I'll come with you – I have a couple of last-minute things I want to get.'

Scene 3

Meanwhile, her mince pies safely in the oven, Mrs Partridge had unearthed the Christmas decorations from some distant part of the Castle and carried them into the Great Hall. Freya sank to her knees, opening the boxes and exclaiming at the glass baubles, the delicate angels, the ribboned reindeer, the tinkling silver bells. 'Oh how this brings back memories. It's amazing that they've survived.'

Babs, who hadn't shown much interest in the proceedings until now came in to see what was going on. She took charge of the decorations and Freya noticed how carefully she placed the ornaments as she hooked them on to the tree. Georgia and Polly were inclined simply to hang them anywhere, but Babs, when they weren't looking, removed the ornaments and arranged them with more style and finesse.

Georgia and Poppy were arguing about what was going to go on top of the Christmas tree. Babs held up a shimmering star, which she said was the right thing to go on top of a Christmas tree. Polly had found an angel. 'It has such a melancholy expression, it looks as though it would like to be on top of the tree.'

Georgia wasn't having it. She was arguing the case for a silver dragon, an exquisite piece with intricate overlapping scales.

Babs said, 'Whoever heard of a dragon on top of a Christmas tree?'

Polly said, 'I don't know, he's kind of cute. But the angel looks unhappy and deserves a break.'

Georgia said, 'We don't want something unhappy at the top of the Christmas tree. It's supposed to be a cheerful festival.'

Mrs Partridge came through a little later to find the two of them still squabbling. Asked for her opinion, she settled the matter by saying, 'What'll go on top of Christmas tree is what always goes on the top of Christmas tree at the Castle.'

Polly said, 'Which is what?'

'You ask Miss Freya. She'll see to it for you.' She put down a plate of mince pies. 'Hot from the oven so eat them quickly. If you want some orangeade to go with them, you have to come along to the kitchen.'

By mid-morning, the tree was as gaudily dressed as a tree could be. Babs's efforts had made it look, Freya thought, a little bit less like an offering from Woolworths, but it was still rather overburdened. She said as much to Hugo, who grinned and said, 'Isn't that what Christmas is all about? Light and colour and fun and not taking anything too seriously?'

Sonia, drifting through the Great Hall, raised her eyes to heaven as she saw the Christmas tree, muttered, 'How vulgar.' Then she said to Gus, who was telling Polly he was going into town to visit the electrical store, 'You'd do better to call Mr Trusby. You really don't need to do that sort of thing yourself.'

Gus said, 'I like doing that kind of thing.'

Sonia said, 'It'll cause quite a lot of gossip in town. They'll think that the new Earl is an electrician.'

Polly said fiercely, 'Well, he isn't.'

'I doubt we could get an electrician so close to Christmas,' Gus said. 'It will need proper work, with new wiring; the whole thing needs to be replaced, but for the moment it'll be better if we can get it working. There are some tender plants in there that are going to suffer if the thermostat doesn't work.'

Scene 4

Martha Radley was reading the tea leaves. Seated at a round table in the Daffodil Tearooms with Mrs Partridge and Mrs Svensson, she expertly tipped her cup upside down and examined the soggy remains.

The other two drew closer, and Jamie came sauntering over, trying to affect an air of disbelief but as the three women well knew, with his ears pinned back to catch every word.

'What do you see, Martha?' Mrs Svensson said. 'You've got that dark look on your face.'

Martha said, 'That's because I see a death.'

Mrs Partridge leaned forward. 'Whose death?'

Mrs Svensson said, 'You don't need the tea leaves to tell us that. There's old Mrs Gilbert fast approaching her end.'

Mrs Partridge agreed. 'Only hours to go I hear. Dr Rogers was up again this morning, and they say the vicar's been called. So there's your death, Martha. And as Mrs Svensson says, that's no surprise to anyone. Mr Trusby has been sharpening his spade these last two days.'

Martha said, 'She may rally.'

Mrs Svensson said, 'At the age of a hundred and three she's no business to be rallying. It's time she went to her Maker.'

Martha prodded at the tealeaves with an experimental little finger. 'This is nothing to do with Mrs Gilbert. This is a death at the Castle.'

Mrs Partridge poured herself another cup of tea. 'That's looking into the past, not the future, Martha. That's all over and done with.'

Mrs Svensson said, 'Not necessarily. Look at what happened in the museum, with his lordship nearly getting thumped in the head with a crossbow bolt.'

Martha said, 'It missed his lordship, and that's not what I'm talking about. I see a death up at the Castle, not here in the town. It's quite definite, just look at this grouping here. And there's some strange force involved in it.'

This was too much for Jamie. 'Really, Martha! Strange force, indeed. What nonsense you do talk.'

Martha poured some more tea, swirled her cup round and put it down defiantly. 'You know perfectly well, Jamie, that the tea leaves never lie. You mark my words, something's amiss up at the Castle.'

'Plenty amiss for Freya and the Hawksworths,' Jamie said. 'Having to leave and find a new place.'

There was silence for a minute and then Mrs Partridge said, 'Nightingale Cottage has been let over Christmas.'

Jamie had gone into the back of the tearooms, and Martha said, 'Are the Pearsons away for Christmas then? How did you hear about it?'

'Irene told me.' Irene worked at the telephone exchange and was a fount of knowledge about what was happening in Selchester. 'She said it was all fixed up on the telephone. You know they put an advertisement in *The Times* about letting the cottage? They went off yesterday. They're going to Cornwall for Christmas, no doubt to practice some heathen rites or other. A Mr Sampson has taken the cottage. He rang them up and it was all fixed up there and then, on the telephone. He's paying £10 for the week.'

The three women looked at one another, lips pursed. 'And who is this man? Apart from knowing his name is Mr Sampson, did Irene find anything else about him?'

'No, except he'll be coming by train.'

There was a further silence, and then Mrs Svensson said, 'It's a strange choice to spend Christmas by yourself.'

'Perhaps he won't be alone. Is there a Mrs Sampson?' Martha said.

'Irene said he's on his own.'

They turned their attention to Dinah. 'I hear she's been asked to spend Christmas Day over with those cousins of hers in Berkshire.'

Martha said, 'There's bad weather coming, she won't be able to get over there.'

'In which case, Miss Freya will invite her to the Castle,' Mrs Partridge said.

'You'll have quite a party there over Christmas,' Martha said. 'I saw Lady Sonia in a car with a gentleman beside her and another one squashed in the back. It was one of those sports cars.'

'That's Mr Dauntsey's car,' Mrs Partridge said. 'He's engaged to Lady Sonia, and the other gentleman is a Mr Seynton, come about the pictures.'

Jamie brought a fresh pot of tea. 'They don't look like an engaged couple to me. Lady Sonia looks thoroughly discontented.'

Mrs Partridge said, 'Her nose has been put out of joint, that's what it is. No longer lady of the Castle.'

Jamie raised dramatic eyes heavenwards. 'And may we thank God for that. Of course we don't know what Lord Selchester's plans are. He may decide that he can't keep the Castle and estate going and is going to sell up after all. But it seems from what Mr Jonquil says that he intends to settle here.'

'I hope so,' Mrs Partridge said. 'Sugar, Lara? I don't think he's finding the Castle comfortable, though, and his daughters don't like it. He needs to take a look at Lady Mathilda's wing. Of course, it's all shut up, but it was modernised in the war and it wouldn't be much trouble to make it habitable.'

'He'll settle,' Martha said confidently.

Scene 5

Gus was enchanted by Hodges Emporium.

'It never changes,' Freya said. 'It's exactly the same as it was when I was a girl. I used to love coming here. All these mysterious objects hanging on hooks or stored away in boxes. And how Mr Hodges knows where every item is, however small or unusual, is another mystery.'

Gus said, 'It's straight out of Dickens.'

Freya said, 'I expect it was here in Dickens's day and no doubt kept by a shopkeeper called Hodges. It's certainly been here a good long while, isn't that right, Mr Hodges?'

Mr Hodges, clad in his habitual brown overalls, was searching with grubby, capable fingers among his boxes for the requisite thickness of fuse wire. 'That's right, Miss Freya. I'm the fourth generation of my family to keep this store, and there's my son will take it on after me.'

He found what he wanted and laid it on the wooden counter for Gus to see. Gus handed over the fuse he'd brought with him, and they looked at it together. 'I reckon that's the one you need, my lord.' He paused and then said, 'If there's trouble with the fuses and so on, I'm sure Mr Trusby would be glad to come up and have a look at them for you.'

Gus said, 'I think I'm okay with the fuses. I won't bother Mr Trusby until after Christmas. The trouble's in the hothouse, and if this doesn't work, I'll isolate it. Not good for the plants, but at least that way we won't be plunged into darkness in the rest of the house.'

Mr Hodges went up the ladder to replace the box on the shelf. He came down and called out to the girl at the till, 'Ninepence, please, Gloria.' Gloria, who had been gazing vacantly into space, flicked a brassy curl behind her ear and rang the amount up on the till which gave a loud ping as the drawer opened. Gus handed over the money.

Georgia, too, loved Mr Hodges's shop and she been wandering about, picking up things and peering into the gloom at strange objects hanging from the ceiling. 'You put that down Miss Georgia, that's sharp, that is.'

'What is it?' Polly said.

'It's a widget,' Mr Hodges said. 'Not something any of you will be needing.'

With a chorus of 'Good afternoons' and 'Happy Christmases', they filed out past the other customers patiently waiting their turn. Freya knew they would all have taken in every word, and the news would be flying around Selchester that the new Earl had been buying fuse wire and was planning to use it himself. She could hear the comments as she went through the door.

'Hothouse fuse,' he said.

'Mr Trusby says that old fuse box outside the Castle kitchen needs a proper overhaul. His late lordship died before he could finish the work and those trustees said it wasn't necessary.'

'Good thing there's a new Earl to set things right.'

'Let's hope so. He might sell up like Lady Sonia was planning to do, and go back to America.'

'Shame, if he does.'

Chapter Eight

Scene 1

In addition to helping her mother with her bed and breakfast, Pam worked two or three days a week at the Dragon. She was in the bar early that afternoon, helping Mr Plinth, the landlord. He was checking over the contents of the bottles while she was busy polishing the long wooden bar. There was only one customer in the saloon, a man in a trench coat with a trilby hat who was sitting in the corner reading a newspaper.

Pam glanced at him, decided that she needn't bother about him and in a low voice said to Mr Plinth, 'I won't be coming in tonight, because I'm wanted up at the Castle again. Just with preparation for Christmas dinner tomorrow because there's only a light supper tonight, but there's a lot to be done. I'll be up there tomorrow as well. I really like working up at the Castle. You should see the great big Christmas tree they've got, with electric lights and everything. I was up there this morning, taking some extra eggs for Auntie and they were putting all the decorations up on the tree.'

Mr Plinth, who had been butler to the previous Lord Selchester, was longing to hear more about what was going on up at the Castle, but he considered it beneath him to let Pam see how curious he was.

She didn't need any encouragement. She said, 'It's ever so nice being up there, with all those guests for Christmas. Lady Sonia and there's a Mr Dauntsey. He's her fiancé, but you wouldn't know it they don't seem affectionate together at all. He's a gentleman as knows his worth, but perfectly polite. The one who's really nice is his lordship. He's got ever such a kind smile and he always has a please and thank you when you do anything for him. Auntie says he should to be a bit more distant and mindful of his position, and behave a bit more like the last Earl, but these days it's all different, we're all equal now, after the war.'

Mr Plinth said, 'It was a pleasure to work for the late Lord Selchester. He knew his place all right and expected everyone else to know theirs. Aloof is what he was.'

Then, remembering some of the things that he knew about the late Lord Selchester, he thought it better not say any more. Instead, he said, 'What did Mrs Partridge serve?'

Pam launched into a lavish account of the meal. She was keen to learn to cook, and described the meal in great detail.

'Was everything amicable at the dinner table? You never know with these families.'

'They didn't argue, but there was quite a bit of excitement. First of all a parcel came for his lordship.'

Mr Plinth said, 'A parcel at the dinner table?'

Pam said, 'It came earlier in the day. I wanted to see what it was. At first I thought it was some kind of black book.'

She stopped and looked suspiciously at the customer in the corner, but he was only folding his newspaper back.

'It wasn't though, it was black tissue paper wrapped round an old photograph in a frame. It was a photograph of his mother. She died when he was born, that's what Auntie told me. His lordship looked quite upset.'

'Who sent it to him?'

'The solicitors did. They'd posted it to him in America but it arrived after he left. So it was sent back to England, to the Castle. Only imagine, it'd been all the way across to America and then back.'

'Was there a letter from his father, the last Lord Selchester?'

'No, just a note from the lawyers.'

The man in the corner folded his newspaper, thrust it into his coat pocket and came across to the bar. He said to Mr Plinth, 'I won't be staying any longer. Get my bill ready for me and I'll settle up.'

'Right away, sir, if you like to come through,' Mr Plinth said, lifting the hinged part of the counter. 'You stay here, Pam. I'll be back in a minute.'

Scene 2

Mrs Partridge served an early light supper that Christmas Eve. While they were eating, Lady Sonia asked what people's plans were for the evening. 'I suppose you'll be ringing your wretched bells, Freya?'

Freya, her mouth full of coronation chicken, nodded. And when she finished her mouthful, she said, 'Yes, we're ringing a quarter peal before the service. Normally we'd ring a much longer one, but quite a lot of people in the town have got colds, and we're a bit of a scratch band.' She looked at Hugo. 'I suppose you and Georgia will be going to the Cathedral for the midnight service?'

Georgia said, 'You bet.'

Lady Sonia sighed. 'I suppose it's down to St Aloysius for me. You'll be going to Mass, Gus?

Gus nodded. 'Yes, we'll all be there.'

'What about Father Leo?' Polly said. 'He'll have to go to Mass? Where is he?'

Hugo said, 'He went down to the Presbytery. He said he'd be helping celebrate Mass tonight.'

Lady Sonia said, carelessly, 'What about you, Rupert? And Oliver?'

Oliver, who had sat rather silently through the meal, said, 'I'm no churchgoer. I'll probably turn in early.'

'I suppose I'd better come along and experience some of your bells and smells, Sonia darling,' Rupert said.

'Are you going to convert when you marry Aunt Sonia, Mr Dauntsey?' Polly said.

'Just Sonia will do, Polly,' Sonia said.

Rupert said, 'I'm not certain. I don't have to, do I, Sonia?'

Polly knew all about that. 'You don't, though it's better if you do. But Aunt Sonia will have to get special permission. And your children will have to be brought up Catholic. She'll have to agree to that and so will you.'

Gus said, 'I don't think your aunt needs a lecture on this, Polly.'

She looked at him indignantly. 'It's not a lecture. Those are the facts. It's always best to know the facts.'

Sonia whose eyes had narrowed, chose to take this in good part and laughed. As she got up from the table she gave Polly's cheek a careless flick. 'You be careful with your facts, sweetie. You'll find an awful lot of people in life will do anything rather than face facts. You'd better come to Mass, Rupert. It'll be good for your immortal soul.'

Rupert said lazily as he got up from the table, 'I don't think I have one of those.'

Polly was about to speak again, but this time a quelling look from her father succeeded in silencing her.

Sonia and Rupert drifted out of the dining room. Babs, like Oliver, had said very little during the meal. Now she said, 'I don't believe they're ever going to get married, Polly. So it doesn't matter what Rupert is, he can be a tree worshipper for all it will matter to Sonia.'

Oliver said, 'Why do you say that, Lady Barbara?' He gave her name an ironic formality.

She shot him a swift, angry look, then shrugged. 'Oh, just because.'

Scene 3

Hugo drove Georgia down to the Cathedral and parked the car on the other side of the Green. It was brilliant moonlit night, frosty and bitterly cold. 'Too cold for snow yet,' he observed as he slammed the car door shut.

Georgia huddled into a tweed coat and scarf wrapped round her neck and a woolly hat on her head said, 'Why do people always say that? How can it be too cold to snow? If it was too cold to snow why is there any snow at the Arctic and the Antarctic?'

Hugo said, 'You'd better ask your uncle, he may have an answer to it. I just speak from experience that when it's been cold, clear and frosty like this, it usually gets a bit warmer before you'll see any snow.'

Georgia walked alongside him, her feet scrunching on the frosty ground. 'Oliver looks awfully fed up at having to be here. He should come to the service and sing a few hymns and carols. It's always lovely on Christmas Eve, and that would be much better for him than being alone at the Castle. Listen to the bells, there's Freya's heaving away. She rings Number 4, it's the G sharp one.'

'You have a better ear than I have; it's all a jangle of sound to me. Pleasing, but unintelligible.'

'Freya said I could learn to ring. I might not be quite tall enough, but you can stand on a box. After the New Year. They quite like learners.' She paused and they walked on in silence. 'If we're still here, that is.'

Hugo caught the note of anxiety in her voice. 'We'll find somewhere to live, don't you worry about it.'

The service was indeed magical. It was a long time since Hugo had been to a Christmas service. He had spent the previous years in all kinds of places, but never expected to end up celebrating Christmas in this English cathedral town. There was a beauty and peace to it; a continuity with the past and his roots that he had never felt before, and it tugged at his heartstrings. He looked down at Georgia's clear young face beside him and felt a surge of affection. He put an arm round her and gave her a hug. She looked up at him, surprised. 'What was that for?'

'I just felt like giving you a hug,' he whispered. 'Happy Christmas.'

Georgia said, 'Happy Christmas to you.'

Although they were in good time, the candlelit Cathedral was nearly full. Freya joined them when the calling bell began to ring, slipping into her seat as the choir assembled at the rear of the Cathedral. A boy's pure, cold voice began the first verse of 'Once in Royal David's City', and then the long procession made its way down the nave, the choir in red and white and the clergy in the embroidered vestments that the Cathedral was famous for.

They sang lots of favourite carols, although Georgia grumbled that they didn't include 'In the Bleak Midwinter'. 'That's my number one favourite.' The infant Jesus was laid in the crib in the sanctuary by a solemn little girl, the Blessing was given, the procession made its solemn return journey, the bishop nodding to either side and the service was over.

The congregation gathered its wits and scarves and streamed out towards the big west doors, wide open to night. The Hawksworths' progress was slowed by Freya, who was greeted with warmth and smiles and 'Happy Christmas' by dozens of people.

'You know everyone,' Georgia said. 'It must be nice to belong.' She yawned as climbed into the back into the car. 'Polly won't be back till after us. Their service doesn't actually start till midnight. She'll be awfully tired. She won't want to wake up early and open her stocking.'

Hugo said, 'And I hope you won't either.'

Georgia said, 'In all the children's books, that's what Christmas is about, waking up very early and feeling the stocking at the end of your bed and so on. I don't usually wake up specially early at Christmas.'

Freya and Hugo looked at one another. Freya said, 'I used to love opening my stocking at Christmas, as I always knew I'd get a pink sugar pig. I never actually ate it, because I hated the taste. But the pink sugar pig meant Christmas to me more than anything else.'

Georgia said, 'You should have told me. They had some for sale in the sweet shop.'

Freya said, 'Much better spend the money on some sweets for yourself.'

'Quite,' Georgia said. 'That's exactly what I did.'

Hugo felt guilty about those years of Georgia's lost childhood. She had been born in the Blitz, bombed, orphaned and then brought up by their Aunt Claire, a kind and capable woman, but a busy one. While he had been enjoying his life. He'd relished the danger and excitement and lack of routine and barely spared a thought for his young sister. If he was in England, he'd nearly always chosen to spend his Christmases among his own friends, salving his conscience with lavish presents for the sister he hardly knew.

He'd only got to know her at all these last few months, and she was still a conundrum to him. Sometimes she reminded him so much of his mother, and that still caused him a pang of anguish. Yet there was a steeliness to her character that was more like his father. And, damn it, now he was all she had, and he couldn't even provide a decent home for her.

Freya, sitting beside him, caught the change of his expression and said, 'Penny for them?'

He'd keep his melancholy reflections to himself. After all, Freya had nowhere to live either. 'Just hoping that I've got the right number of presents and cards.'

Freya said, 'Pity poor Oliver. Coming not planning to spend Christmas here and finding himself in a big household. He took himself off down into town to do some Christmas shopping. I said no one would expect it, but he was worried about it.'

Georgia said from the back, 'Oliver's all right but he does smoke those disgusting cigarettes.'

Freya laughed. 'His cheroots? They are rather horrible. But at least he doesn't smoke them in the Castle.'

Georgia said, 'I expect he would, if he could. Only Sonia won't have it, she's so bossy. He goes and lurks in the hothouse and puffs away.'

'How do you know that?' said Hugo.

'I've seen him, from my bedroom window. He switches on the light and I can see him standing there in clouds of smoke. Poor plants; I don't suppose they like it at all.'

Scene 4

Freya hadn't spent the last few Christmases at the Castle. If she was in Selchester, Aunt Priscilla always invited her to Veryan House, and if her parents were in the country she spent Christmas with them. So she woke on Christmas morning happy to be in the Tower. She looked at the bedside clock. Eight o'clock.

She stretched, wondering how long Georgia had been awake, and at that very moment there was a knock on the door and Georgia's head came round it. She was wearing a red flannel dressing gown, which her aunt had sent from America. Freya remembered that when she'd first arrived at the Castle, she wore a rather elegant robe that had belonged to her mother. It always upset Hugo to see her in it. Red flannel was much more sensible for warding off the chilliness of the castle.

'Good heavens, Georgia, bare feet. You must be frozen. Hop into bed and get them warm.' She moved over, holding the covers aside and Georgia jumped in, snuggling her cold toes against Freya's legs. 'I won't stay; I've come to get you. You've got to come and open your stocking.'

Freya said, 'Don't be ridiculous, I don't have a stocking.'

Georgia said, 'Much you know. Father Christmas called by to leave a filled stocking for you. It's downstairs in the library, hanging over the fireplace.' She giggled. 'Uncle Leo's got a stocking too, and he looks quite perplexed by it.'

Freya knew that Georgia had planned a stocking for Hugo. She had put in some things she'd made at school and had laid out some of her pocket money at Woolworths. Freya had helped out by adding a couple of items of her own.

Georgia pushed Freya out of bed.

She put on her dressing gown, ran a quick comb through her hair, thrust her feet into her slippers and rummaged in the draw for a pair of woolly socks. 'Where are your slippers, Georgia?' She handed her the woolly socks. 'At least put these on.'

Georgia sat on the edge of the bed and pulled them on. She wiggled her toes. 'These are nice. I left my slippers somewhere. They'll turn up, they always do. Meanwhile, these will do nicely. Thank you.'

Hugo had lit the fire in the library, firmly chasing Mrs Partridge away when she came in with a basket of logs. 'I'll take those; you've enough to do today without worrying about the fires. My uncle and I will see to them.'

Leo wished Freya a happy Christmas and kissed her on the cheek.

Freya said, 'Is it just us?'

Hugo said, 'Gus and the girls aren't up yet. They didn't get in until half past one; I heard them come in. So I thought we'd go ahead.'

Georgia, pleased, said, 'Good. Just us, just family.'

Freya looked at the three Hawksworths. Yes, they were like family. Georgia handed her a lumpy worsted sock. 'It isn't really a stocking. Mrs P found it for us. I wanted to give Mrs P a stocking, but she wasn't having any of it. The minute she knew what I was up to she said I wasn't on account to think of a stocking for her.' She imitated Mrs Partridge's indignant tones to perfection: '"I can't be doing with that kind of thing on Christmas morning. I never could, and I'm not going to start now." Bit Scroogish and bah humbug, but I don't think she meant it like that. Anyhow, Hugo's got her a lovely present. He's bought her a new handbag.'

Freya said, 'I know. A very handsome one, and I got her a scarf and gloves to match.'

Georgia was diving into her stocking with cries of pleasure. Hugo watched her, a faint smile on his lips. 'Don't think of the past,' Freya whispered to him as Georgia unwrapped a pencil. 'She's happy now, and that's what matters.'

Chapter Nine

Scene 1

Sonia had informed Gus and the Hawksworths, with no more than a nod in Freya's direction, that they would follow the old Castle custom on Christmas Day. 'A decent breakfast, and then a cold lunch. Tea at Veryan House for those invited, and opening Christmas presents round the tree before dinner.'

Gus had no objections to this plan. Georgia, a rebellious glint in her eyes, said, 'I usually open my presents in the morning.'

Sonia gave her a cool look. 'Really? It's not of the slightest interest to me what you usually do. Since you and your brother are still at the Castle, you'll follow our ways.'

'Our ways?' Georgia muttered to Magnus the cat. 'Our ways, nothing.'

Gus, having given each of his daughters a present to start the day, thought that he should spend some time in the morning with Oliver. He felt sorry for him, since he was obviously so distressed at not being able to get back to London.

'How were you intending to spend Christmas? Are your family in London?'

'I don't really have any family. My parents . . . My parents are both dead and I never had any brothers or sisters.' Oliver's voice was unemotional. 'I had planned to spend Christmas with friends. Still, it can't be helped, and, to be honest, I don't care much about Christmas. Shall we start in the South Drawing Room? You've seen the paintings in there, but perhaps you don't know what they are. There's a fine Reynolds and a Gainsborough. And the boar hunt tapestry, of course.'

Gus was amused by the change in Oliver when he talked about art. He no longer seemed an ill-at-ease young man, but an expert, speaking with authority. Gus was impressed by his enthusiasm and knowledge. Although he worked for an auction house, and obviously money and value was always at the back of his mind, he came to life as he pointed out details and delights of each painting.

Gus said, 'I wonder if I'll ever get used to all this. It's like living in a museum; so many works of art, so many beautiful things.'

'Of course, the best items of the collection, the really important pieces, are on loan. They couldn't have stayed here – the insurance would be impossible. When it was obvious that it was going to be just Miss Wryton living here, with the housekeeper and that handyman, the trustees arranged for all the major works to go to various public galleries.' He paused, gazing up at a serene Constable landscape. 'It's none of my business, although obviously I do have an idea of what the valuations are, but I assume you'll be planning to give quite a few of the most valuable items to the nation. To be set against death duties.'

'That's what the lawyers and accountants say I should do.'

'Your predecessor – your father – the late Lord Selchester was very good about loaning pictures for exhibitions and the national

collections. So some of them haven't been back here for years. You'll
find you have to deal with a lot of requests for that kind of thing.'

In addition to all the other duties that would fall on his head?
His inheritance was beginning to seem a poisoned chalice.

'You'll need to call in advisers if you want to know more about
all the rest of the collection,' Oliver said. 'A lot of it is outside my
area of expertise. I only have a superficial knowledge of the ceramics
and the silver and so on. And then there are the tapestries. They're
famous, and again very valuable, but since they were woven for the
Castle and haven't been moved since they were first hung, I doubt
if you'd want to dispose of them. Lady Sonia was planning to sell
them to an American collector but in my opinion, it would be a
shame for them to go.'

They were standing before a magnificent tapestry depicting an
elegant Renaissance landscape. Gus said, 'It would be rather like
taking down the walls and selling them. Besides, I like the classical
themes.'

'And there are the Bellini bronze medals. They were acquired
by your great-grandfather. Apparently in a slightly dubious way: a
payment for a gambling debt. A lucky turn of the cards, as they're
worth a lot of money. No, I can't show them to you. Apparently,
Lord Selchester didn't care for bronzes, so they've been on display at
the Victoria and Albert for years.'

They walked on, and Oliver said, slightly hesitant, 'Of course,
although the inventory was thoroughly done, it might turn out that
there are items that were for one reason or another never included.'

'Why would that be?'

'They could have been overlooked, stored away in a cellar or an
attic or even an outhouse. In a place this size, with so many treasures
. . . If that were to be the case, and you were thinking of disposing
of any such items . . . Privately, you understand, not in the auction
rooms, then I might be able to help you.'

'Help me?'

'Dispose of them. Find you a buyer. I do know people who are always on the lookout for something special. For their own collections.'

It had taken a few minutes for Gus to understand what Oliver was hinting at. He frowned. 'The idea being that I could pocket the proceeds?'

'There would be the usual commission, of course.'

'And your employers allow this?'

Oliver gave a deprecating laugh. 'Let's say they would turn a blind eye. It's quite usual; tax rates are so high that many clients are anxious to do what they can to make the most of their assets.'

'If I come across any such items, I will add them to the inventory, Mr Seynton. And if your firm is lax on such matters, I doubt if I'll be using their services for anything I do need to send to an auction house. I believe I've seen everything I want to. Thank you.'

He turned to go, and didn't see the look of anger on Oliver's reddening face.

Scene 2

Sonia came in at the far end of the room and said, 'Gus, Babs was looking for you. And if you've finished with Oliver, I want to pick his brains about something.'

There was something of Lady Priscilla in Sonia's ruthless removal of Oliver, but Gus, still overwhelmed by his new responsibilities and the decisions he would have to make, was glad to get away from the Selchester collections and from Oliver.

Once Gus had gone, Sonia became even more brisk. She produced a key and waved it under Oliver's nose. 'There are these other paintings I want you to look at. The ones you haven't seen before. And this is as good a time as any.'

'Exactly what are these other paintings, Sonia? Not those Russian ones that were left to Selchester's godson, surely? I thought those were removed and given to him a while ago. The trustees weren't too happy about that.'

'Never mind those, they weren't worth making a fuss over,' Sonia said. 'I'm going to show you something much more interesting. No, not that way. We're going up, not down.' She led him into a part of the house that Oliver was unfamiliar with, along several passages, up some stairs and then up another flight of much plainer stairs.

'Are we going up into the attics?' Oliver asked.

Sonia was impatient. 'Do stop asking questions and just come along. We don't necessarily have a lot of time. And this is a good opportunity, since there's no one about.'

They were now walking along a narrow passage with a slanted ceiling on one side and small oval windows on the other. Oliver reckoned they must be above the central courtyard. Peering through one of the windows, he could see lead flashings and crenellations.

This had been one of Sonia's favourite parts of the castle when she was a child. It was where she'd hide from her nurse or from her mother, and it also brought back other childhood memories of games. Of running feet and laughter and voices. All gone now; the Castle was silent and cold and it felt as though no other footsteps but theirs had sounded here for years.

They went past some closed doors, but she didn't pause. She was heading for the door at the end of the passage. She fitted the key in the lock, turned it and pushed open the door.

Oliver was looking distinctly uneasy. 'Sonia, what are these pictures? Who do they really belong to?'

Sonia said, 'They belong to me, I said they did. Don't worry about it. I told Gus about them; he knows that some of my possessions are stowed away here. None of these paintings are recorded anywhere on the inventory. They were never included in the insurance or anything. It was something private between my father and me.'

Oliver was still doubtful. 'Questionable ownership? That makes handling them risky.'

Sonia said, 'Don't get all stuffy with me, Oliver. Selchester told me, when he acquired his paintings and showed them to me, after the war, that if ever I needed any advice about artwork or if there was anything I needed to sell without it being too much in the public eye you were the man to go to. He told me quite a lot about you, so don't you think he'd want you to help me over this?'

Oliver blanched. 'Is that a threat? You shouldn't speak like that, you could ruin my career.'

She gave a very direct look. 'It's true though, isn't it? The pay you get from the auctioneers is hardly going to keep you in the style of life to which you've become accustomed. Besides, I know all about you from other people. The Ancasters, for instance, and the Latimers. They all had paintings they needed to dispose of discreetly, no fuss about them going abroad or that kind of thing. No trail for the beastly tax people to follow.'

Oliver said stiffly, 'I may have done some private deals, but those people were fully entitled to dispose of the items in question. They'd been in their family's possession for many years.'

'Well, these pictures have been in my possession since Selchester died. Oh, do get a move on just have a look at them, Oliver, and tell me what I can do with them.'

Reluctantly but quite curious by now, Oliver went over and removed the wrapping from the first of the paintings. His eyes widened. 'This is a Monet.'

Sonia said, 'Yes, that's what Selchester said it was. I think there are a couple of other Impressionists and then there's a picture of the Virgin, which he really liked. I asked him why he didn't hang it in the

Victorian chapel, but he said he hadn't made up his mind what to do with these paintings. After all, there isn't actually much room here in the Castle to hang more paintings, not without taking some others down.'

Oliver was still uncertain if these paintings really had been a gift from Lord Selchester to Sonia, but in the end he thought it probably didn't matter. If the new Earl was happy about Sonia's claim to the paintings, it might be best not to enquire further. Because if the Impressionists were genuine, his commission would be substantial.

He took out the pair of spectacles he needed to wear for close work, polished them with his silk handkerchief and propped them on his nose. Then he said to Sonia, 'With paintings of this quality, prospective buyers will want to know what their provenance is.'

Sonia said, 'What do you mean, provenance?'

'Buyers want to know the history of a painting and how it came into the possession of the person selling it. There's no problem with the provenance of all the rest of Selchester's collection. They'll have been in the family for generations, or were purchased by various members of the family. All the paperwork is there; I had to check that after I'd done the inventory. Receipts, valuations all that kind of thing. So when a painting is up for sale the buyer is quite sure that the title is proper and what the history of the painting is.'

Sonia said, 'Surely there are people who aren't too fussy about that kind of thing.'

Oliver hesitated, and then asked, 'Do you know how and where Selchester acquired these paintings?'

'I think Rupert put him on to them. He said that art was a good investment and there was a lot of good stuff floating around after the war. He was sure that some of these paintings would increase in value.'

'So he bought them. Do you have any paperwork relating to the purchases?'

Sonia said, 'No, and it won't matter, for all your talk about provenance. I know if you put them into the salerooms it might be difficult, and I dare say that way, with all the right bits of paper I'd get more money for them. But that way the government would know about it and I'd have to pay a thumping tax bill on it. No, thank you. Are you going to help me or aren't you?'

Oliver had gone over to the other side of the room and he pulled out the painting of the Virgin. He whistled. 'That's remarkably fine.' Then he drew the cloth off the larger painting stacked behind it.

He stood stock-still, the colour draining from his face.

Sonia came over and stood beside him. 'Quite different from the rest isn't it? It's a Picasso. I can't be doing with all that cubist stuff, but there are people who like it.'

Oliver said in a strangled voice, 'Yes, there are.' Then he swung round on Sonia, a look of such pale ferocity on his face that she took a step back. 'Where did Selchester get this? Tell me!'

'Don't try and bully me, Oliver. I told you I don't know. Selchester is dead, so he can't tell you, and no one else will.'

Oliver said, 'He didn't just go out and buy them in the flea market in Paris, did he? Somewhere there must be a record of how Selchester came by these paintings.'

And with that he flung himself out of the room, living an indignant Sonia irritably drawing the covers back over the paintings.

She went out, locking the door carefully behind her. She'd get hold of Oliver later and talk some sense into him. Rupert was standing at the bottom of the stairs. 'Oliver just shot past me looking like he had seen a ghost and had the hounds of hell after him. What have you been doing to upset him?'

Sonia shrugged. 'Oh he's being a complete bore. I can't think what made him lose his rag like that. He's always so meek. When he saw one of the paintings, a Picasso, he went all peculiar. Perhaps he isn't feeling well.'

Scene 3

Fuelled by too much bad whisky, Saul Sampson's festering rage came to a head on that Christmas afternoon. He put on warm jersey under his overcoat; he felt the cold acutely after years in a hot climate. He knew it wasn't a sensible time to go to the Castle and confront Lord Selchester, but his resentment was so strong that he couldn't wait any longer.

The cold walk up the long drive did nothing to calm his temper. When he reached the archway, he didn't go up to the front door; he knew from what he had overheard in the town that the back door, which led off the stable yard and into the kitchen quarters, would almost certainly be open.

He didn't know that family and visitors parked their cars in the stable yard. Otherwise, he would have known that, since there were no cars there, Lord Selchester was probably not at home.

After trying a door that led into some kind of storeroom, full of old harnesses hanging on hooks, he tried another door, which opened on to a passage. He could smell cooking, and so guessed he was in the right place. His feet made no sound on the stone flags; silence was one of the skills he had learned in the desert. He noted the fuse box on his left with a kind of detached interest. There had been talk in the pub last night about Lord Selchester mending his own fuses; a bit of a comedown for the high and mighty Earl.

Saul had no idea where he was, but found himself in what he realised must be the older part of the castle. It was a high stone chamber, with another passage leading off it, and a couple of arched doorways. There was a telephone there, and above one of the entrances words in Gothic script: '*Deo Gratias.*'

He gave this no more than a cursory glance. His eyes were fixed on the portrait that hung over the stone fireplace. Lord Selchester to the life: cold and arrogant and manipulative.

So intent was he that he didn't at first realise that someone else had come into the hall. He swung round, every nerve taut. It was a youngish man, with a tired, drawn face. Saul had never seen him before. Saul said, looking back at the picture, 'That man ruined me.'

'I know who you are,' the man said unexpectedly. 'You're Saul Ingham. You were in the art transport business after the war. Getting all those looted paintings out of Berlin without people asking awkward questions.'

How did this man know about his activities in Berlin after the war?

'Did you never wonder,' the man went on, 'how Lord Selchester found out about what you had done? I'll tell you, he learned about it from me. My name is Oliver Seynton. It won't mean anything to you, but back in 1946, when you were making money hand over fist insuring and transporting valuable works of art, I had just started working at Morville's, the auctioneers. I was in a van owned by your company, taking a painting to a client. A porter came with me. He was resentful of how successful you were, and he told me that, as a private in the army, he had helped you with your despicable trade.'

Saul knew who that porter must have been. Private Wilkinson had been resentful even in 1946. After he had his demob, he came to Saul, asking for a job. Which Saul had given to him, even though he suspected that a fondness for the bottle would make him unreliable. It did. He fired him, but for old times' sake gave him a reference. An act of kindness that had rebounded on him.

'Why did you tell him? What was it to you what I had or hadn't done?'

'You don't suppose that you were the only one that Lord Selchester wanted a hold over, do you? He knew something about me, and in return for his keeping quiet about it, I passed on any information that might be relevant from the art world.'

A casual word, without a thought of what might be the repercussions for a man Oliver didn't even know.

'I don't regret telling him,' Oliver went on. 'I didn't then, and I don't now. Because of you and your kind, you made it possible for a man like Selchester to acquire paintings he had no right to. He didn't buy them because he loved them or wanted them, but simply because he thought they were a good investment. If he knew those paintings were tainted, he didn't care.'

'How do you know they were tainted, as you put it?'

'German labels on the back of a Monet. A Picasso looted from my family.

The sound of a car, voices: a man and a woman.

'They're back,' Oliver said. 'You'd better go, or I'll tell them to call the police.'

Saul hesitated. The last thing he wanted was an encounter with a policeman. With a shrug he headed for the door – but not the one he'd come through. He closed it behind him. Then waited on the other side, listening.

Oliver didn't leave. Instead, Saul heard the slight ping as he picked up the telephone receiver. Slowly and quietly, Saul lifted the latch and opened the door an inch. Was he calling the police after all? No. He was asking for a London number. There was a brief conversation, and then Oliver left by the other door.

Saul was about to come back into the room when another man came in. He went straight to the telephone and got through to the operator.

Odd, but Saul had little time to think about it as that man, too, left the room. Silence.

But as Saul stepped back into the hall, he saw a thin woman in an apron standing at the other entrance, hands on hips.

Scene 4 .

Dinah joined them for dinner that Christmas night, but Oliver excused himself, saying he wasn't feeling well. He did look ill and Gus, kind and concerned, asked if there was anything they could get him.

Oliver shook his head.

Freya was secretly relieved that he wasn't there; he was behaving strangely and surely the fact that he was obliged to stay at the Castle didn't account for it.

She was glad to see Dinah. She'd told Gus that Dinah hadn't been able to go away for Christmas and he at once said she must come to the Castle.

'Is she on her own?' he asked. 'She isn't married?'

'She's a war widow. Her husband, Toby, was a pilot in the RAF. He was shot down and killed during the Battle of Britain. They'd only been married just over a year.'

'And she never met anyone else?'

'No one she liked well enough to marry.'

Mrs Partridge had roasted a sirloin of beef. 'They have turkey for Thanksgiving at Christmas in America so Lady Polly told me. So I thought we'd go for something olde English.'

It was a relaxed, pleasant evening. A leisurely meal, rounded off with Mrs Partridge's Christmas pudding, complete with silver ornaments. And then they drank port and played games in the library.

'A perfect Christmas day,' Georgia said when Hugo came in to say goodnight to her. 'Thank you for my French horn, it's a super present. The best one I ever had. I can't wait to start lessons next term.'

Hugo was relieved and pleased that she'd been so thrilled with the horn. It seemed an unlikely present, but Freya and Mrs Partridge had urged him to talk to the music teacher at her school, who had been encouraging and helpful. He had had no idea that musical instruments were in short supply, like everything else.

'I'm glad it isn't a trumpet,' he'd said when he collected the one she'd managed to acquire for him. Stone walls and a beginner's brassy hoots wouldn't make for comfortable listening.

'She'll make a good horn player, she's a musical girl,' the teacher said, and he was amazed at the sense of pride these words gave him.

Georgia yawned. 'I'm so sleepy. And there's still a lot of the holidays left; hooray. Boxing Day tomorrow; let's hope something exciting happens.'

'Like what?'

'Oh, I don't know. Something unexpected.'

Chapter Ten

Scene 1

To Sonia's indignation and Mrs Partridge's relief, Gus had put his foot down about breakfast in the dining room. 'It's too far from the kitchen for the food to be hot and it's too much trouble for Mrs Partridge. I've asked her to serve breakfast in the kitchen. There's plenty of room for everyone.'

Sonia said, 'In the kitchen? Oh Lord, how very suburban.'

Freya said, 'Do shut up, Sonia. As if Mrs Partridge didn't have enough to do. And I don't see you volunteering to cook the bacon and eggs and carry it all to the dining room.'

Sonia shrugged. 'The answer is obvious: get more staff. She's only got that dim-witted niece helping her.'

'Pam isn't dim-witted. And your last-minute decision to spend Christmas here, with two other guests, was bound to put a strain on the arrangements.'

Gus intervened. 'Mrs Partridge does need more help, and I'll be seeing to it. But it's not something that can be fixed up at Christmas.'

So on the morning of Boxing Day, they drifted down one by one for breakfast in the big kitchen. Rupert accepted a plate of eggs, bacon and sausages from Mrs Partridge with a courteous thank you, took his place on the bench and said that it reminded him of school. 'Except, of course, the food at Eton was never as good as this. Tasty sausages, Mrs Partridge. That's the advantage of being in farming country, not like in London where we have to scrabble for every mouthful.'

Mrs Partridge set the pan to one side. 'That's all of you, except Mr Oliver. Perhaps he's overslept. Or maybe he's feeling poorly still, he didn't look at all well when he came back from his walk yesterday, dreadfully pale he was.'

Sonia said, 'I expect he's packing. I know he was hoping that the weather would be better and he'd be able to get away today.'

Mrs Partridge said, with a kind of satisfaction, 'He won't. I listened to the weather forecast ~~on the radio~~ on the wireless this morning, and there's been a hard frost, icy conditions on top of the snow. The announcer said roads are hazardous and there'd be few trains in or out of London today. I was telling Georgia and Lady Polly that there'll be no chance for them to go and watch the Boxing Day meet set off either, not with the ground as iron hard as it is.'

Hugo folded up the copy of *The Times* he had ruthlessly appropriated when he came down for breakfast and said that he was going out to get some fresh air. Freya rose from the table. 'I'll come with you.'

They left through the kitchen door, went out through the stable yard across the other courtyard and into the walled garden. 'We can get out on to a track through there,' Hugo said. 'Hullo, the door to the hothouse is ajar. That can't be right, letting all the heat out and the frost in.'

'I expect Gus's in there, he's probably looking at the wires again.'

Hugo held the door open for Freya to enter. She took a step inside, sniffing the scent of wet earth and greenery, and called out, 'Gus?'

Then alarmed, she said, 'Hugo, there's someone in here, lying on the ground.'

Two strides and Hugo was beside Freya. He crouched down beside the still figure that lay on the wet earth.

'Oliver!' Freya said. 'He must have fainted.'

Hugo laid his fingers on the side of Oliver's neck. 'Dead, and for several hours I'd say.'

Freya knew Hugo was right. She'd known it from the minute she'd seen Oliver's face. For a moment, horror and panic threatened to overwhelm her, then she fought them off. 'You stay here; I'll go and ring for the doctor. Poor man, he must have had a heart attack.'

Hugo was used to men who had met their end in various untimely ways. Six years of the war and his work as an intelligence officer in the field had accustomed him to sudden violent deaths. There was no sign of anything on Oliver's body. No signs of strangulation, no bruising, no bullet hole, no blood spattered or seeping from a wound.

Freya ran back to the house. As she headed for Grace Hall, she met Leo. He took one look at her face, and said, 'What's happened?'

Freya took a quick look around to make sure that there was no one within earshot and said, 'There's been an accident.'

'Gus?'

Freya shook her head. 'No, it's Oliver.'

Leo said, 'Where is he? Does he need help?'

'No.'

'Is he dead?'

'I'm afraid he is. He's in the hothouse. Hugo's with him. I'm just going to telephone the doctor.'

'Do that. I'll go to the hothouse.'

Scene 2

Dr Rogers had just come back from delivering a baby, and was tucking into a belated breakfast. He pulled a face when the telephone rang. 'Now what?'

His wife answered the phone, listened for a few moments and then, putting her hand over the receiver, said, 'Alan, you need to get up to the Castle. Somebody's died.'

'Good God, who? Not Lord Selchester, I do hope.'

'No, no, it's a Mr Seynton, who's not one of the family. A guest, Freya Wryton says.'

Dr Rogers took a last mouthful of his breakfast, wiped his mouth with his napkin and got to his feet. He went into the hall, picked up his medical bag and went out into the frosty air. Good thing the car engine was still warm, he'd had a lot of trouble starting it this morning, what with the heavy frost. Although if Freya said this Mr Seynton was dead, then there was no real urgency, a few minutes one way or the other wouldn't do any harm.

Scene 3

Hugo left Leo with Oliver and went back into the Castle to look for Gus. He found him in the library.

Gus saw from Hugo's face that something was amiss. He put down the book he was reading and stood up. 'What is it? Has something happened?'

Hugo told him, and a look of consternation came over Gus's face. 'Poor man. I would have said he was the picture of health. He seemed to me an extremely fit young man, unusually so for someone with his kind of occupation.' Then he said, frowning, 'What's the procedure? Who deals with this kind of accident?'

Accident? Hugo sincerely hoped that was what it would turn out to be. He said, 'Freya's called the doctor and he's on his way.'

Gus said, 'Do you have any idea how he died? I mean there's no question of someone breaking in, of him being attacked?'

Hugo said, 'No, no sign of violence.'

'You haven't just left him there? Surely—'

'Leo's there with him.'

'Good.' As they went out of the library, Gus said, 'What was he doing in the hothouse?'

This was a question that had occurred to Hugo, and to Freya, who now joined them.

She said, 'Did it happen this morning?'

Hugo said, 'Leo thinks not. He agrees with me that he's been dead a few hours.'

'Did anybody see him last night after we'd finished dinner?' Freya said. 'He said he was going to his room and I supposed he was intending to go to bed. I have to say, he looked pretty bad.'

Hugo and Gus looked at one another. 'We were the last up, I think,' Hugo said. We didn't see him; I assumed he was in his room, asleep. It was quite late by then. We'd had a game or two of billiards and then talked for a while. It must have been past one when we went up to bed.'

Mrs Partridge, her face alight with ghoulish concern, came to meet them. 'Dr Rogers is here. He said you'd telephoned him, Miss Freya. Is someone ill?'

'Mr Seynton's met with an accident, Mrs Partridge,' Gus said and then, as if to prove that he was already acquiring English ways, he said, 'Perhaps you could make some tea.'

Gus shook hands with Dr Rogers and led him out to the hot-house. The doctor looked down at the body and Hugo put down a piece of matting for him to kneel on. Leo's knees bore the signs of the damp earth and he brushed his trousers down as he watched the doctor making his examination.

Dr Rogers had been looking intently at Oliver's right hand and now he laid it back on the ground. Then he stood up.

'Was it his heart?' Gus said.

'In a manner of speaking, yes,' Dr Rogers said. 'But there was nothing wrong with his heart; I suspect he was electrocuted.'

Leo nodded. 'I noticed the burn mark on his hand.'

Gus moved towards the switch that was just a foot or so above where Oliver's body lay. He stretched out a hand, but Hugo said, 'Don't touch it.'

Gus jumped back, startled, then he nodded. 'Yes, how stupid of me.'

'I'll go and take the fuse out and make sure there's no current,' Hugo said.

He was back in a few minutes. 'All off, that should be all right now.'

Gus looked intently at the switch. He produced a small screwdriver from his pocket and unscrewed the casing. He peered at the inside and then stood back frowning. 'Someone has tampered with this. The earth and live wires have been wired wrongly.'

Dr Rogers said, 'So that old metal casing would have been live?'

'Yes,' Gus said. 'It would have been.'

'And if Oliver had been standing on wet earth with leather shoes and touched it, he would have received a considerable shock,' Hugo said.

The doctor nodded. 'Yes. It's a very short distance from the hand to the heart and I think that's what killed him. Have you had any wiring work done recently? It looks as though someone has been criminally careless.'

Gus said, 'I was in here yesterday afternoon. I checked the wiring in the switch and socket and I assure you it was correctly wired.

Perfectly safe. And no, even though I am an American, I am familiar with English electrical wiring and I would never have connected the earth instead of the live wire. I made sure everything was working, and I was coming back this morning to check the circuit.'

'In which case you've had a lucky escape, Lord Selchester. Because I dare say you would have reached out for that switch without a second thought. You would have been lying here, not Mr Seynton.' He was looking grim. 'You are sure the wires were correctly connected?'

'I am quite sure.'

'Then I am afraid this is a matter for the police. If I can use the telephone, I will ring the police station.'

Scene 4

Hugo felt a sense of déjà vu as the police car drove up to the entrance and came to a smooth halt in front of the house.

Superintendent MacLeod got out, followed by a young constable. Gus came forward, and before he could say anything the Superintendent said, 'You'll be Lord Selchester. You've a strong likeness to his late lordship. I'm pleased to meet you, my lord. I am Superintendent MacLeod. This is a distressing thing to happen, particularly at Christmas.'

Last time Superintendent MacLeod had come to investigate a body at the castle, the circumstances had been quite different. For one thing the body had been a skeleton and for another, it had lain under the flagstones for several years. There had been no urgency and little of the paraphernalia of a current murder investigation.

The Superintendent asked everyone to leave the hothouse except for Dr Rogers. Watching from the outside Hugo could see the two men in earnest conversation.

Leo said, 'Hugo, was the fuse in place?'

'Yes.'

'It hadn't blown?'

'No. I'd have noticed if it had been, when I removed it.'

Gus was looking at Leo with keen interest. 'I know what you're getting at. Why didn't the fuse blow when the poor guy touched the switch?'

Scene 5

Mrs Partridge had gone into Selchester; to get a few things, she said. In fact, as Freya knew perfectly well, she had gone to spread the news.

Freya was drying the last of the plates when the door opened and there was Dinah. She had a parcel wrapped in brown paper under one arm. Hugo, who had been doing *The Times* crossword puzzle, looked up and said, 'Good morning, Dinah.'

Dinah said, 'Is it true? Somebody's died?'

Freya turned round and said, 'Yes. There's been a fatal accident.' She couldn't bring herself to say the word, murder.

Dinah caught her lip. 'The town is full of rumours. It isn't Gus, is it?'

'Thankfully, not. He's fine. Just as well, two Earls being hustled into the next world in the Castle would really be a bit much. No, it's Oliver, a friend of Sonia's who'd come to advise Gus on the pictures.'

Dinah said, 'I didn't see him at dinner last night.'

'He wasn't feeling well and kept to his room,' Freya said. 'I can't think why none of us mentioned him. It was awkward having him here because he wasn't invited for Christmas; he was supposed to go back to London on Christmas Eve. He was marooned here because of the snow.'

More footsteps. Heavy, official footsteps. Policeman's footsteps.

The door opened and there stood the burly figure of Superintendent MacLeod. 'Good morning, Miss Wryton. I'm looking for Mrs Partridge.'

Freya said, 'I'm afraid she isn't here. She went into Selchester.'

The Superintendent's eyebrows rose. 'I dare say she did. Eager to spread the news around, although it'll have been all over the town before we had the car brought round.' He gave Dinah a severe look 'Miss Lindsey. May I ask what you're doing here?'

'I have a book for Father Leo Hawksworth.'

'And it was so urgent you felt a need to deliver it, in person, on Boxing Day?'

'I wanted a walk and I thought I'd come in this direction.'

The Superintendent regarded her thoughtfully. 'It wasn't that you'd heard that there been a death and came up to see what was going on?'

Dinah said with dignity, 'Miss Wryton just told me that a guest met with a fatal accident. I'm appalled, naturally. It's an inappropriate time for me to be here, so I'll take myself off.'

'We're here to investigate a suspicious death,' the Superintendent said, 'Hold on for just a minute, if you don't mind.' He produced his notebook, opened it and flipped to a page. He looked at it with pursed lips. 'You were one of the guests at the castle on Christmas night?'

Dinah said, 'I was.'

The Superintendent said, 'The deceased is one Oliver Seynton. A guest here at the Castle, but not present at dinner on that evening. Do you know him?'

There was just tiniest pause, before Dinah said lightly, 'Oliver Seynton? No.'

'Did you know he was staying at the Castle?'

Dinah shook her head.

Freya saw that Hugo was regarding Dinah intently, a slight frown on his face.

The Superintendent closed his notebook with a slap. 'Nonetheless, we'll need a statement from you, as we will from everyone who was here on Christmas night. If you care to come along to the study with me, I'll have a constable take down your statement.'

Silently, Dinah got up and followed him out of the kitchen.

Hugo and Freya looked at one another.

Hugo said, 'Why is she lying?'

'You noticed, did you? I don't know. She was obviously relieved that it wasn't Gus who was dead.'

Hugo nodded. 'So you've noticed that those two get on well together.'

'Yes,' Freya said. 'But this is hardly the time to think about that. Dinah said she'd come to bring a book for Leo.' She gestured to the parcel, which lay on the table. 'I dare say she did, but I don't think it's the main reason she's here.'

Freya hung up the damp tea towel above the range and said, 'Do you know where Georgia and Polly are? I'm not sure how Polly will take the news. Georgia wasn't shocked when they found Selchester's body, because she'd never known him and besides, bones aren't quite like a body.'

'Not when they're your uncle's bones?'

'We aren't talking about me, but about Georgia. And Polly, too. You never know how they'll take things at that age.'

'Babs has come out of her reverie and with great good sense taken them up to play skittles.'

'Skittles?'

'Yes. You told her you used to play skittles up in the Long Gallery at the top of the Castle.'

Freya said, 'Yes, of course, it just seems that at a time like this—'

'Inappropriate? Callous? Nothing of the kind. It's much the best thing. The police won't want them underfoot, although they will have to question them at some point. And it'll take their minds off what's going on. The ambulance will be here for Oliver, and it's best that they keep out of the way until he's gone.'

'Is Dr Rogers still here?'

Hugo said, 'No, he left a little while ago; he had a patient to see. Leo and Gus are seeing to everything.'

'Poor Oliver. The unwanted guest, carted off in an ambulance to the mortuary. And I'm just glad it wasn't Gus.' Freya sat down, resting her head in her hands. She looked up, taking a deep breath and pushing her hair of her forehead. 'It's horrible. There he was, and then a jolt of electricity and he's no longer with us.'

Hugo said, 'It's odd. During the war we got so used to death and yet when it comes close to home suddenly and violently like this it's such a shock. Even though none of us knew Oliver well.'

Dinah was back. She sat on the bench, gratefully accepted a cup of coffee and said brightly, 'Well, that's that. What I had to say to the police was no use to them, but I suppose they have to be meticulous.'

'Dinah, you did know Oliver, didn't you?' Freya said.

Dinah looked from Freya to Hugo and then down into her cup. She said nothing.

'You can talk in front of Hugo. He's capable of keeping secrets and confidences to a remarkable degree.'

And that was true; it was one of thing she liked about Hugo. You'd expect him not to talk about the work he did up at the Hall, or about the secret life that she suspected he'd led before he came to Selchester. She had her own secrets to keep, and so respected him for it. But she also knew that if you said something privately to Hugo it would go no further; it was a safe as talking to Leo.

Dinah give a big sigh. 'I'm not exactly lying. I didn't know Oliver Seynton; I never met him in my life. And I certainly didn't know that he was here.' A long pause, and then she said slowly, 'Let me put it this way. If I'd known that he was a guest at the Castle and if I had thought that I would meet him at dinner on Christmas night, I wouldn't have come.'

Freya looked at her, puzzled. 'You didn't know, him but you feel that strongly about him?'

Dinah hesitated and then said, 'It's to do with Marcus.'

'Marcus?' Hugo said.

Freya answered for Dinah. 'Marcus was Dinah's twin brother.'

Dinah said, 'He died in the war.'

She looked at Freya, 'You know we were brought up speaking French fluently, because Pa was keen on all things French. Come the war, people with good French were in demand.'

'Marcus was in the Special Operations Executive,' Freya said to Hugo.

'And so,' said Dinah, her voice cold and bitter, 'was Oliver Seynton. I assume he had some French connections and spoke French like a native, or they wouldn't have taken him.'

Freya said, 'I know nothing about him, or his background.'

'None of us do,' Hugo said. 'Except perhaps Sonia. So your brother and Oliver were both in the SOE during the war?'

Dinah looked down at her hands. 'Marcus died in France. He was helping the Resistance, and he was turned over to the Germans. Who killed him.'

There was a world of story behind those stark words. Freya wondered how much Dinah knew of the details. 'Do you know how he died?'

'Not much. They never tell you the gory details. But we all have a fair idea of what happened to people like Marcus if they were captured. It went with the job. Marcus took risks – he had to. You could say he was just unlucky. People were.'

Dinah looked up and her eyes were full of anger, 'Only this time it wasn't a matter of bad luck. Marcus was betrayed. By Oliver Seynton.'

Hugo said, 'Are you saying that Oliver was a traitor?'

Dinah shook her head. 'Not exactly. It was something to do with a Jewish girl who worked in the Resistance. A mixture of mistake and cowardice. It doesn't matter because the result was that when the war ended, Marcus was dead and Oliver was alive.'

Hugo said, 'If, as you say, they didn't give out many details of what happened to anyone who died while on an operation, how do you know this?'

'It was pure chance. Last time I was in Paris I was at a dinner party, and I sat next to a Frenchman who had been in the Resistance.' She managed a smile. 'I mean really in the Resistance, not claiming to be, in the way that most of the population did once the war had ended. The ones who joined in 1946, as they put it. Of course, my name isn't the same, but he noticed the resemblance and asked if I was related to Marcus.'

Freya said to Hugo, 'It was remarkable how alike Dinah and Marcus were. When they were younger – and you were a terrific tomboy, Dinah, weren't you? – people took them for identical twins. And even when you were grown up anybody would have known you for brother and sister.'

'Yes, and that's why the Frenchman recognised me. He told me what Oliver had done.'

Hugo said, 'Once you knew that, did you make any attempt to find out what had happened to Oliver, whether he'd survived the war? Or try to contact him?'

'In a mad moment I might have done that. Tried to find him and accuse him. Tell him that he had been responsible for the death of the person I loved most in the whole world. Marcus was part of me; he was my other half. You wouldn't understand; you never had a brother. And there's a special link with twins. I knew. I woke in the night and I knew something terrible had happened to Marcus.'

Tears were running down her face, and she opened her handbag to take out a hankie. She dabbed at her eyes. 'I'm sorry. It's one of those things I don't think I'll ever get over. But that's why—' She took a deep breath. 'That's why I say that if I'd known Oliver was going to be at dinner here, nothing would have brought me to the Castle. I couldn't have sat down at table with him.'

Hugo was looking thoughtful. 'How much of this have you told the police?'

Dinah said, 'I answered all the questions that the police asked me truthfully. I didn't tell them anything about Marcus, why should I? I've no intention of doing so. It can't have any bearing on Oliver's death.'

Didn't she realise this might give her a motive for murder? Freya exchanged glances with Hugo. He was thinking the same. But no, Dinah was flooded by memories of Marcus and wasn't thinking clearly about the present situation.

Hugo said, 'It doesn't seem to be relevant. If it is, you'll have to come clean. You can't supply any information about Oliver's present circumstances or family or anything like that, can you?'

'No.'

'Besides,' Hugo went on, 'I don't know what theory the police are going to come up with but I suspect that Oliver wasn't the intended victim.'

Freya said, 'I've come to the same conclusion. I know that's what Leo thinks.'

Dinah stared at them. 'I'm so glad it wasn't Gus. But why would anyone want to kill him?'

Hugo said, 'That's what we have to find out.'

Scene 6

Lunch that day was a subdued affair. It was mostly leftovers from Christmas Day. Mrs Partridge had come back from the town with several loaves of bread to make sandwiches for the police.

Gus had suggested the police might care to join them in the dining room, but Mrs Partridge wasn't having that. 'They've taken over his late lordship's study and sitting room; they can eat in there.'

Hugo didn't like to say that the policeman weren't going to sit down at table with a group of people who were all suspects for a murder.

Sonia was in a disgruntled mood. She wanted to leave, but the police had told her that she couldn't. 'It's too bad. Are they going to arrest me? Why on earth should I want to murder Oliver? Why should anyone want to kill Oliver? It's a complete mystery to me.'

Leo said, 'You must know more about him than any of us, Lady Sonia.'

Sonia disagreed. 'Hardly. I know him because he does useful things with pictures for all kinds of friends. But that's not knowing him. I mean, we meet occasionally at cocktail parties, that kind of thing, but we don't move in the same circles. Or didn't, I should say, since any circles he's now moving in aren't anywhere I plan to be.'

Hugo said, 'What circles did he move in?'

Sonia threw a glance at Rupert. 'Do you know?'

'Oh, for heaven's sake, Sonia. I hardly met the guy until we were all squashed into my car.'

Was this indifference assumed? Was Rupert really just the smooth and superficial man he appeared to be? Hugo suspected a trickier, more complex nature. He'd need it, if he were going to climb the greasy pole of a political career.

Sonia said, 'I think he's part of Ricky Armitage's set. All those arty people who live on the fringes of what used to be called

Bloomsbury. The Superintendent asked me for his address. How should I know where he lives? I suppose he has lodgings somewhere. The police will have to find out for themselves. Isn't that what they're paid to do, investigate?'

'You don't know anything about his family?' Leo said. 'Did he have any brothers or sisters?'

Sonia said, 'I never asked, and I don't care.'

'Careful, Sonia,' Rupert said. 'Don't sound too ruthless, or they'll start to think that you're exactly the kind of person to stick a knife into somebody's ribs.'

The whole table fell silent. Sonia gave Rupert venomous look. 'No, darling, no knife this time. That was what happened to my father, if you remember. And I wasn't the one who did it.'

Rupert held up his hands in a gesture of mock surrender. 'My apologies, I spoke without thinking. One shouldn't talk of rope in the house of the hanged and so on. Sorry, Gus.'

That brought the meal to an uneasy close. Gus, rising from the table, summoned his daughters with authority. 'Get your coats on, we're going for a walk.'

Babs scowled. 'Not me thanks, Pops.'

Gus said, 'I didn't ask you, Babs, I told you. You haven't seen anything of the surrounding countryside except from the windows of the car. You've been cooped up indoors, and a walk will do you both good.'

Freya said, 'It's a pity the weather is so frosty because otherwise you could have gone to watch the Boxing Day meet.'

Babs shuddered. 'A lot of people in red coats all set to gallop after foxes? That's not my idea of fun.'

Georgia said, 'They're called pink coats and it's not done just for fun, even though the people who do it enjoy it. It's jolly useful because if the foxes weren't kept under they'd have all the hens and lambs. Besides, it's very English and you're English now. You have to get used to that kind of thing.'

It was clear from Gus's face that he wasn't going to take any rebellion from his daughters. So they went off to wrap up in the coats, scarves, hats, gloves and walking shoes necessary for any expedition at this time of the year.

Georgia went upstairs to have a happy tootle on her horn, while Freya and Hugo and Leo decamped to the kitchen to have their post-lunch coffee. Mrs Partridge was there with Pam, who had come up from the town again to help out. She was full of excitement after being interviewed by the police.

Mrs Partridge was quelling Pam. 'It doesn't do any good to tell the police any more than you have to. That's a rule in life you'll do well to follow, my girl.'

Pam said, 'But it's a murder inquiry.'

Mrs Partridge said, 'It makes no difference. Do your duty as a citizen and nothing more. What needs to be found out, they'll find out without your help.'

Freya said, 'I suppose they've finished questioning all of us now. Not that it's much help, except they've established that no one saw Oliver after eight o'clock.'

Pam said, 'What they wanted to know from Auntie and me was about that strange man who called on Christmas afternoon.'

Leo, Hugo and Freya all stared at her. 'What strange man?'

Mrs Partridge closed the oven door with a slam. 'Oh, it had quite left my mind. I never even mentioned it to his lordship. But Pam here let on about it to the police and they were on to it like dogs pouncing on a rat.'

'Did they question you together?'

Mrs Partridge said, 'They did. Pam here is only sixteen and underage. No call to be questioning her without someone else being present, and seeing as how I'm her aunt, that was me.'

Hugo said, 'Tell us about the stranger.'

'It was Christmas afternoon, when all of you except Mr Seynton had gone off over to Veryan House for tea. And he wasn't here, either, since he'd gone out for a walk. I went into Grace Hall and there this man was, standing there. I knew who it was, it was the gentleman that has rented Nightingale Cottage. Mind you, he looked right out of place here; I've never seen anyone with such a tan on him. So I called out to Auntie.'

'What did he want?' Hugo said.

'He wanted, no, demanded to see his lordship,' Mrs Partridge said indignantly. 'He wouldn't believe it when I said he wasn't here, and I thought for a moment he was going to turn quite nasty. I told him straight out, it was outrageous coming up on Christmas Day demanding to see his lordship and did his lordship know him?

'He said, "Oh, his lordship will know me right enough." He sounded angry, that sort of cold anger that makes one nervous. But I stood my ground and I told him he'd have to write a letter asking for his lordship for an appointment like any normal gentleman would. The sauce of it, coming marching in like that. I asked how he'd got in. Well, of course, the doors and everything are all open here, so I knew he hadn't needed to break in. But that's no excuse, as I told him.'

'And that was what the police were interested in?' Freya said.

Pam said, 'That and the phone call Mr Seynton made when he came back in from his walk.'

'Phone call?' Hugo said.

Mrs Partridge said, 'That's right, he came in here and said he needed to make a phone call, could he use the telephone. Very abrupt he was. I told where him where the telephone is, although I'm sure he knew. And off he went.'

Hugo said to Pam, 'Did you get any idea who he was telephoning?'

Pam shook her head. 'That's what the police wanted to know. No, I wasn't really listening. I'd just gone to Grace Hall because Mrs Partridge said I could ring up my mum to say I'd be back a bit later than expected, as there was so much to do here. Of course, my mum isn't on the telephone but I knew Irene at the exchange would be coming off duty and she'd drop in and give Mum a message.'

Leo said, 'Only you couldn't make the call because Mr Seynton was using the telephone?'

'I didn't want him to see me, so I waited for a few minutes. It wasn't a long call, but just when he put the receiver down, I could hear they were all back from Veryan House. I heard Lady Sonia's voice and I thought she might not like me using the phone. And then I saw that Mr Dauntsey had come into Grace Hall and so I made myself scarce. I didn't call Mum until later, but I just managed to catch Irene so it was all right.'

'It seems have been an eventful afternoon here while we were all taking tea at Veryan House,' Leo said.

'Did you hear what Mr Seynton said, Pam?' Hugo asked.

'I wasn't paying much attention, just hoping he didn't notice me and that he'd get off the line so I could make my call.'

Freya said to Mrs Partridge, 'I suppose the town is abuzz with the news?'

Mrs Partridge said, 'You may be sure it is. Two bodies in the space of a few months? That's excitement, that is.'

Freya said, 'Three, Mrs P. You forget about Jason Filbert.'

Mrs Partridge said, 'Forgetting about Jason Filbert is the best thing to do, the dreadful old reprobate. Well, his death was as near as natural as can be for somebody as wicked as that. I dare say Old Nick came in person to carry him off, begging your pardon, Mr Leo.'

Scene 7

Georgia spied the brown-paper parcel on the kitchen table and said, 'What's that?'

Freya said, 'It's a book that Dinah brought for Leo.'

Georgia said, 'I saw her going off down the drive. Is that why she came? Or was she being nosy?'

'Georgia!' Hugo said automatically.

'Okay, don't bite me. I didn't think she'd be a rubbernecker.'

Freya said, 'A what?'

'Polly says that's what they called in America, people who want to have a look when there's been an accident or something's happened. I think everybody in Selchester would be a rubbernecker if they got the chance. You could charge them half a crown to come up and look at the hothouse. Put some extra money into Gus's pockets.'

Hugo couldn't help laughing. 'Georgia, you are a wretch.' But he was relieved that she didn't seem to be too upset. Of course, she had had her own brush with death and, like all children who'd lived through the war, knew something of the imminence of the Grim Reaper.

Freya said, 'Where are Babs and Polly now? I thought you were playing skittles.'

Georgia said, 'We were. But it's no fun. They do something called bowling in America which is like skittles. They're awfully good at it. They smash the whole set of skittles in about two goes and when I roll the ball and I hit just one. Anyhow, they've gone off to tell the bees.'

Hugo said, 'Tell the bees?'

Georgia said, in her most patient voice, 'It sounds odd, doesn't it? But they say you're supposed to tell the bees what happened in the house, so that's what they've done. And Polly said it had to be her or Babs to do it, seeing as how, it's their home now.' She pulled a face. 'So I thought I'd come to the kitchen and see if there's anything to eat.

Freya said, 'You didn't feel inclined to go along to the bees?'

Georgia gave her a dark look. 'You know jolly well I didn't. Those bees don't like me. I got stung three times last time I went anywhere near them. I think Polly and Babs are brave to go. In fact, I call it foolhardy. And they're not planning to put on all those veils and things either. Polly says that when you go to tell them something they all sit quietly and listen. I think that's a lot of hooey, they'll probably come in any moment stung all over.'

Hugo said, 'How's Polly taking it?'

Georgia shrugged. 'She feels nervous about being in the Castle anyway, always wondering if there's a ghost around the next corner or thinking something is going to happen to her father. But as he's perfectly all right, I don't think there's any point making a fuss about it.'

Georgia took the biscuit tin down from the shelf and helped herself to one. 'I bet that whoever did it didn't intend to kill Oliver. After all, the person who'd been fiddling around with electricity and would be likely to go in there and get electrocuted was his lordship.'

'You didn't say that to Polly?' Freya said.

'No, but—' She rammed another biscuit into her mouth as Leo and Gus came into the kitchen.

Hugo looked a question and Leo nodded. 'All done. I think we could both do with a cup of coffee if there's any in that pot, Freya.'

Gus asked Georgia, 'Do you know where Polly and Babs are?

She told him, and he smiled. '*Principio sedes apibus statioque petenda.*'

Georgia regarded him suspiciously. 'That's Latin.'

Leo obligingly translated. 'First find a settled home for your bees. Vergil, Georgia.'

'I like all that farming stuff in Vergil, though he gets it all wrong about bees. It's much more fun than those bits of the *Aeneid* we have to do with old *pius Aeneas*.'

Hugo thought how bizarre it was that they were sitting round the kitchen table talking about Latin poetry.

Gus said, 'Hugo, the Superintendent wants you to ring Sir Bernard. I don't know why.'

Hugo wasn't going to tell him. He got up from the table. 'Does he? I suppose I'd better do so.'

Scene 8

Hugo left the kitchen and went out to Grace Hall. He lifted up the receiver and asked to be put through to Thorn Hall. He knew why Sir Bernard needed to be told. Standing orders were that anything untoward which happened in Selchester, especially if it had any connection to the Castle, had to be reported to Sir Bernard. Hugo couldn't see that the death of Oliver would have anything to do with the Service, but orders were orders. He got through to the Duty Officer, told him what had happened and said that the police wanted Sir Bernard to be notified.

Roger Bailey was the Duty Officer, a man who had taken a dislike to Hugo for reasons which escaped him. He said, 'Sooner you than me, Hugo You haven't been here long enough to know that when Sir Bernard's off he's off.'

Hugo said, 'Has he gone away for Christmas?'

'He has. Not far, well, nobody could with the weather the way it is. He's in the next county. I have his number, and if you feel like braving it, you can telephone.'

Hugo took the number down, got the exchange to connect him again and finally an irascible Sir Bernard came on the line. 'Hugo?

Why are you ringing me? You're not the Duty Officer. Is something up?'

Hugo explained. 'Superintendent MacLeod said you had to be informed. So I'm informing you.'

There was a silence, and then Sir Bernard, sounding slightly less irritable, said, 'Quite right. I shan't be back at the Hall the till the end of next week. We need to be kept informed. You liaised with the police very capably over Selchester's death. You can do the same now. Tell the Superintendent so, on my authority. Goodbye.'

'And a merry Christmas to you too,' Hugo said to himself as he put the receiver down. How would the Superintendent feel about him tagging along? They hadn't worked too amicably together over Selchester's death, and he wasn't sure that the Superintendent would welcome his intrusion into the present case.

He went to find him. The police had taken over the late Lord Selchester's study, which Hugo supposed made a kind of sense. A constable at the door announced Hugo and the Superintendent looked up from the desk.

'Ah, Mr Hawksworth. Do you have something to tell me?'

Hugo passed on Sir Bernard's message.

As he'd expected, the Superintendent didn't look pleased, but he said in a resigned voice, 'Always the way with the Hall. Well, I'll tell you where we've got with our investigations, which is not very far. It being Boxing Day doesn't help. I'd like to have the Yard take over on this, but with the weather conditions there's no way they can.'

Good. MacLeod had his faults, but he would be easier to deal with than someone from Scotland Yard.

'We put a call through to London, and they've said we're in charge of the case. I've put in hand inquiries at the London end, because it seems that nobody here knows much about this Mr Seynton at all. Merely that he was here to advise Lord Selchester about paintings and the person who recommended him to his lordship was Lady Sonia. She says she knows practically nothing about him, except that a lot of her friends use him for business to do with pictures, and he works for the auctioneers. She knows nothing of any family, and,' he added, 'clearly is not in the slightest bit interested.' He became more human, 'You'd think since she was here as a guest that she'd show a little more feeling.'

Hugo said, 'You can't always judge people's feelings from what they say. And after all, Oliver wasn't invited for Christmas. He was due to leave on Christmas Eve.'

The Superintendent grunted. 'I wish he had.'

Hugo said, treading carefully, 'I suppose you are quite sure that Oliver Seynton was the intended victim?'

That earned him a sharp look from the Superintendent. 'Do you have any reason to think it should be anyone else?'

'There have been two or three incidents which in the light of what's happened here might indicate that somebody wanted to kill Lord Selchester.'

That earned him a hard look from the Superintendent 'Go on.'

The Superintendent listened in silence and then asked Hugo to write down an account of everything he remembered from the time the fuses went until the body was discovered.

'We've questioned everyone, of course, and I'm putting together a fairly accurate picture of where people were, and when, but in a place this size over the Christmas season it's not going to be a great deal of help. And it's just as likely to have been an outside job, to be honest. Particularly in the light of what you just told me.'

Hugo was surprised. 'An outside job? It doesn't seem likely. Who would know that there'd been a problem with the electricity in the hothouse and that Lord Selchester was dealing with it?'

The Superintendent said, 'Most of Selchester, after he'd been into Hodges's for fuse wire. The fuse box is there in the passageway and any number of people know about it. The back door into the kitchen wing at the Castle is rarely locked and everyone knows that's the case. But at the moment, we're particularly interested in the man who turned up demanding to see his lordship on Christmas Day. It sounds like it might be the man staying at Nightingale Cottage.'

'The mystery tenant, Mr Sampson.'

'Yes. He's still there; I was a bit worried that he might have done a flit but he hasn't. I sent a constable along to check and we're keeping an eye on him. I'll get him in for questioning when I'm back in the town. But he's not the only one. In view of what's taken place at the Castle, I don't like what I hear about these other attempts on his lordship's life. It's not likely that some local person in Selchester was also on the liner. So any strangers about the place warrant further investigation.'

Hugo retreated to the library to write a precis of events for the Superintendent. Leo was in another alcove writing letters and Freya had taken Last Hurrah out for some exercise. Georgia was helping Mrs Partridge in the kitchen. Although, as Hugo remarked to Leo, 'I'm not sure what she means by helping. I think it mostly consists of licking the bowl from the chocolate cake that Mrs Partridge is making.'

Scene 9

When Hugo had finished his report, he decided to walk down into the town and give it to the Superintendent, who'd driven off in the police car a little while ago.

Since he'd moved to Selchester, Hugo had grown used to walking in the darkness of the countryside. His life up to then had been essentially urban, spent in either in London or in the various capitals and mean streets of occupied and then post-war Europe. He'd come to like the intense stillness of the countryside, the inky velvet darkness of the night, the stars and the sounds that carried so far and so clearly on still nights like this.

The moon was only just waning and so in the bright, if eerie, moonlight, he had no difficulty finding his way down to the Castle gates. He turned right to go over the bridge and into the town. It was very quiet in Selchester, with most people still indoors and enjoying the last few hours of the Boxing Day holiday.

It wasn't quiet inside the police station, which was a positive hive of activity. Murder wasn't a usual crime in this town. He told the Sergeant on duty at the desk that he had something to leave for the Superintendent and then looked around as a tall man in a belted mackintosh, shaking his shoulders as though to slough off his surroundings, came out of the Superintendent's office. He glared at the Sergeant, glanced at Hugo and then strode out of the door.

Hugo was about to follow him out of the police station when the Superintendent came out of his office. The sergeant handed him Hugo's envelope.

'Quick work, Mr Hawksworth. Thank you,' the Superintendent said. 'I dare say that'll be very valuable to us. Like I said, there's nothing so useful as a trained eye.'

Hugo said, 'That man who just left – is he the one who went up to the Castle on Christmas Day?'

'Yes, that's Mr Sampson, although I have a feeling that when we look into it we'll find it's an assumed name.'

'Does he have a explanation for his visit to the Castle?'

'None that he's willing to share with us. He just said he had his own reasons for seeing his lordship. Did he return to the Castle later that evening in another attempt to have an interview with Lord Selchester? No, he was in his cottage all evening. Is there anyone who could vouch for him? No.'

'You're not holding him?'

The Superintendent shook his head. 'We don't have grounds. There's no evidence and nothing to connect him with Mr Seynton. He won't be going anywhere. We've put a watch on the cottage and I've told him he's not to leave Selchester at present. Besides, with the weather closing in the way it is, he won't get far if he does try to get away. No, he'll stay put, and in good time I'll get the truth out of him about that visit.'

Looking at the Superintendent's implacable face, Hugo suspected he would. 'If the intended victim was the Earl, an angry man turning up demanding to see him must be presumed to have a motive for doing him a mischief.'

'Exactly so,' the Superintendent said. 'But Lord Selchester wasn't killed. He's not the subject of this inquiry, although I'm inclined to agree with you that his lordship's a more likely victim than Mr Seynton. Suspicion isn't fact. I can't hold Mr Sampson on suspicion. Once I have more information as to who exactly he is and why he's in Selchester, then we'll see.'

Hugo left the police station with something vague tugging at the back of his mind. Back at the Castle, he told Leo about the encounter with Mr Sampson. 'The infuriating thing is I'm sure I've seen him before. Or seen his photograph somewhere. I recognise his face.'

'You've a good memory for faces. You always did have, and your work has sharpened the faculty. Don't worry about it, I'm sure it'll come back to you.'

Hugo walked around the library, picking up an inkstand here, and a book there. 'I don't think I've met him, I think it was a photograph of him somewhere. The name doesn't mean anything to me. Sampson. Have you ever known anybody called Sampson?'

Leo had gone back to his letters. 'Not outside the Bible, no.'

'It has a P in it,' Hugo said, but Leo wasn't listening.

Chapter Eleven

Scene 1

Reason told Hugo that even with a murderer on the loose, it was unlikely that anyone other than Gus could be in danger. A policeman was on guard at the Castle, Leo was keeping an eye on Georgia; they should all be safe.

So he told himself as he picked up his briefcase and set off for the Hall the next morning. Would he ever get used to the routine of a desk job, instead of using his time to the best advantage?

He was beginning to doubt it.

The tea lady came round with the cup of weak coffee and the plain tea biscuit that was his lot mid-morning. As he dunked the biscuit in his cup and gazed out of the window, it suddenly came to him where he had seen Sampson's face before.

He left his half-eaten biscuit and his half-drunk coffee and limped out into the corridor. Mrs Clutton was, as usual, standing in front of her rack of index cards, sorting with nimble fingers. 'Do we still keep old newspapers at the Hall?' he asked.

Mrs Clutton looked round in surprise. She pushed a drawer back in its place and said, 'Such as the back copies of *The Times*? We do. There's a plan afoot to get rid of them, London saying there's no need for us to have duplicate copies here, but we're fighting them. I don't want to have to ask Archives every time I need to look something up in a newspaper, thank you. Is there anything in particular you're looking for?'

Hugo was about to say he'd go and have a look, and then he remembered that if he had a good memory for faces, it was nothing to Mrs Clutton's for details and facts. 'I'm trying to recall something that happened soon after the war, I think in late 'forty-six. Some man, whose name I can't remember, embezzled a lot of money in rather scandalous circumstances. He was going to be prosecuted, but before he could be arrested he fled the country. There was quite a flap about it at the time. Possibly there were political implications.'

Mrs Clutton's face took on the eager attentiveness of a truffle hound who has just spotted a fine example of that delectable root under a tree. 'I do indeed remember the case. Would you like me to go and find the relevant newspapers?' She hardly waited for an answer but was off out of the room.

Hugo returned his own room confident that he'd have an answer before the end of the day. Which he did, and since Sir Bernard was still away, so there would be no summons from Mrs Tempest, Hugo decided to finish work for the day. He wanted to tell Freya and Leo what he'd found out. He put on his tweed overcoat, plucked his hat from the hatstand in the corner of his office picked up the folders on his desk – memo from Sir Bernard to all senior staff: *No files or papers are to be left overnight in or on desks* – and went along the corridor to hand them over for safekeeping. 'Here you are, Mrs Clutton. They're all there.'

He caught the bus to Selchester. As he got off, he saw Last Hurrah tied to a railing outside the post office. Good, that meant Freya was here. He waited for her beside her horse, and in a few minutes she came out.

'Hullo, is something up?'

'I left work early. I think I've found out who the man in Nightingale Cottage is. Or rather my admirable Mrs Clutton, an Archivist at the Hall, has.'

Freya looked interested. 'Mr Sampson?'

'Mr Sampson, nothing. His name is Saul Ingham.'

Freya frowned. 'That name rings a faint bell. Nothing recent though.'

Hugo said, 'It was headline news in 1946, a big financial scandal. Saul Ingham was in the thick of it. It seemed an open and shut case and he faced several years imprisonment.'

Freya said, 'I remember now. He vanished.'

Hugo nodded. 'Yes. He did a flit. Like Lord Selchester. Unlike him, he hasn't been seen since, dead or alive. He simply disappeared, presumably to another country and a new identity.'

'Didn't it turn out later that he wasn't guilty after all?' Freya said. 'Someone spilled the beans and it turned out that he had been falsely accused for? Set up as a fall guy?'

Hugo said, 'Quite right. I've been looking at the newspaper accounts of the time.'

'So why,' Freya said, 'didn't he reappear and take his place in society? If he were living abroad under another name, he'd surely have kept an eye on what was happening in England. Hadn't he left a wife and a child behind?'

'He had. Difficult for her, and it seems he never got in touch with her. She thought he was dead, but as with Selchester's wife, there was no possibility of getting a divorce or anything legally settled. She thought he was so shocked by the accusation, which he'd always denied, that he'd taken his own life. Anyhow, the whole point is, I think this is our man and for some reason he's turned up here in Selchester.'

'Desperate to see Gus,' Freya said. 'Why? And where and when?'

'Gus has travelled on the continent quite a bit, especially in Italy and Greece. It's possible that their paths crossed. I telephoned Gus to ask him if he had heard of the man under either name and the answer is no. Not that it means much, as this guy could have been using an entirely different name. I'm getting a copy of the photo that was in the papers, so we can see if Gus recognises him.'

'Have you told the Superintendent?' Freya said. 'Shouldn't you pass on this information?'

Hugo said, 'The police took him in for questioning, but haven't held him. They have their own ways of finding out things and what I have is only supposition. Meanwhile, I thought it might be useful to go along and have a word with him. He's not cooperating with the police and even if they find out who he is and what he's up to, then he may not be willing to talk.'

'So you're planning to call on him?'

'I am.'

Freya untied Last Hurrah. 'You do realise we might be going to call on the murderer?' She shoved her horse to one side and made him walk on.

That had occurred to Hugo. 'The prospect doesn't frighten you, does it?'

'I'm more curious than alarmed.'

'There's safety in numbers. If he is a murderer and he makes a habit of it, I doubt if he's going to try and take two of us out. That really would hit the headlines,' Hugo said.

Scene 2

They walked past the Cathedral, Hugo struggling to keep up with Last Hurrah, who was dancing along on impatient hooves. Then across the Green to Nightingale Cottage. 'Even if it is a wild-goose chase,' Hugo said, 'it gives me a chance to see inside the cottage, which I never have.'

'There's Fred Camford. I suppose he's on duty to watch the cottage,' Freya said. 'I'll get him to hold Last Hurrah.' She walked her horse across and handed the reins over to the constable. He held them with one hand and touched his helmet to her with the other. Last Hurrah gave an impatient jerk and lowered his head to get at the grass.

There was a brass knocker on the door, in the shape of a bird. 'Doesn't look like a Nightingale to me,' Hugo said, as he rapped on the door. 'Much too burly; it should be called Cuckoo Cottage.'

At first it seemed that nobody was at home or, if Mr Ingham aka Sampson was there, he wasn't going to answer the door. Then they heard a bolt being drawn back and the door opened and there was the man that Hugo had seen in the police station and whose picture had been all over the newspapers.

'Mr Sampson?' Hugo said. He put a foot inside the door before the man could close it, and he and Freya were inside in a flash.

The man did not seem happy to see them. 'Who the hell are you? What are you doing here?'

Freya said, 'Consider it a courtesy call, to a new neighbour. We're from the Castle.'

Hugo's astonished eyes were taking in the surroundings. Clutter didn't begin to describe it, and what clutter! Corn dolls hung from the beams together with crystals and bundles of feathers and a contraption of small mirrors clinked strangely together. The walls had bookshelves interspersed with paintings of a peculiar kind: a single eye gazing out from a blue triangle; a red shore with strange figures walking along it; a black square with a swirling black pattern in its centre.

The man caught Hugo's expression and gave a laugh. 'Ghastly, isn't it?'

Hugo said, 'Your hosts seem to be people of rather eclectic tastes. I knew that they had a reputation for being eccentric and interested in folklore, but I had no idea they went in for all this sort of stuff.'

Sampson said, 'Don't look at me. I don't know them from Adam. I simply answered an advertisement in the newspaper because I wanted to be in Selchester.'

Mrs Partridge was right; this man's tan was striking. Hugo would be prepared to bet that he'd spent time in a very hot country. Asia? Or maybe in the Middle East. Put that together with his straight carriage and the kind of taut fitness that went with hard physical activity and it spelled soldier. A mercenary?

In a moment of inspiration he said, 'You joined the Foreign Legion. That's what you did when you vanished, isn't it? You're Saul Ingham.'

Saul said with a wry laugh, 'How clever of you. So you know who I am. I suppose you'll tell the police, and I'll be carted off for embezzlement. And a murder charge on top of it, judging by the way the police were interrogating me.'

Hugo said, 'I don't know about murder, but nobody will be arresting you for embezzlement. If you were with the Foreign Legion, no wonder you never got to know that your name had been cleared. You could have been back in England a free man any time these last five years.'

Saul looked at him in astonishment and at last said, 'You're making that up.'

Freya said, 'He's not.'

Saul sank into a chair at the table. Under his tan his face had gone completely white. Hugo went over to the sideboard, picked up a decanter, eyed it doubtfully and poured some into a glass. 'It's whisky. Not very good whisky, but you need it.'

Saul made as though to refuse the glass held out to him, and then he took it and swallowed the whisky in a gulp. Colour began to come back into his face. 'Five years? I could have come back five years ago?'

'Yes,' Hugo said.

Freya said, 'Why did you come back now, if you thought that you would still be arrested?'

'I signed up for seven years with the Legion, and that's enough for any man. I went through the war serving in the Army, but that was a picnic compared to the Legion.'

Hugo said, 'It has a reputation for tough soldiering.'

Saul went on, 'I came back for revenge. Selchester ruined my life and deprived me of my wife and my child. They emigrated to Australia to start a new life. I don't suppose I'll ever see them again. He destroyed my reputation and my livelihood, and on his word I'd have been locked up in prison for something I never did. Why do you think I'm in Selchester? Revenge. I want to take revenge on the bastard who ruined my life.'

'You're talking about the Earl of Selchester?' Hugo said.

'Yes, I am. With his ancient name and his impeccable reputation and devoted government service. All true, and yet what kind of a man is he really? What about the private man? I can tell you that as well as his cold heart and ruthless ways, he's infinitely cunning. He's a man full of subtlety.'

Hugo looked at him, puzzled. Gus? Cold heart and ruthless ways? Then it dawned on him.

Freya was already there. 'You're talking about the last Lord Selchester.'

Saul's head shot up. 'What do you mean, the last Lord Selchester? Lord Selchester is very much alive and up at the Castle. I wish he weren't. I wish he were dead and six foot under.'

Freya said simply, 'He is. The one you're talking about was the seventeenth Earl. He died more than seven years ago, although they didn't discover his body for a long time.'

'The present Earl, the one at the Castle now, is the eighteenth Earl,' Hugo said.

'You're lying,' Saul said.

'No,' Freya said. 'The seventeenth Earl was my uncle. Dead and buried.'

'How did he die? He wasn't old and was fighting fit the last time I set eyes on him.'

Hugo said, 'He was murdered.'

Saul let out a shout of bitter laughter. 'Murdered? Well, I'll raise a glass to that; it's not often men get what they deserve. Good riddance to him.'

Scene 3

Hugo and Freya came out of Nightingale Cottage, and stood on the Green together. Hugo said, 'I think in all honesty I must go and tell MacLeod what we've just learned.'

Freya said, 'Will he be annoyed at you for talking to a suspect?'

'Let him be annoyed, I'm supposed to be liaising on Sir Bernard's behalf. I haven't threatened the witness or frightened him away.' He nodded at the stolid figure of Constable Camford, who was standing under the solitary lamppost, still holding Last Hurrah. 'He'll know I've gone in there anyway. Our names will have been duly written down in Fred's notebook.'

'I'll ride back to the Castle, and tell Leo what we've found out.' Freya said.

Superintendent MacLeod was still at the police station. Hugo didn't think the Superintendent looked exactly overjoyed to see him, but he listened attentively while Hugo told him what he and Freya had found out.

MacLeod thought for a while, and then said, 'That clears up the mystery of why he went tearing off to the Castle. But from what you say he had a grudge against Lord Selchester, not realising that the present Lord Selchester isn't the same one. He went up to the Castle to do violence, so who can say what he did while he was there?'

Hugo said, 'If he was in such a temper, it seems unlikely that he would go to all that effort to rig the wiring. Without any idea who might go into the hothouse.'

The Superintendent said, 'I don't know much about the Foreign Legion. It's one of those things you read in the boys' own papers, all sounds very dramatic and romantic, but I don't suppose it's a bit like that.'

'It's a tough life.'

'So,' MacLeod said, 'he's the kind of man who'd be quick-witted, good in an emergency and swift to grasp any opportunity that was offered. He came in through that back door; he might very well have seen the fuse box and taken an idea into his head.'

Hugo said, 'It's a big leap from seeing a fuse box as you go past in a temper and returning under cover of darkness to set up a trap that might kill anyone in the household.'

'Risky. But from what you say the kind of man who's been in the Foreign Legion is one inclined to take risks. As to the whole business with fuses, like I said, his lordship's intention to fix the electrics in the hothouse was common knowledge. Even so, I'm not sure the timing's right. I think the wiring job was done much later.'

'He could have gone back to the Castle.'

'He could.' The Superintendent made a note of Saul Ingham's name. 'I remember the case. Caused quite a stir. I'm grateful to you, Mr Hawksworth. I'll get on to London right away and they can find the records from the time. At least we now know who the man is. And he won't be going anywhere, as I told you earlier.'

Hugo left the police station wondering why MacLeod hadn't asked what had caused Saul's animosity towards Lord Selchester, or what he had to do with the financial scandal that had ruined Ingham.

Of course, the Superintendent didn't know what kind of a man the last Lord Selchester really was. He knew little about Selchester's very private life. His secret life.

Damn it, the man had been dead these seven years, and his secrets still haunted the present. In the eyes of the world, the late Earl had died with his reputation intact. Hugh knew better.

When they'd found out who had murdered Selchester, Freya had said, 'What's the point of blackening a man's reputation when he's been dead these seven years?

Leo had agreed with her. Time passed, and the people whose lives had been affected by Lord Selchester would undoubtedly prefer to let sleeping dogs lie.

Perhaps the dogs had woken.

Chapter Twelve

Scene 1

Babs, sitting across from Freya at the kitchen table the next morning, asked if she could draw her. 'You've interesting bones and a kind of old face.'

Freya said, 'I'm not sure that's a compliment.'

Babs said hastily, 'Hey, I'm not saying you look old. I mean you have a face that seems to belong to a different time. I've been looking at the portraits in the gallery, all those ancestors. I suppose everyone has exactly the same number of ancestors as everyone else, but most people don't have so many of them hanging on the wall. And though the styles and fashions of the clothes and the way the artists portray the women, you see the same features again and again. The way the eyes are set, shape of the nose, slant of the jaw.'

'The Selchester face. And the blue eyes. You've got those.'

'Yup. I'm loving using these charcoal crayons you got me for Christmas. I've drawn Polly and Pops so often that it would be I'd like to have a new subject. If you don't mind.'

Freya said, 'I noticed you sketching when we were in the Daffodil Tearooms. That's what made me think you might like those.' She obligingly sat still while Babs, her head on one side, utterly absorbed, worked her charcoal over the page. Occasionally she smudged a line with a finger as she looked up at Freya and down at the page, working with a swift professionalism that took away all her habitual world-weary languor.

University? That might be Gus's plan for her daughter; Freya doubted if it was what Babs wanted to do.

Babs finished, in a remarkably short time. Freya said, 'May I look?' and Babs handed the sketchbook over.

Freya she was impressed by how Babs had caught not only the physical structure of her face but also a look of wariness in her eyes. It wasn't something she ever noticed in her looking glass, but she recognised from the inside what Babs had seen from the outside.

'Can I look at some of your other sketches?'

Babs nodded and Freya began to work her way through the sketchbook. There were some very well-drawn sketches of objects, little miniature still lives, but obviously what most attracted Babs were people. People in motion, people's faces and expressions. She had drawn three women consulting the tea leaves, a sketch that gave them a witchy quality that made Freya laugh. 'Mrs P to the left, and look at Martha peering into her cup.'

Babs came round to see what she was laughing at. 'I saw those when I dropped into the Daffodil Tearooms for cake. Those three were wonderful to draw. I thought if you were doing a modern production of Macbeth that's what three witches should look like.'

Freya said, 'You could be nearer the truth than you imagine.' She turned the page and let out an 'Oh!' of astonishment.

'Whatever is the matter? You look as though you've seen a ghost.'

'Not a ghost. But I know this man. At least I don't know him but I met him. Once, on a train.'

Babs turned the sketchbook round to look. 'He was in the tea-rooms when we were in there with Pops and Polly. Sitting still and quiet in the corner. Watching everyone and listening hard.'

Freya said, 'I can see that from your drawing.'

'I wonder about people when I draw them, and I kind of see inside them, see what they really are. It's not a facial thing. I couldn't put a profession to people, I can't say, he's a doctor, he's a lawyer, she's a secretary or an accountant or whatever. But even so, the drawings say something about what kind of a person they are. If it's a good drawing, that is. He was a bit weird. If you asked me about him, I'd say he's a blank.' Babs took back the sketchbook and looked at the man's picture thoughtfully. 'You met him on a train, is he a local?'

'No. Can I borrow this?'

Babs looked surprised, 'What, the whole sketchbook?'

'No. Would it be possible to take this this drawing out? I'd like to show it to someone.'

Babs obligingly removed the page, and she turned to the one she'd done of Freya. She said, 'I can take this one out too. I think Hugo would like to have it.'

Freya looked at her. 'Why would Hugo want a sketch of me?'

Looking down at her sketchbook and making another slight adjustment with her pencil, Babs said casually, 'He likes you.'

'I hope he does. We're good friends. Not in a romantic way, though. He has a girlfriend in London.'

Babs waved a dismissive pencil. 'Oh, girlfriends in London. That's quite another thing.' Back in existential mode, she reassumed her bored expression and mooched out of the kitchen.

Freya found a newspaper in one of the drawers and spread it on the table. She laid the sketch on it and was about to wrap it up when Mrs Partridge came in.

'What are you doing with that newspaper?'

'I'm only using it to protect this sketch. Why, is it special? It's several days old.'

Mrs Partridge whisked it away from her and rummaged in a basket under the table for a copy of the *Selchester Gazette*. She smoothed out the pages of the one from the drawer and pointed to a photograph. 'I want to keep this one, it's a picture of his lordship coming down the gangplank of the *Queen Mary*, with their ladyships. When he arrived in England.'

Freya looked, not much interested, and then she almost snatched the sheet from Mrs Partridge. She took it over to the window. Yes, there was no doubt about it. Never mind Gus and the girls; what interested her was the man coming down the gangplank several paces behind them. She glanced at Babs's sketch. There was no doubt about it; he was the same man.

Scene 2

Freya pulled on boots, hacking jacket and mac, and went out to saddle Last Hurrah. He was pleased to see her, but snorted and made a fuss about having his girth tightened by cavorting across the yard. He needed a good gallop, but the ground was too hard for anything brisker than a trot.

Ben came out to watch her go. 'You take care of him, Miss Freya, and yourself. He's in a right grievous mood, that horse.'

That was nothing unusual; Last Hurrah's bad temper was habitual. But Freya loved him for all his faults and wickedness, and it was good to be the saddle. Even if all she could do was walk and trot, it was a relief to escape from the Castle and its conundrums.

Except she wasn't exactly escaping from them. She trotted over the bridge and turned into the alley that ran behind the Daffodil

Tearooms. Richard, who did the baking, worked in the kitchens at the back and he would keep a watchful eye on Last Hurrah. She looped his reins over the gatepost and went in through the back door.

Richard greeted her with a brief wave of his hand. He was doing something finicky with a piping tube and said, 'Go on in. Jamie's out front.'

The tearooms weren't busy. 'Post-Christmas lull,' Jamie said. 'Sit anywhere.'

'I've not come for coffee, but to ask you a question.'

Jamie looked interested. 'Advice on how to persuade Lady Babs to wear more becoming clothes? Lady Priscilla was quite cutting about her, so I hear.'

'Nothing to do with her.' She took out Babs's sketch and handed it to him.

Jamie looked at it. 'That's the man who was here last year. That stranger who came into town. Came and went, about the time Jason Filbert got his come-uppance in the woods.'

Come-uppance was a delicate way of putting it, given Jason's violent end; he'd been found dead in the woods with a gun beside him. Freya said, 'Have you seen him again since then?'

Jamie blew out his cheeks. 'Now you come to mention it . . .' Then he shook his head. 'I couldn't say yes or no. There was a man in here just before Christmas, might have been him. I didn't serve him, we had Ivy helping out and she waited on his table. No good asking her, the Archangel Gabriel could come in for tea and cakes, complete with feathered wings, and she wouldn't take any notice. Is it important?' His voice lowered to a conspiratorial whisper. 'Is it anything to do with the murder up at the Castle?'

'I just want to track this man down.'

'I wouldn't bother if I were you, not from what I remember of him. He gave me the creeps. Pale eyes, watchful. Not a nice man.'

Scene 3

Freya came out of the tearooms and stood in the street, uncertain what to do next. When she'd met the man with pale eyes on the train, he'd known who she was. He hadn't given her his name and she hadn't asked. He'd worked for her uncle, he'd said. So there was the Selchester connection. What was he doing here now? He might know people here, why should it be anything to do with Gus? Yet he'd been on the liner, when Gus had nearly gone overboard, and he'd been here when that crossbow bolt had just missed the Earl.

Her time was limited, for in a little while Last Hurrah would get impatient with the meagre tufts of grass available in the alley and become restive. He was securely tied, so he wouldn't break loose, but he might lash out at anyone going past. Although most inhabitants of Selchester were familiar with Last Hurrah and had long ago learned to give him a wide berth.

She'd try the Dragon. If he'd spent any time in Selchester, he must have stayed somewhere, and the Dragon was the most likely place.

It was quiet at this time of day, soon after opening time. Mr Plinth was behind the bar, his shirt sleeves caught up in elastic arm-bands. He greeted Freya like an old friend and she sat on a stool at the bar.

'I won't have anything thank you, Mr Plinth. I've really come to ask you something.' She took out the drawing and passed it to him. 'I don't suppose this man has stayed here recently, has he?'

Mr Plinth went on polishing a glass, glanced at it and said, 'That's the gent as came for a couple of days before Christmas. A Mr Jenkins.'

Bingo! 'How long did he stay?'

'Hold on,' Mr Plinth said. He vanished and reappeared a couple of minutes later with the hotel ledger.

He ran a stubby finger down the names. 'We were very quiet then, you don't get many folk coming before Christmas and not with the weather the threatening the way it was. Yes here we are. Mr Jenkins, London. He arrived on the twenty-second and checked out on the twenty-fourth.'

Freya said, 'Had he booked in advance?'

Mr Plinth shook his head. 'He walked in and asked if we had a room. He said he wasn't sure ~~he said~~ how long he was going to stay, and in fact I wasn't too keen on him staying over Christmas, because I'd hoped to take the day off. Still, business is business. As it was he took himself off after lunch on the twenty-fourth. Quite sudden.' He looked up at the ceiling, reflecting. 'That was the day that his new lordship and Mr Hugo came in to have lunch. Mr Jenkins was sitting in the corner there. Having a sandwich and a half pint. And then, just before his lordship came in, he got up, ever so abrupt, went upstairs, packed his bag, came down, paid his bill and off he went. He must have been heading west or down south, because he wouldn't have got very far otherwise, not with the snow.'

Freya said, 'Was he in a car?'

'Not that I knew. If he had been, he'd have parked here in the car park at the back. I reckon he came on the train.'

Freya thanked him, waved at Pam who was just coming in and left. She rode back to the Castle, mulling over the implications. A rabbit hopped out in front of them, and Last Hurrah shied, nearly throwing her. She gathered him up, patted him on the neck and pulled her mind away from strangers with pale eyes, murder and all the rest of it. Time enough to think about that again when Hugo was back and she could talk it over with him and Leo.

She'd wondered before she came back whether she should tell the police, but they would simply say that she was interfering in things that were none of her business. No, if the police needed to be told, Hugo could do that.

Freya grinned. She knew that Hugo wasn't best pleased at the way that Sir Bernard had once again left him with a watching brief, as he had done over the murder of her uncle. She didn't feel sorry for him; he might protest, but he was the kind of man who liked to get to the truth of things. And he knew that the authorities didn't always go about their investigations in the best way.

Not for the first time, Freya wondered exactly what Hugo had done before he injured his leg. She didn't believe for a moment that he'd been injured in a bicycle accident. Perhaps one of these days he would trust her enough to tell her. After all, she, too, had her secrets.

Chapter Thirteen

Scene 1

To Hugo's surprise, when he got off the bus in Selchester that evening, planning to walk up to the Castle, he saw Gus standing by the bus stop. He was wearing a voluminous tweed coat, of a most un-English cut, and his hat and horn-rimmed glasses would have made him stand out in Selchester or anywhere else in England.

Hugo climbed down from the bus and went over to Gus. 'What are you doing here?'

Gus's eyes were on the bus. As it trundled off, Hugo could see all the faces turned to watch them. No, not them: Gus.

Gus said, 'Sometimes I feel like a freak show.'

Hugo said, 'It's simply polite curiosity. And novelty. You're not yet the familiar figure around here that your father was.'

Gus said, 'Freya told me you usually caught this bus, and I thought I might walk back to the Castle with you. They're are a few things I wanted to ask you and it seems impossible anywhere in Selchester to have a conversation without it being known by everyone within the half hour. I'm not even sure in the Castle that someone isn't above or to one side listening in. Intentionally or otherwise.'

Hugo laughed. 'Including Polly's ghosts?'

Gus's expression was serious. 'Those ghosts of hers worry me. And they worry her, too.'

'I get the impression that you haven't exactly taken to the Castle.'

'I find it strange. Perhaps I'm spoiled, having been brought up in America where we're used to our creature comforts, but the stone walls and flagstone floors aren't what I'd call cosy. It's almost as though the place breathes history at me. Of course, you could say it's my history and I must get used to it, but the truth is, I'm not familiar with English history.'

'You'd probably be more at home in a Roman villa.'

Gus grinned ruefully. 'And isn't that the truth? You haven't been at the Castle for long. Did you find it oppressive when you first came?'

Hugo hadn't ever considered this. 'No. I've lived in far worse places, and there's such a housing shortage in England that I was too relieved to have a roof over my and Georgia's heads to care where I was.'

'I suppose one becomes accustomed to almost anything,' Gus said. 'After all, I didn't feel out of place in Oxford and the rooms I had in college went back a good many centuries.'

They came to the bridge and paused to look down into the black, swirling water. 'It's quite a river,' Gus said. 'Does it ever flood?'

'Yes, apparently, although it hasn't while I've been in Selchester. The locals all treat the river with respect, there are some evil currents.'

They took the turning to the Castle drive. Hugo said, 'In daylight and in good weather I sometimes take the shortcut. I wouldn't venture on it at this time of year and in the dark. Too likely to slip.'

Gus said, 'I gather your lameness is due to a bicycle accident. Will you always have to walk with a stick?'

Hugo said, 'Probably. I'll certainly always be lame. But my leg's getting stronger month by month.'

'Does it cause you much pain?'

Hugo said, 'From time to time. That, too, is getting better.'

They walked on again a little way in silence and then Gus said, 'I was talking to the police today. They came up to the Castle to see me. I gather from what the Superintendent told me that they're inclined to think the intended victim of the electrical contrivance was me and not Oliver.'

'Yes. The Superintendent is working on that theory.'

'Who would want to kill me? Why?'

'That's what the police are trying to find out. The other question is who would want to kill Oliver? No one knew he was coming; he has nothing to do with Selchester, other than a single previous visit. No one here except for Sonia knew him.'

Gus said, 'And it seems it was a last-minute decision of Sonia's to bring him. So the police are asking why would any of those present want to kill him? Myself included, for if he were the victim I would be as much a suspect as anyone else.'

Hugo said, 'Did you have any particular animosity towards him?'

Gus dug his hands deeper into his coat pocket and said slowly, 'I was kind of annoyed with him over one thing. He told me that if I found I had any items not listed on the inventories, he could arrange for a private sale. He seemed confident that I'd be happy to go along with such a scheme, even though it was dishonest and dishonourable. I don't like paying tax any more than the next man, but however unfair and however high taxes seem, I reckon it's a citizen's duty to pay them. I don't like cheating.'

'You told him so?'

'Yes.'

'Did he think you might report him to Morville's?'

'Not in so many words. I could do that, and I certainly won't use them when I do come to sell anything, because they should be more careful about the people they employ. On the other hand, they may be aware of what Oliver got up to and chose to turn a blind eye, because it could bring them more business. But I'd like to feel I was dealing with people that I could trust.'

'From what I know of the art world you might find it quite difficult to find people to trust. What you need is an expert who doesn't stand to make any money from what you decide to do.' An idea came into his head. Emerson would know someone, or might even be prepared to advise himself. 'With regard to that I might just know the very man. Leave it with me.'

'I'd be obliged to you. That's not really what I wanted to talk about though, although I suppose it might be connected with the murder. What I am kind of concerned about is that the police think that somebody had it in for me. They brought up that stuff about the liner, when I nearly went overboard, and it seems they're looking into the incident in Oxford when I was almost a hit-and-run victim.'

'And the crossbow. The convenient crossbow.'

'All of those, if they were intended to harm me, were supposed to look like accidents. Although at first sight what killed that unfortunate young man might have been taken to be an accident, the fact that the wiring had been tinkered with was bound to be discovered. It seems to me a very different kind of thing.'

Gus was no fool. He had thought this through. Hugo decided to take the bull by the horns. 'There's a man staying in Selchester who it turns out had a grudge against your father. He wasn't aware your father was dead and you're now Lord Selchester. So he can't be ruled out as someone with a motive for attempting to murder you.'

'Any idea what the quarrel was between him and my father?'

'He's not saying at the moment, but he might, once he's adjusted to the new reality.'

'Lady Sonia would benefit financially were I to pass on and therefore I suppose Rupert as her fiancé might be a suspect. Only I don't buy this fiancé business. Do they seem to you like an engaged couple?'

'The person to ask about that is Freya. She knows Sonia better than anyone. They grew up together. I hardly know her, but from what little I do know of her, I would never expect her to behave as other people do.'

Gus said, 'Rupert? He seems to me a smooth fellow, rising in the world, an ambitious well-connected politician. We have a lot of those in America. He's a familiar type.'

'Yes, Rupert is smooth. Although what goes on behind his well-mannered exterior is not obvious.'

Gus drew his tweed coat more firmly around him and pushed a stone out of the way with his shoe. 'I don't like to think that somebody hates me enough to want to do me in. I have academic enemies, what scholar doesn't, but they slay me in print, in the columns of the learned journals, not in person.'

Hugo, trying to lighten the mood, said, 'Georgia suggested that somebody has it in for Earls.'

Gus laughed at that and said, 'I'm beginning to think I have it in for Earls. I don't think I'll ever feel like one or learn how to behave like one.' He shrugged his shoulders. 'Priscilla give me the name of a tailor in Savile Row, she says I need new clothes, that I can't go around looking like an American. I am an American.'

'Not entirely. Not now.'

Gus said, 'I'll always be an outsider. Look at Freya, she grew up here, like Sonia. They understand the Castle and its ways and the town and its people, although Freya tells me the Castle and town never really mingle.'

'It's always been that way for the English aristocracy. They often don't make their lives where their country houses are. Your father's centre of his life was really London – Parliament and his government work. The Castle was a duty and obligation and a place where he liked to be from time to time. I think he had very strong feelings about it. But that's quite another proposition to moving to a new place and a new life. Where you have to establish yourself and put down roots.'

'Tell me about it,' Gus said. 'In the small town where I grew up, if you hadn't been there for thirty years or so, you're a new-comer and an outsider. There's more to it than that here, isn't there? I wouldn't have thought in this day and age that this whole business of being an Earl and rank and so forth could mark one out as being so apart from most people.'

Hugo said, 'It could take you half a lifetime to accustom your-self to the English class system. It's all changing now, thank God. It started to be shaken up after the first war and now after this war, things are very different.'

'I hope you're right.'

'You can make yourself into whatever kind of Earl you want. You have responsibilities to your tenants, of course, but I can't see you falling down on that. Your father was, from what I heard, an excellent landlord.'

'It seems such a tremendous task, looking after this Castle and everything that goes with it.'

Hugo said, 'Delegate. You have plenty of people who know what they're doing. As long as you choose the right people and keep an eye on them in the right way, they'll run things for you. It doesn't have to be a full-time job.'

'That's what my father did?'

'I never knew your father but I do know that his wife, virtually ran the estate and the Castle in the thirties. Before she went off to Canada.'

'Are you suggesting I should marry an Englishwoman and pile all these responsibilities on her shoulders? I can't think any woman worth her salt would be prepared to take that on.'

Hugo laughed. 'Not if you put it like that, no. Somebody might be willing to take you on, Gus, simply because you are you.'

The darkness made it easy to speak of things two Englishmen probably never would. They were both outsiders, which is why Gus could talk to him like this.

Gus went on, 'I sometimes think I should have married again. For the sake of Babs and Polly. It's hard for girls to grow up motherless. But of course you know that with your Georgia. She's quite a character.'

Hugo said diplomatically, 'I'm glad that she and Polly seem to be getting along better.'

Gus said, 'They've got some scheme going. I'm not sure what it is, but it seems to be taking up a good deal of their attention. Babs is helping them, which is good. I can't say that she seems to be settling here, but it's early days yet.'

'It's disconcerting to have a murder inquiry on your doorstep within a few days of arriving here.'

'Georgia seems to take it in her stride.'

Hugo said quickly, 'It isn't callousness, I assure you. I think because of the manner of our mother's death and the hardship of growing up during and after the war, she's developed something of a carapace. It doesn't mean that she doesn't feel things, but I think she's learned to cope with them at an earlier age than most girls do.'

Gus sounded horrified. 'Heavens, I would never accuse the young lady of being callous. I do worry that it's affected Polly. She's had another nightmare, although not such a noisy one.'

'Isn't it better now that she's sharing a room with Babs?'

'It is, but she still complains that the room is creepy. I agree with her, with the big fireplace all those rooms have and the full-length windows and the panelling – it is like something out of a horror movie. But there you are, at the moment it's our home and I don't see what I can do about it. I just have to hope that she can grow accustomed to it. And not get fanciful about these ghosts she claims to see.'

Scene 2

As they drew near to the top of the hill and went through the great archway with its portcullis, the moon was obscured by a passing cloud. Hugo looked up into the night sky. 'The weather is changing.'

Gus said, 'I thought it wasn't feeling quite so cold.'

'I don't think there'll be a frost tonight.'

When they went into the kitchen, Mrs Partridge greeted them with a weather update that confirmed this. She'd listened to the forecast on the wireless and there was a front coming across the country. 'It's going to get warmer, and there's already a thaw with possible flooding from the melting snow,' she said with relish. 'It's only a lull, mind you, they say a few days of wet and windy weather and then, come the New Year, there's going to be a big freeze and a lot of snow.'

Gus and Hugo were glad to get into the warmth and light of the kitchen. Freya was sitting at the kitchen table with Magnus on her lap. 'It's a shame the thaw didn't come sooner; think of all those people who couldn't get away for Christmas.'

In which case, Oliver would have left the Castle on Christmas Eve and would still be alive. Hugo knew that Freya was thinking just the same, but the thought was left unspoken.

Mrs Partridge said, 'I told Lady Sonia, and she's in a right paddy about it. She said that she and Rupert would leave immediately, but Superintendent MacLeod says they can't for the moment.'

Freya looked dismayed. 'Oh Lord! Where is she?'

'She's gone off to take a bath, one of those long ones she has that use up all the hot water. Full of potions and lotions, and she'll come out smelling like a film star.'

Freya said, 'If it puts her in a better temper then let's be glad of it. What about Rupert?'

'He said he had letters to write and some work to attend to.' Mrs Partridge paused, a disapproving look on her face. 'He's installed himself in his late lordship's study. Lady Sonia said it would be all right.'

She looked at Gus, who said cheerfully, 'He's welcome to it. I don't think it's a room that I'm going to want to use much. Where's Polly?'

'In the dining room, along with Georgia and Lady Babs. They've taken over the dining table and they've got long strips of paper laid out all over it. They carried off a roll of lining paper they found in a cupboard and that's what they're using. Don't ask me what they're up to, because I don't know. I just told them there was to be no scratching the table, because that table's murder to get scratches off.'

Intrigued, Freya, Hugo and Gus went along to the dining room, which was a hive of activity. Leo was there, consulting a large leather-bound volume and Polly was sitting beside him. There was a big pile of books between them. She looked up as they came in. 'Hi, Pops. You'll never guess what we're doing.'

'A spot of decorating?'

Polly looked at him severely. 'Don't be frivolous. I'll tell you exactly what we doing; we're drawing up a family tree. I asked Freya this morning she said she thought there was one somewhere in a Bible but when we looked it's all very dull. Just names and things, doesn't tell you about anything, and so I thought since they're your ancestors, Pops, and ours too, you ought to know about them.' Then she said to Freya: 'You're just the person we need. You've been writing a history of Selchester, you must know all about it.'

This could be awkward. 'So far I've only covered a small part of the family history. It takes a lot of time to go through family letters and records as they're often hard to decipher.'

Polly looked at Freya disapprovingly. 'Georgia and Mrs Partridge say you tap away at that typewriter for hours and hours on end. You write reams and reams of stuff and that has to be more than going through a few letters and so on. You must have the whole thing at your fingertips. You've been at it for years.'

Freya said, 'I'm sure your father will tell you that it doesn't quite work like that.'

Leo came to her rescue. 'History does take many different forms, Polly.'

'A family tree sounds interesting,' Gus said. He moved over to the table and saw that Babs was drawing the stem and the branches of a large oak tree with numerous branches. 'This looks as though it's going to be very decorative, Babs.'

She muttered under her breath, 'It'll amuse the kids. Take their minds off things.'

Freya, watching her clever fingers, knew that Babs was, in fact, enjoying herself.

Babs stood back and said, 'I can put in the faces from those portraits upstairs and maybe there are more portraits elsewhere. In books? Family drawings and photos?'

'I'm sure there are,' Freya said.

'Polly and Georgia can add information about them. Father Leo says he'll help.'

'Hugo's the one who'll be most use to you,' Leo said. 'He read History at university and I daresay he's used to old records.'

Polly said, 'I'm starting with the Fitzwarins right from the beginning. I can tell you, Pops, they were a fairly wild bunch. Always pushing and shoving to get their hands on the Castle and the Earldom. All kinds of mischief they got up to. And you're not the only one to come in from outside and not brought up in the Castle, in case you had any thoughts that way.' She pointed to the book. 'There are heaps of them who didn't expect to inherit or simply inherited in some doubtful way. Like when Henry IV banished one of the barons, as we were then, and gave the title to his nephew. The nephew had the original Earl killed in France because he thought he might come back and claim the title. Not very familial.'

Freya said, 'You'll find quite a lot of lively family history there. Polly's right; our Fitzwarin ancestors were a violent and lawless lot.'

Polly said disapprovingly, 'A lot of them were apostates. It's quite shocking the way they gave up being Catholic. I thought all these old families were recusants and stuck to the true faith through thick and thin.'

Leo said, 'They did that for a reason, Polly. If you look you'll see it's the eldest son who apostatises. Until the late eighteenth century, Catholics couldn't own property and they couldn't sit in Parliament until 1829. So if they wanted to keep the Castle in the family, then at the time of his inheritance the eldest son had couldn't be a Catholic. So he became a member of the Church of England, and once he'd inherited lands and titles he reconverted.'

Georgia said admiringly, 'I never knew that. And they let them get away with it?'

'It was easier in some times than others. But the Selchesters were by and large true to their faith.'

'You'd think,' Georgia said, 'that there'd be a priest hole or two in the Castle.'

'There's supposed to be one,' Freya said. 'Tom and Sonia and I used to spend hours searching for it, but we never found it. Wherever it is, it's hidden so well that it's completely lost. It is mentioned in some of the records, though. It was known as The Room That Has No Ears.'

Gus said, 'That's quaint.'

'It makes sense,' Hugo said. 'If it was more than a priest hole, if it were a secret chapel where a priest could hold Mass then it would be essential that nobody could overhear them. They would have been careful about the household, the servants and so on, but even so those were difficult times for Catholic families, as Leo said.'

'And a lot of them came to sticky ends,' Polly said. 'You'd be amazed, Pops, how many of our ancestors were murdered or killed in battle.'

Georgia said, 'To be fair, that was in the olden days.'

Polly came back swiftly, 'Well, my grandfather didn't exactly die in his bed, did he?'

Freya said, 'No, but his father did. With great pomp and ceremony from what I gather. All the family gathered about his bed. Mind you, his dying words were, "Damn you all."'

Polly was shocked. 'That's no attitude to take with him into the next life. Whatever did the priest say?'

'I think the priest had momentary deafness,' Freya said. 'Officially he died fortified by the rites of Holy Church, so that was all right.'

Polly said, 'Are they all here in the Castle?'

'Ghosts, you mean?' Georgia said.

Gus said quickly, 'I'd rather you didn't talk about ghosts, Georgia. Your Uncle Leo will tell you that there are no such things.'

'I meant their remains.'

'Many of our forebears do lie in the Castle vaults, Polly. And that's where they stay,' said Freya.

Georgia said, 'Not your grandfather though. He was buried in Oxford, wasn't he, Freya? Lady Sonia didn't want him here in the Castle.'

Scene 3

Gus and Hugo left them to it and adjourned to the library, calling in at the kitchen on the way to ask Mrs Partridge if they could have some coffee.

'You go along, my lord, and I'll bring it to you there.'

'Do you think I'll ever get used to being called "my lord"?' Gus said as they walked through the Great Hall.

'You aren't the first person to have inherited a title unexpectedly. Give it few months and you won't notice it.'

Gus wanted to see the old drawings and engravings of the Castle. Hugo went across to the far corner where a deep cabinet with slender shelves housed albums of prints and photos.

Meanwhile, Gus was cruising along the shelves. He extracted a small black book from two leather volumes of poetry and said, 'This looks as though it doesn't belong here.'

As Hugo looked round to see what Gus was talking about, there was a slight sound from the gallery above his head.

Was someone moving about up there? Maybe it was just the sunlight filtered by branches outside the window which had given him that impression. Yet instinct, training and experience told him that somebody was there.

The gallery ran round three sides of the library and was accessed by a wooden spiral staircase within the library and another staircase outside. The library was arranged in sections marked with antique busts placed on pillars, and these busts were level with the gallery railing.

Hugo's eye swept along the line of classical emperors and ancient worthies. It stopped at Cicero. Was there a slender shadow along one edge of the base? At that very moment, the marble bust toppled over and crashed to the floor.

Gus and Hugo were there in a flash, looking down at Cicero, who now had a broken Roman nose. Bits of marble lay strewn around.

'Stay right here, Gus,' Hugo said, and he limped over to the spiral staircase. It was awkward, with his leg, but he made it up to the gallery. There was nobody there. He hadn't expected there to be. He walked along the gallery till he came to the pillar on which Cicero had stood.

He leaned over the railing and said to Gus, 'I can't see any reason why it should have fallen. It's lucky that neither of us was underneath it.'

The door opened and Leo came in. He looked at Gus, at the broken bust and then up at the gallery. Hugo beckoned to him and, moving much more nimbly than his nephew, he went up the spiral staircase to join him. Hugo pointed silently to the plinth on top of the pillar.

'Did you see anyone?' Leo said.

'No, but I'd swear somebody was up here.'

'It could have been dislodged for a while without anyone noticing it.'

Hugo said, 'It's heavy, but it wouldn't take too much effort to rock it towards the edge. But I don't think it could have happened while somebody was flicking a feather duster over it, and I don't suppose these busts ever get more than that.'

Leo ran his fingers over Caesar's nearby bald pate. 'This hasn't been dusted for some time.'

The others were coming into the library now. Polly said, 'That was the most awful crash. Are you all right, Pops?'

Georgia said, 'Golly, look; one of those old Romans has come down.'

Sonia came in, interested but not alarmed, followed by Rupert. She surveyed the scene and said, 'I always said that those marble busts perched up there were dangerous. I'd get rid of them all if I were you, Gus.'

Freya, who had come in on her heels, knelt beside the marble head. She said to Gus, 'It'll be possible to have this repaired. How odd that it should suddenly topple over like this. None of them have ever done that, and they've been here for about two hundred years.'

Hugo had been going round from Trajan via Ovid to Horace at the end of the row, methodically checking each bust. He looked down and called out, 'All the others are perfectly secure. I can't think why that one fell.'

Polly was holding her father's arm. 'You weren't anywhere near it? It wasn't intended for you?'

Gus put his arm round her. 'No, Polly, I'm fine. No one was trying to drop a bust of Cicero on me. I was nowhere near it. I was standing over there, I was looking at a book I'd taken from the shelf that seemed interesting.' He looked around the library. 'Where is it? I must have dropped it when the bust came down. See if you can find it, girls, it's a black book.'

Georgia and Polly hunted for it, going down on hands and knees and peering under chairs. 'It's definitely not here,' Georgia said.

Gus frowned. 'How odd.'

Leo said, 'Do you know what it was?'

'I'd only just opened it. There were drawings of rustic scenes and ruins. And a poem or two written in copperplate.'

Sonia, who'd been watching him intently, let out a long breath. 'No other writing? Was it a notebook?'

'It looked to me like a commonplace book, I should think from the last century.'

Sonia said, 'Whatever it is, it seems to have vanished.'

'Maybe in the excitement of the moment I flung it away from me and it caught on a shelf or something. It will turn up.'

Mrs Partridge came stalking in. 'Now what?' She looked severely at the fallen Cicero. 'I never could hold with all these marble heads. They take a deal of dusting and do no good to anyone. Now my fine gentleman here has come crashing down and lost his nose. I'll have to fetch a dustpan and brush.'

Hugo grinned at her. 'I don't think you can sweep him up with a dustpan and brush, Mrs P.'

Mrs Partridge gave him a scathing look. 'No, and I wouldn't try to, as you very well know, Mr Hugo. There's a lot of dust come down, and look at the dent it's made in the parquet. That'll all have to be put right.'

Between them Gus and Hugo shifted the bust and propped it up against a shelf.

Georgia surveyed it with a look of contempt. 'Serves him right. They're always making me read Cicero at school; he writes a lot of rot. Come on, Polly, let's get back to the family tree.'

Chapter Fourteen

Scene 1

'Just like it used to be,' Georgia said happily, as she helped Mrs Partridge lay the table.

Most of the Selchester clan plus Rupert had gone over to dine at Veryan House. Gus willingly, as he felt that he needed to get to know his aunt better. Babs and Polly, who had been intimidated by their great-aunt, with less enthusiasm. Sonia with a kind of resignation. At first she said she wouldn't go. 'Let Priscilla shake Gus inside out, which is what she wants to do.'

Rupert, mindful of how influential an MP Lady Priscilla's husband, Sir Archibald, was, said, 'Rude not to go, don't you think?'

Freya was definite; she wasn't going. 'No, thank you. When she's finished with Gus, she'll start again on me, and I had enough of that on Christmas Day.'

Hugo said, 'What have you done now?'

'It's not what I've done; it's what I'm not doing. Aunt Priscilla is a great organiser of other people's lives, and she considers that now that I have to give up my tower here, it's time for me to leave Selchester and go to London. To make a life for myself.'

'Preferably,' Georgia put in, 'by finding yourself a suitable husband and settling down? Isn't that what aunts always want their nieces to do?'

Freya laughed. 'She's not the only one, because my parents nag me, even from Washington. They send me letters saying how I mustn't let myself sink into provincial life and what wonderful opportunities are opening up in London.'

Georgia said, 'That's what Valerie says to you, Hugo, all those opportunities she goes on about.'

Sonia said, not sounding particularly concerned, 'Priscilla will be annoyed; an invitation to Veryan House is a equivalent to a royal command.'

Freya said, 'Tell her I'm starting a cold or something.'

Sonia cast her eyes heavenwards. 'That would be lying, which would be wrong, wouldn't it, Father Leo? And lucky you not to be invited, only I happen to know it's because she plans to have you to dine on your own – what an honour.'

Leo said, 'I'm keeping out of this, but I have to say I think Freya is wise to stay away. Her reluctance to do what Lady Priscilla wants is bound to end in recriminations and a family argument. Which are always best avoided.'

So there they were having supper in the kitchen. Mrs Partridge had said that she'd get food on the table and then would be off, if they didn't mind. 'It's my evening for whist.'

'Watch how you bet,' Georgia said. 'You know last time you lost three shillings and sixpence.'

Mrs Partridge said, 'I feel my luck will be in tonight.'

They ate their stew and baked potatoes. Georgia was right, it was like old times. Not so old; it was hard to remember they'd only been at the Castle since September.

It felt like home, that was the trouble.

He'd never imagined that home sweet home might come in the shape of a castle. A London flat, possibly; not this huge, cold and ancient pile. Nor could he have foreseen that three women – Georgia, Freya and Mrs Partridge – were what made it feel like home. As did the presence of Leo, who was feeding a scrap of meat to a pleased Magnus.

When they were eating the excellent trifle Mrs Partridge had left for them, Freya said, 'We need to talk things over.'

Hugo opened his mouth to suggest that Georgia should remove herself, but she was having none of it.

'You've got that look on your face, Hugo, that means you're planning to talk about things to do with the murder. You think it might upset me and so I'd better go off and do something else. Well, I won't. For one thing I intend to have a second helping of pudding. And for another I'm just as interested as you are. And if you're worried about me being of a nervous disposition, it'd be a lot more worse for my nerves for me to be by myself all in this great big frightening castle while you're sitting cosily in here discussing interesting things. Besides, I was very helpful last time, when we were solving Lord Selchester's murder. I shall keep notes and make lists; I'm good at that.'

Hugo admitted defeat. There was no point in trying to reason with Georgia in this mood. And there was some justice in what she'd said. They could wait to talk until she went to bed, but by then the others might be back from Veryan House. So he launched into an account of what they'd discovered about Saul Ingham, aka Sampson.

Georgia unscrewed her fountain pen, wrote 'Suspects' at the top of a sheet of paper, underlined the word carefully and then looked round expectantly. 'Shoot.'

They looked back at her and she said impatiently, 'Somebody has to have killed Oliver, so we need a list of suspects. Of course, if any outsider could have crept in and done things to the fuses and switches and things, then it could be a long list. Only who'd want to kill Oliver? Nobody knew him.'

'An accidental murder, perhaps.'

'Means, motive and opportunity, that's what we want for whoever the victim was meant to be. You are lucky, Hugo and Freya, to have got into Nightingale Cottage, because I've heard that it's very strange in there. Can we put the man there down as a suspect?'

Georgia wrote down all the names. Then she put crosses beside their four names. 'None of us did it. Gus and his daughters? I can see Babs murdering someone for a philosophical reason, but I don't think she'd know anything about all the electrics and nor would Polly. Child murderers are interesting, of course, but I don't think Polly is one. Then there's his nibs, he knows all about the electrical stuff, and he's clever, but why on earth would he want to kill Oliver? He'd never set eyes on him until he came here, and he didn't even invite him. And he wouldn't go electrocuting himself, he's not bonkers. So that leaves Hugo's mysterious stranger who sounds like he was certainly out for blood, even if it was the wrong blood. And Rupert and Sonia.'

Freya had been in a bit of a dream, but she now came to and said, 'I have someone to add to the list of suspects. At least a kind of suspect; I don't see how he could have fiddled with the electrics on Christmas Day, but you never know. And he could certainly have been responsible for all those other things that happened to Gus.'

They listened in silence, while Georgia added the name Mr Jenkins to her list.

Leo said, 'Can we see the sketch?'

Freya had put it in the drawer together with Mrs Partridge's newspaper. She said to Hugo, 'I thought of telling Superintendent MacLeod, but it's going to come better from you.'

'It's an interesting face,' Leo said. 'Babs has managed to capture the blankness of his expression. This is a man who doesn't want to be noticed, the kind of man who blends into the background.'

'He was in Selchester in the autumn,' Freya said. 'We thought he might have had something to do with Jason Filbert's death, but the police said they knew him, he was a private investigator.'

Georgia added a star beside Jenkins. 'What could he have been investigating in Selchester just before Christmas? He has to go down as a suspect.'

Leo said, 'Except that he seems to have left Selchester on the 24th.'

'Laying a false trail,' Georgia said promptly. 'Muddying the waters, queering the pitch, that kind of thing.'

'Or maybe,' Leo said, 'he had something to do with what did seem to be attempts on Gus's life, but nothing to do with Oliver's murder.'

'Other than this mysterious Mr Jenkins, who doesn't seem to have been in the neighbourhood at the time,' Georgia said, 'it's Lady Sonia or Rupert.

Hugo said, with a glance at Freya, 'Both of whom are the only people who stand to gain in any obvious way from Gus's death.'

'Money is always a motive for murder,' Leo said. 'Yet neither Lady Sonia nor Rupert are in any way desperate for money – didn't you say Rupert had recently come into a considerable inheritance of his own? It seems odd that they would want to dispose of the Earl, especially since Lady Sonia is the only one who'd benefit directly.'

Georgia said, 'I did suggest there might be a maniac out there with a grudge against Earls. Or some unknown enemy who wants to take revenge on any Lord Selchester. There could be an ancient feud and they won't be content until the line dies out.' She added practically, 'Although unless Gus gets married again and has a son, the Earldom will finish with him in any case. So it all seems a bit pointless.'

Freya sighed. 'It seems awfully cold-blooded to think of Sonia wanting to kill Gus. I know she's infuriated by his coming into the title, but if she had any murderous intentions, why make her discontent so widely known? She'd be the obvious suspect, especially inviting herself here. Could she be that stupid?'

Hugo said, 'Whatever Lady Sonia is, she's not stupid.'

'I can see her bumping someone off,' Georgia said, 'only I think she'd do it in some insidious way. Poison, for instance.'

Freya gave her a sharp look 'Why do you say that?'

Georgia shrugged. 'Poison's supposed to be a woman's weapon. And it's detached; you can poison people at arm's length. You slip something into their tea, so it isn't the same as bashing them on the head. I suppose wiring up a switch so that somebody gets frazzled is also distant, but it's sort of contrived, and can you see Lady Sonia messing around with fuses and wiring?'

'What did Sonia do during the war, Freya?' Hugo asked. 'If she worked as a driver in the ATS as a driver or anything like that, she might have acquired skills that would make electrical circuits child's play to her.'

Freya's face lightened and she laughed. 'Need you ask? Nothing like the ATS for Sonia. She married to avoid being called up, and then once she was widowed she managed to get herself a cosy billet in some charitable outfit attached to the Navy. Which meant she came and went very much as she wanted and went on living the life that she was used to. No, Sonia was never one to get her hands dirty.'

Georgia said, 'That sort of leaves Rupert.'

'The difficulty there,' Leo said, 'is that as far as we know, Rupert has nothing to do with Gus. He hadn't met him and except the connection with Lady Sonia, why should he have any animosity against

216

him? The same applies as it does with Lady Sonia: why come to the Castle and commit a murder where you'll be a suspect? His only motive is Lady Sonia's inheritance if – and it's a big if – he really is going to marry her. And I'm not at all convinced by the engagement or the motive.'

'We're forgetting about the other attempts on Gus's life. Sonia or Rupert weren't on that liner, and even if you count that one a genuine accident neither Sonia nor Rupert were in Selchester that afternoon in the museum. One or other of them might have been in Oxford; that can be checked.'

'Hired assassins,' Georgia said. 'They paid a hitman to do the job.'

Leo said, 'You've been going to the pictures too much, Georgia. It's not as easy as you think to find assassins.'

'London's full of people shooting each other; all those gangs. Although I don't suppose Rupert moves in those circles.'

'What line are the police taking, Hugo?' Leo asked.

'Gus, rather than Oliver, as the intended victim.'

Georgia said, 'Perhaps it was meant to be Oliver all along.'

Freya said, 'That's even more improbable. The only person who knew him was Sonia and she claims she hardly knew him at all.'

Georgia, with a sly look at her brother said, 'Maybe they'd had a love affair. Maybe it was a *crime passionnel*, like in France.'

'Stop right there, Georgia,' Hugo said.

Leo took her suggestion more calmly. 'I think we can discount that. There was nothing in their behaviour to suggest that there'd been any degree of intimacy between them. It's a difficult thing to conceal; they'd have to both ~~have to~~ be consummate actors to pull that off. Either there's hostility or there's some kind of friendly regard. Such liaisons always leave an emotional impression.'

Freya said, 'Apart from coming to do the inventory in the autumn, when he was only here for a few hours, Oliver has no connection with anyone here or with the Castle or Selchester at all.'

Georgia said, 'That's not true.'

They all looked at her. 'What do you mean?' Freya said.

Georgia got up, went to a drawer of the dresser, withdrew a large book and plonked it on the table. 'This is the housekeeper's book. Of course it hasn't been kept up for years, but it was still being used when Lord Selchester was alive. So when we were having all these guests for Christmas, Mrs Partridge said she would get out the book and put them in and she showed it to me. The housekeeper used to write which guests were coming, what servants they'd bring with them – maids and valets and things these days – and which rooms they were in. And if they didn't bring servants, who was going to wait on them. All that kind of information.' She opened the book. 'Look, this is way back before the war.'

Freya reached out and took the book. She said in an awed voice, 'I'd completely forgotten about this. Yes, of course, everything was meticulously recorded.' She riffled through the pages and put her finger on an entry. 'There's me coming back for the holidays. I was in the Peony Room, which was the room I always had. And that Mabel was to wait on me. She was Sonia's maid and we shared her when I was here for the holidays.'

Hugo took the book from her in his turn, 'Where does it mention Oliver, Georgia?'

'Go to the very last entry, in January 1947. There's a list there of who was invited for the weekend that Lord Selchester was murdered. Only there are lines through most of them since they never came on account of the snow. There you are, second from the bottom. Oliver Seynton. He was going to be put in the Randolf Room.'

There was utter silence for a few moments and then Hugo let out a low whistle. 'So your uncle did know Oliver, Freya.'

'And,' Freya said, 'since we know he had some hold over those four' – she pointed to the top names in the list – 'maybe he did over the rest of them as well.'

Leo looked annoyed. 'I remember saying at the time that we should find out about the people who were invited and didn't come. How remiss of us not to have followed up on that. Except that we didn't need to know about them, as things turned out, because we identified the murderer.'

Hugo said, 'Selchester's puppets.'

'Puppets?' Freya said. 'Oh, he was pulling their strings.'

'And, if the four we knew about were typical, they danced to his tune.'

'So just what did he know about Oliver Seynton?' Leo said. 'He wasn't over-scrupulous about his dealings in the art world, but I doubt if that would have given Selchester much of a hold over him.'

Freya got up and began clearing the dishes from the table. 'No, I don't need help, thank you.'

She wanted to think.

Scene 2

Georgia stroked Magnus, who had leapt on to the bench beside her. Hugo took her notes and studied them, while Leo sat wrapped in calm silence. When Freya came back to the table he said, 'You know something about this, don't you, Freya?'

'Yes and no. I didn't know that Selchester knew Oliver. What I do know is that Oliver had something disgraceful in his past. To do with the war. And if my uncle had found out about it, then he would certainly have had a hold over him.'

Hugo was looking at her with some surprise. 'Why didn't you mention this before? You told us you met Oliver for the first time when he came with Sonia to do the inventory.'

'I didn't know anything about it at that time, and I hadn't met Oliver until then. I only learned about it recently.'

Caught between a rock and a hard place was what she was. She couldn't pass on what Dinah had told her, not without her permission. At the same time, if it had anything to do with a murder, then she couldn't just keep silent.

'I can't tell you about it in any detail, because it was told to me in confidence.' She looked at Leo. 'You'll know about that.'

'There are secrets one has to keep,' Leo said. 'Not just the famous ones bound by the seal of the confessional. If this information was entrusted to you on the understanding that it would go no further, you feel it a matter of honour not to pass it on.'

'You should tell the people of Selchester that,' Georgia said. 'A Selchester secret is one only half the town knows about. Can't you tell us anything about it, Freya? Did this person have nasty habits? Did he keep mistresses or was it one awful guilty secret from the past, like he himself killed someone? Perhaps this was a revenge killing.'

That struck home. If Dinah had a motive, it would be revenge.

She addressed herself again to Leo. 'Would you say that any one of is capable of killing in certain circumstances?'

'Yes, unfortunately human experience bears that out.'

'I know revenge is a dish best served cold, but I think if that was the reason for a murder, it would be done impulsively. I'd expect in those circs that someone would lash out, not plot a subtle crime.'

'Someone here in Selchester might have wanted to kill Oliver out of revenge, is what you're saying?'

Hugo's voice was impersonal. Had he guessed?

Leo said, 'Would this person have the knowledge to be able to tinker with the wiring?'

Dinah had worked as radio operator in the war. Didn't they all have to know about wiring?

'I can't honestly say. During the war, almost everyone learned to do a lot of things that they wouldn't have done before.'

Hugo was looking again at the entry in the ledger. 'It's extraordinary how your uncle's influence reaches out from beyond the grave. I can't help feeling that Oliver's presence here and the motive, whatever it was, for his murder, is connected to your uncle.'

Georgia said, 'What about that phone call Oliver made on Christmas Day?'

'When he was so distraught?' Hugo said. 'I'd forgotten that.'

'Would the local telephone exchange have kept a note of numbers called?' Leo said.

Freya shook her head. 'They aren't supposed to. I mean if you asked Irene, she might remember a name or a conversation.'

'That's not something that she should pass on,' Leo said firmly.

'Of course not, but Selchester has its own rules; Irene and the other operators are great spreaders of news,' Freya said.

'The police could question her,' Hugo said.

'They could,' Freya said, 'but it's fifty-fifty as to whether she'd tell them anything.'

Hugo made a face. 'Having told the police I thought someone wanted to murder Gus and Oliver's death was a mistake, I wonder whether they'll take any notice when I turn up and say, "Actually, we think the murderer did want to kill Oliver." And,' he looked directly at Freya, 'they'll start to dig for dirt, looking for motives and in the end they'll find out the information you want to keep secret, Freya.'

She said in a sudden burst of temper. 'I wouldn't shield a murderer. But I don't think the person in question, however much hostility they felt towards Oliver, would murder him.'

Chapter Fifteen

Scene 1

The next morning, when Hugo had left for work, Freya button-holed Leo, 'We need to talk to Sonia.'

'Isn't she more likely to come out with any information if I'm not there?'

Freya said, 'You have a lot of influence on her. I don't think it's your being a priest, although that alarms her – maybe somewhere she has vestiges of a conscience. No, she regards you as having extraordinary powers of perception. Which you do. If I talk to her alone, we'll end up quarrelling. I don't get on easily with her, although once I did. She's built such a barrier around herself that it's *hard* to find a way in. Sometimes when you are so familiar with someone you just run along the same tracks. You aren't; you'll pick up things that I won't. And I daresay you're as good as Hugo at telling when people are lying.'

'Oh, I think you attribute too great a skill to me there, Freya. Many people do lie quite consistently. If it's habitual, then their lies don't mean so very much. But I have a feeling that Lady Sonia isn't that kind of a liar. She seems to me the kind of person who skirts round the truth or avoids a direct question. She doesn't really feel comfortable with lies.'

Freya thought about her cousin. 'I think you're probably right. She didn't lie as a girl, but then she didn't tell the truth either. So I suppose she hasn't changed very much. And you're right, some of us tell lies all the time.'

Leo said, apparently inconsequentially, 'It is after all what novelists do. It's a respectable profession, but you could say that they make their living by telling lies.'

Freya said, 'I never looked at it like that. But yes, it is all making up stories, as our nurses used to warn us not to do. Stories told with the express intention of wanting people to believe them, at least until the book is closed.'

'Sometimes in that fabrication, among those stories, there are grains of deeper truths. Reading novels is one of the ways we come to understand our humanity.'

Freya said, 'I remember Hugo buying you an Agatha Christie for your birthday. I was surprised when I found that you were priest, as well as a distinguished scientist.'

Leo was amused. 'Did you think I spent my time reading works of theology, when not catching up on the latest scientific publications? I read a lot of fiction for pleasure and relaxation.' He paused. 'Dinah sent up a book for me that I'd asked her for. The latest novel by Rosina Wyndham. I greatly enjoyed it. An enthralling story written by a first-class author. And one who knows her history. I couldn't put it down.'

'Hardly suitable reading for a priest, I would have thought. Rather too racy.'

He regarded her with amusement.

He knew. He knew she was Rosina Wyndham. How had he guessed?

'I gather the author cherishes her anonymity,' he said.

'I expect she has her reasons.'

'I expect she does.' He smiled. 'Don't worry, I shan't tell anyone your secret. I guessed you weren't writing a family history last time I was here. I know quite a few writers, and I could tell you were writing a novel. And then your delightful Clarissa is so like your seventeenth-century ancestor. I put two and two together and there it was, Freya is Rosina. You must be doing very well from your books.'

That was true. 'I'd have to get a job if I didn't write. My private income after tax would barely keep Magnus in fish.'

'Or you in dashing frocks.'

Freya felt that this conversation had gone far enough. 'Let's get back to Sonia,' she said firmly. 'She's not with Rupert; he's in Grace Hall, making important telephone calls. It's inevitable that the news about Oliver being the intended murder victim is going to come out, and I expect he's briefing the Conservative Party office and everyone else about it. I believe he's more annoyed about being mixed up in a murder than he is sorry for Oliver. He doesn't seem to be a man who cares very much for other people at all. I suppose that's what will make him a successful politician.'

Leo said, 'Where is Sonia?'

'Mrs P will know. Let's go and ask her.'

Mrs Partridge was in the kitchen, having set Pam to work preparing vegetables while she was stirring a pan of something on the stove.

Leo sniffed the air. 'Smells delicious, Mrs Partridge.'

'Do you know where Lady Sonia is?' Freya said.

Mrs Partridge said, 'I do, she's in the South Drawing Room. She's a pile of magazines with her and Pam just took her up some coffee, didn't you, Pam?'

Pam looked up from her potato peelings. Her face was shining, 'Oh, she's got the most lovely magazines, *Vogue* and *Tatler* and all sorts. She said she'd leave them here when she goes back to London, and I can have them.'

'Get on with you,' her aunt said scornfully. '*Vogue*, indeed!'

Pam went back to her potatoes.

Sonia was indeed in the South Drawing Room, stretched out on a sofa and flicking through *Vogue*. She had a cigarette tucked into her long holder and a discontented expression on her face.

She looked up at Freya and Leo. 'Do you want Rupert? Because he isn't here.'

Freya sat down, and Sonia, clearly not wanting to be interrupted, ostentatiously held her finger to mark her place on the page. 'What is it?'

Freya said, 'Tear yourself away from *Vogue* for a few minutes, Sonia. There's something we need to know.'

Sonia's eyes narrowed. 'We? Who's this we? You and Father Leo?' She gave him a baleful look. 'What about?'

'Oliver Seynton,' Leo said.

Sonia heaved a loud sigh. 'I know nothing about Oliver, at least no more than I already told you. And I don't see why it's any concern of either of yours, or Hugo who seems to have a propensity for putting his nose in where it's not wanted, or that irritatingly curious sister of his.'

Freya tried another tack. 'Did Selchester not give you any idea how he came by those pictures you claim are yours? Did Oliver have anything to do with them? You took him up to the attic, didn't you, on Christmas Day? And it was after that that he started to behave so strangely. What upset him so much?'

Sonia waved her cigarette holder in the air and closed her eyes in exasperation. 'I really don't know how my father acquired those paintings and I don't much care. It was a canny move, because they're worth a lot of money, thank goodness. And don't start saying they should go to Gus and not me, I don't want to hear any of that again. They're mine and I won't let anyone take them away from me. As to Oliver, who knows what made him go all peculiar. He'd never seen them before. At least,' she added thoughtfully, 'he might have seen the Picasso; he came over all odd when he saw that one.'

'Did you know that Oliver was invited here the weekend your father was murdered?' Leo said.

Lady Sonia's eyes flew open. She stared at Leo. 'What do you mean, Oliver was invited?'

'Come on, Sonia,' Freya said. 'You must know that there were about a dozen guests asked for that weekend. Who would all have been here that night if it hadn't been for the weather.'

Sonia said, 'I have no idea who else was invited. It's not the kind of thing that my father spoke about, and he was in such a foul temper that weekend anyway, over Tom. And once my migraine had started, he could have invited the whole of the bench of bishops and half the saints in heaven for all I knew or cared. What makes you think Oliver was invited?'

'His name is in the housekeeper's book. The names of all the guests were listed there. You know that's what was always done.'

Sonia said, 'Who's been snooping in the housekeeper's book?'

Freya was finding it difficult to keep her temper. 'No one. It's in the drawer in the kitchen where it's been ever since Selchester disappeared. Mrs Partridge had a fancy to put down the guests this Christmas, so she took it out. Oliver's name is there. My uncle would hardly have invited him if he hadn't known him.'

'I have no idea how he knew him, if he did. And he can't tell you, unless you want to have a séance to find out.' She glanced at Leo. 'Sorry.'

'I can think of more efficient ways of getting information,' was all Leo said.

'Anyhow, whatever Oliver was doing in 'forty-five or six, I don't think he was dealing in pictures. But you'd have to find out from his colleagues and people who know him better. I scarcely know him. I just know that he's very good at this kind of deal, that's why I asked him to come up.'

Leo said, 'Who told you that he was good at this kind of deal?'

'I can't remember. Word gets about – you know how it is. Maybe it was the Ancasters. I really can't remember. Does it matter?'

'You really didn't have anything to do with Oliver?'

Sonia took a long draught on her cigarette and looked up at the ceiling, a deliberately bored look on her face. 'Oliver Seynton and I did not move in the same circles. End of story. I'm not a bohemian. I do number a few artists and musicians among my friends, but I don't have a wide circle of acquaintance in that world. I prefer to stick to my own kind.'

Freya exchanged a glance with Leo. Then she said, 'Did you feel the slightest sorrow at Oliver's death?'

Sonia's lip trembled slightly. 'Oh, for heaven's sake, so many people die every day, so many people died in the war. Everybody dies. I didn't know him, I didn't care particularly about it, but I wish he hadn't died here because it's such a damned nuisance.'

Freya could tell from Leo's face that he was no more shocked by Sonia's apparent callousness than she was. There was a note of defiance in Sonia's voice. She didn't care particularly for Oliver, that was true, but something about him had upset her.

Scene 2

Hugo rang Emerson from his desk at the Hall. It might be unorthodox and not according to the rule book, but to hell with that. He was supposed to be checking up on Zherdev and Emerson was a valid source. He wasted no time with preliminaries, but as soon as he was put through said, 'This isn't about our Russian friend. It's something quite different, a question to do with the art world. Have you heard of, or come across one Oliver Seynton?'

Emerson replied instantly. 'Seynton? He works for Morville's. Paintings are his main thing. Rising in his career, well thought of.'

Hugo knew that this was only half the story. 'And?'

Emerson said, 'And nothing. Why do you want to know about Oliver?'

'Because he was found dead two days ago. And his death was what you might call suspicious.'

There a long silence and then Emerson said, genuine sympathy and his voice, 'Oliver dead? Poor fellow. How did it happen?'

'He was electrocuted. It wasn't an accident; it was murder. It's been in the newspapers. He died at the Castle.'

'I never look at the newspapers over Christmas. I suppose you're besieged by reporters.'

'The weather kept the newshounds from London at bay, but I imagine they're on their way here now.'

'Electrocuted. Poor guy. Yes, I knew Oliver. What do you want to know?'

'He may or may not have been the intended victim. That's why I'm trying to find out more about him. Nobody seems to know much about him. He was at the Castle on behalf of Morville's and couldn't get back to London because of the snow; he hadn't intended or expected to spend Christmas in Selchester.'

'He was the kind of chap who kept himself to himself. That's true.' There was a slight hesitation in Emerson's voice.

Hugo said, 'Look, Oliver is dead. If you know anything about him that might be a reason why anybody would want to kill him, for goodness' sake, tell me.'

Emerson didn't answer directly, but instead said, 'What's it to do with you, Hugo? Surely if he's been murdered, it's a police matter.'

'Let's just say I'm working with the police on this.'

Emerson was making thoughtful noises at his end. Then he said, 'I don't wish to speak ill of the dead, and I certainly don't have any direct experience on that side of the art world, but the word in the business was that Oliver was the man to go to if you had anything you wanted to dispose of discreetly.'

'Do you mean stolen property?'

'Good Lord, no. At least not as far as I know. More the kind of thing where someone inherits and there are various items they want to sell without the tax authorities getting wind of it. With taxes the way they are today, and some of these old families sitting on priceless treasures and so on, it happens.'

Hugo said, 'But you have nothing to do with this?'

Emerson said, 'I've very little to do with the business end of the art world. I'm a specialist. Quite a different area from what goes on with the dealers and the salerooms. Although they rely on our expertise.'

'So Oliver wouldn't come to you for advice?'

'He might, as part of Morville's. For anything he was handling privately, no.' There's was a moment's silence and then he said, 'I know that a lost heir has appeared, who'll inherit the Castle and title and all the treasures belonging to the family. Is the new Earl pukka?'

'Definitely.'

'So he'll be dealing with all the problems of his inheritance. Do you think he asked Oliver there? Is he the kind of man who would like to see if something could be sold privately and with no questions asked, no publicity?' He made a tapping sound as though he was rattling a pencil on his desk. 'On the other hand, the Selchester collection is well recorded. We were called in to advise on the pictures on loan to the national collection. Some fine pieces that'll no doubt be offered to a grateful nation in lieu of death duties. No one could do any secret deals on those, of course.'

'I don't think the new Lord Selchester would want to do any secret deals. He's a straightforward and honourable man. But there are some pictures at the Castle which apparently belong to Lady Sonia. That's why she brought Oliver up with her.'

'Do you know anything about these paintings?'

Hugo said, 'No, nothing. All I can tell you is that my young sister saw Oliver and Sonia going up to the attic where the pictures are locked away and after he'd seen them, he was in a strange mood and he behaved very oddly.'

'I can't see there being stolen paintings hidden in Selchester Castle, if that's what you're suggesting. A man of the late Lord Selchester's reputation would hardly be likely to have anything to do with that kind of thing. And Lady Sonia? I doubt it. However, if Oliver was murdered on account of anything of that kind, then stolen pictures sound possible. Art theft is a murky world, with criminal connections, and where there are criminals there can be violence.'

Hugo hadn't thought of that. 'Don't tell me that gangs have got into art?'

Emerson laughed, a deep rumbling laugh.

'Wherever there's money and valuable property, there will be gangs and crooks. It's a wicked world we live in. Go to Sotheby's or Christie's or Morville's and it all seems very civilised. People in evening dress, all perfectly correct. That's the public face. There are other parts of the art world that operate very differently. If Oliver was dabbling in those, then he could have got himself into trouble.'

Hugo said, 'On the other hand I really don't think any members of art theft rings or any other crooks were going to be in Selchester on Christmas night, particularly when half the country was snowbound.'

'You do have a point there. I'll tell you one other thing. I don't suppose it has anything to do with this, but you should probably know. There was a particular painting that Oliver wanted to trace. No, I don't think it was anything to do with his dealings on the side. This was a picture that he had a particular interest in. It was a Picasso that had belonged to a member of his family.'

'You told me about a missing Picasso last time we spoke. So your client was Oliver?'

'Yes. His painting was last seen in France in nineteen forty-one. I told him that the paintings that disappeared under the Nazi occupation would fill several aircraft hangers, but I added the Picasso to our list and said we'd do our best to find out what we could.'

Hugo said, 'I don't pretend to know anything about much about art, but didn't the Germans go in for burning a lot of decadent artists like Picasso? Isn't that most likely what would have happened to a painting? Wouldn't Oliver have known this?'

Emerson said, 'You're right to some extent. But there were Germans who had an eye for a good painting, who weren't quite such zealots for that extraordinary ugly form of art approved of by the Third Reich. So, either because they liked the artist or because they had the sense to see that at some point these works of art would be very valuable, they made it their business to see that instead of being destroyed they were shipped back to Germany.'

'Including Picassos?'

'Yes. They sometimes removed paintings from museums, but a lot came from private individuals. Of course, all property belonging to the Jews or anyone with the Jewish connection was forfeit. We've actually spent quite a lot of time identifying pictures that have turned up in strange places. But that won't be why he was at the Castle.'

'It seems unlikely.'

'I'm pretty sure the reason he was in Selchester will have been to advise the new Earl about his paintings. You want me to see what I can find out?'

Hugo said, 'Tactfully. The police will be making inquiries, I don't want you to tread on their constabulary boots.'

Emerson laughed. 'I know I wasn't much good at my job when I was in the Service, but I do remember enough of what I learned to be quite careful how I handle the civil authorities. Who have they got in their sights? Not the new Earl, I trust; that would be a scandal indeed.'

'I think the chief suspect is a man calling himself Saul Sampson, who's rented a cottage for the Christmas period. He came up to the Castle on Christmas Day when the family were out and Oliver was alone there except for the housekeeper and a girl. The police can't get him to say why he was there.'

'Calling himself Sampson, you say?'

'His real name is Ingham. You may remember—'

Before Hugo could finish, there was an exclamation from Emerson and the line went dead.

Damn the telephone connection. The weather might have brought lines down but it was infuriating to be cut off like this. Hugo got through to the Hall exchange and asked them to try the number again.

It rang and he got the same woman who had answered the phone in the first place. No, she couldn't help him. No, Mr Emerson wasn't there; Mr Emerson had just that minute left the building. 'In rather a hurry'.

Scene 3

Hugo was setting off for the Hall the next morning when he heard a car coming up the drive. A noisy engine that belonged to a dashing, low-slung Morgan. It drew up in front of the house. Hugo limped over to it and saw to his amazement the bear-like figure of Emerson extracting himself from the driver's seat.

'Emerson! What on earth are you doing here?'

Emerson said, 'I had to come and see you. There are some things that can't be said on the telephone; these are dangerous times, Hugo, you must know that as well as anyone. Not putting it in a letter either. There's something fishy going on here and while I naturally associate Her Majesty's Government and the whole of the Service – a pox on it – with every kind of skulduggery, when skulduggery extends to the art world, I feel it is once again my business.'

Hugo said, 'I was just setting off for work.'

Emerson said, 'Blow that. You can be late, don't tell me the Service has turned into a clock-watching establishment? I left London yesterday to get here, had a puncture on the way and had to find a hotel for the night. Left first thing and I need breakfast.'

Hugo gave into the inevitable. 'Leave your car here; it won't come to any harm. Come inside and I'll see what I can rustle up for you.'

Mrs Partridge was nowhere to be seen, but Georgia and Polly were sitting in the kitchen. They looked up with interest as Emerson came in. Hugo said, 'This is my sister, Georgia, and Lady Polly Fitzwarin, Lord Selchester's younger daughter.'

Emerson looked at Polly and said, 'Lord save us, she's going to grow up to look exactly like Lady Priscilla Veryan.' And then his eyes went to Georgia. 'I last saw you when you were a baby, young lady. You take after your mother.'

Hugo was surprised. 'When did you meet my mother?'

Emerson said, 'During the war. Your father gave me a letter to take to England for her. She was extraordinarily civil to me. I landed on her doorstep a bit dishevelled and she let me have a bath and fed me what I feel must have been a fair chunk of rations. Kind woman. Yes, you've a great look of her,' he said benevolently to Georgia.

Polly wasn't pleased. 'I'm not in the least bit like my great-aunt Priscilla.'

Emerson responded at once. 'Yes, you are. Nothing but respect for her ladyship, don't get me wrong. Before you ask, Hugo, I know Lady Priscilla through Sir Archibald, who consulted me about some paintings, rather nice early Dutch scenes.'

Georgia felt that somebody needed to act as host to this unexpected guest. 'Why are you in the kitchen?'

'I want breakfast.'

Georgia said to Polly, 'We could make him breakfast.'

Emerson sat down at the table. 'Yes, please do, or if you don't want to, I can cook it for myself. I'm handy in the kitchen. Since we're in the country, I'm sure you have eggs and bacon to hand.'

Polly and Georgia were rather pleased to cook him breakfast and, squabbling in a friendly way that warmed Hugo's heart, they set about what Georgia described as a fry-up. He was longing to know why Emerson was here, but didn't want to ask in front of the girls.

Georgia said, 'If you want talk secrets, go ahead. We know how to be discreet, don't we, Polly?'

Polly said, 'I'm not too sure. It might be something that you're much worse off for hearing. Let's make him breakfast and then clear off upstairs to play skittles. Then they can talk as much as they like.'

Georgia said, 'I hope you're on important official business, Mr Emerson. Because Hugo should be at work. I don't want him to get the sack, as then I'd starve.'

Hugo said, 'Don't be absurd, Georgia. Hurry along with that bacon now, it looks to me as though it's nearly done.'

Between them Polly and Georgia produced an excellent breakfast which they laid with great satisfaction in front of Emerson, before taking themselves, noses in the air, out of the room. As she went past Hugo, Georgia whispered in his ear, 'I bet this is to do with the murder, and mind you tell me afterwards what it's about.'

Emerson speared a sausage and grinned. 'Quite a character, your sister.'

Hugo said, 'She does have her moments. Do stop eating long enough to tell me why you're here.'

Emerson was having none of it. He finished his breakfast, polished off the toast that Georgia and Polly had thoughtfully made, and finally, with a look of satisfaction, sat back.

'Another cup of coffee and then I'm ready to talk. Calm down, Hugo, you've become devilish twitchy. That's what comes of staying on in the Service. Never a day goes by that I don't thank God I got out of the Service. I don't know why you're still there, Hugo, although I can see why you're no longer in the field.' He gestured at Hugo's leg. 'I assume you didn't get that falling off a wall.'

'No.' Why, having rushed from London, was Emerson being so slow in coming to the reason for his visit?

Emerson finally finished his coffee, put down the cup and stood up. 'Excellent breakfast. Now I need is to see the pictures which Lady Sonia wants to flog under the counter.'

'Is that why you've come?'

'It is. And, if I'm right, you'll find that there's a connection back to Berlin, back to Orlov.'

'They're locked in one of the attics. I don't know where the key is.'

He hadn't noticed that Freya was standing just inside the door, and he said, startled, 'How long have you been here?'

Freya said cheerfully, 'Don't worry about me passing any secrets on. I had to sign the Official Secrets Act, the same as you two did. If you want to get into that attic, Sonia has the key, and it so happens that at the moment she and Rupert aren't here. They've gone off in his car. She's furious about not being allowed to leave the Castle and I wonder if she's taken off for London. Although she's probably got too much sense for that, or at least Rupert has. He'll be anxious about his reputation, being an MP.'

Hugo said, 'Do you think you can get the key?'

Freya said, 'It won't be hanging up with the others. I expect it will be in Sonia's room. I'll go up and have a cousinly look round. If I do find it, you'll have to be quick, because we've no idea how long she's going to be away.'

Scene 4

Emerson and Hugo waited in the Great Hall. Emerson spun round, letting out whistles of delight. 'Lucky man, to live here, Hugo.'

'I don't. Just lodging, and I'll be moving out any day now.'

Freya came down with the key. She said, 'I'll keep an ear open for Rupert's car. Gus is in the library, poor man. Surrounded by papers to do with the estate. Leo is with him. The girls are up in the gallery, so the coast's clear.'

Hugo said, 'I'm not sure where we're supposed to be going.'

Freya said, 'I'll show you, or at least a point in the right direction.'

As she led the way swiftly up and down staircases and along passages, retracing the steps that Sonia and Oliver had taken, Hugo said, 'If these paintings have been up in the attic since your uncle was alive, how come you never knew about them?'

Freya said, 'I've only been up in the attics once recently, a few weeks back. You know, when I had to find some pictures that were left to his godson.'

She guided them up a final flight of stairs. 'The door at the end is the one you want. The one painted blue.'

Hugo inserted the key, opened the door and went in. Emerson darted past him and went over to where the pictures lay swathed in their racks. He whipped the covers off one after the other, with care, but with extraordinary energy and enthusiasm. He then looked at the pictures in their cradles letting out little sounds of astonishment and amazement.

Hugo said, 'Are they what you expected?'

Emerson said, 'These are remarkable paintings, and I can tell you right now that whoever is their rightful owner, I doubt if it's any member of the Selchester family.'

'Lady Sonia said her father bought them. Presumably in good faith.'

'The Lord knows where he bought them because there's no reputable dealer in the world who would have dealt with these particular paintings.' He propped up one of the paintings, which Hugo recognised as a Monet, and stood back to admire it. 'This belonged to the Rousslers, the bankers. And that Degas there hung in a small private gallery in Toulouse. Its owner was deported to Germany.'

Footsteps sounded on the bare boards of the passage. Two pairs of footsteps – one light, one heavier.

'Damn,' Hugo said. 'Now we'll have Lady Sonia to deal with, and probably Rupert, too.'

The door opened, and in came Leo and Babs.

Leo said, 'Freya told me that you were up here and I thought I'd come and have a look at Lady Sonia's paintings.' He shook hands with Emerson and said, 'This is Lady Barbara Fitzwarin.'

Babs said, with an animation she rarely displayed, 'These pictures have something to do with Oliver's death, don't they? I want to see what's up here.'

Leo had moved over to look at the pictures and he was staring at one that Hugo hadn't noticed before. It was a small and exquisite picture of the Virgin and child. Leo looked stunned.

Emerson said, 'That's unquestionably a van Eyck, but I'm not sure where it's from.'

'I can tell you exactly where it's from,' Leo said. 'It's come from the Abbey at Grosmont, in France. I saw it there in 1937. The Abbey was badly damaged in the war, and certainly such treasures as they didn't manage to hide disappeared. I've been in communication with the present Abbot and he mentioned this painting was missing.'

Hugo said, 'Another picture that should not have been in Selchester's possession.'

Babs had gone to look at the Picasso. She stood staring at it, and then she said, in a high voice, quite unlike her usual one, 'This picture belonged to Oliver's family.'

Emerson came as stand beside her. 'He said that his family had owned a magnificent Picasso and this is certainly a fine one, but what makes you think it's that particular one?'

Babs said, 'I'm sure of it.'

'You'd better tell us why, Babs. but not here. Emerson, have you seen enough? Good. Cover the paintings up again. We need to discuss this and I'd rather Sonia didn't know we've been up here.'

As she drew the cover over the Picasso, with a kind of caressing care, Babs said, 'There's something not right about all this, and whatever's wrong, it's to do with Sonia, isn't it?'

'Library?' Leo said as they waited for Hugo to lock the attic door.

'Isn't Gus still there?'

'No,' Babs said. 'He's gone off to talk to those people in the estate office.'

Once in the library, Leo said to Barbara, 'I think you better tell us about how well you knew Oliver.'

She said, 'You guessed early on, didn't you?'

Leo said, 'I could tell that you and he weren't strangers.'

'I met him in Paris,' Babs said.

Hugo broke in, 'Why did you pretend not to know one another?'

Babs looked at her fingernails. 'He was good about it. He realised pretty quickly that I didn't want Pops to know that I'd met him in Paris. Not that there was anything wrong, I didn't have an affair with him or anything like that. It was just that the life I was leading in Paris wasn't quite what Pops thought it was. I was supposed to be there learning French and doing some cookery classes. What I mostly wanted to do was art. And philosophy, the whole Left Bank thing. I want to be an artist, and that's not what Pops wants. I liked spending time with students from the Sorbonne and so on. Everybody went to these cafés: artists, writers, philosophers. It was so exciting and different from America.'

'And you met Oliver.'

'Yes, I was at a café one evening and so was he, and we got talking. I liked him. He was a good listener. Sympathetic. He said he wished he had had some artistic talent, but he'd never be good enough to do it seriously, which is why he had gone into the business end of art. I asked him why he was in Paris. I thought it was possibly to do with the auction house that he told me he worked for. I don't really know much about that side of art. And then, one evening, when I suppose we'd drunk too much, out it all came. How he was in Paris to try and trace this painting that had belonged to his aunt. He had grown up in France, and in fact had spent part of the war in France. His father was an Englishman, but his mother was French. And Jewish. As was her sister, his aunt who owned the Picasso.'

'Yes,' Emerson said.

Leo nodded. 'I thought as much.'

'His mother and his aunt were taken off during the occupation and he never saw them again. But he was determined to find out what had happened to this particular painting; it had become a sort of obsession with him. He'd found out that it had been taken when his aunt was arrested, but he felt sure for some reason it hadn't been destroyed. He told me about a man in England, Victor Emerson, who was tracing missing pictures so that they could be restored to any of the owners or their families who were still alive. I suppose that's you, Mr Emerson.'

Emerson said, 'How can you be so sure that this is the Picasso he was talking about?'

'He described it to me. I love Picasso's work. Oliver had a vivid memory and he described it to me as though it was there in front of him. And I drew it.' She held up her sketchbook. 'Look.' She flicked through the pages and pointed to one, a quick sketch of Oliver sitting at a table in a café She shook her head. 'He was quite happy that day. It's terrible to think of him . . .' She turned over a few more pages, took a deep breath and said, 'There. That's what I drew for Oliver. You can see it's the one upstairs in the attic.'

'Emerson,' Hugo said, 'you think this painting, among others, ended up in Germany and then after the war came on to the market?'

'You're missing a step, Hugo. I'm sure these paintings after the war were still in the possession of some of the people who'd taken them and who then used them as payment to clear their names, get passports or whatever it was they needed to make a new life. Which is what we were talking about; it brings us back to Orlov.'

Hugo was thinking hard. 'If Oliver saw his Picasso up there, wouldn't his first thought be to telephone you, Emerson?'

'When did he see the paintings?'

'Christmas morning,' Leo said.

Emerson shook his head. 'He didn't have my private number. He would have got through to my assistant; all calls were switched through to her over the holiday when we were closed. She wouldn't have given him my number; she'd have taken a message. He obviously didn't leave one, or I'd have known about it. I expect he didn't want to say anything about his painting to anyone except me.'

Chapter Sixteen

Scene 1

Hugo said. 'Georgia, did you see where I left my briefcase?'

'You dumped it at the bottom of the stairs.'

Hugo gave her a quick wink and she got up from the pouffe. 'I'll get it for you.'

Outside the library door, Georgia said, 'Why the wink? Do you really want your briefcase?'

'Not at the moment, no. I want you to watch my back. I need to make a phone call, and I want to make sure no one's listening.'

'I will be,' Georgia pointed out.

'Yes, but I can trust you.'

Georgia was pleased, but said, 'You could trust Uncle Leo. Or Freya.'

'I could, but they're still in the kitchen with Emerson, and this is urgent.'

'You carry on. I can't promise I won't hear, because if I put my fingers in my ears, then I wouldn't hear any lurking footsteps. But my lips are sealed.'

Hugo gave the operator a London number. Thank goodness it was June on duty; he wouldn't have to talk opaquely to his friend Henry Surcoat.

Henry and Hugo went back a long way. Like Hugo, Henry had had to leave the field and now worked at the London headquarters of the Service.

'Henry, Hugo here. Red box, please.'

He put the phone down and grinned at Georgia, who was looking enquiringly at him. 'That's not much of a phone call,' she said.

'Wait.' After a few minutes, the telephone rang and Hugo answered.

'Why am I playing phone boxes? Don't tell me, you're up to some unauthorised skulduggery and you want me to help you.'

'Got it in one. There are a couple of things. I have to arrange a meeting with a Gregor Zherdev.'

Henry made disapproving noises. 'Presently Cultural Attaché at the Russian Embassy. Supposedly a career diplomat. Is this wise, Hugo?'

'Sir Bernard has asked me to look into his pre-war career, as it happens, last part of his clearance, but that's not why I need to see him. Of course, he's no more a career diplomat than you are, but that's not the point. He has information I need, and need urgently. You can set up a meeting for me without anyone knowing about it; I can't. Say Montagu wants to see him, about some bronzes.' Montagu was the cover name he'd used in Berlin. 'He'll know.'

'Hugo, you're getting into murky waters. Where, when?'

Hugo thought for a moment. 'The Holly Bush in Hampstead.'

'That's a bit off the beaten spy track.'

'Exactly. I hardly want to meet him in the Brompton Oratory, do I, under a dozen watchful eyes and doubtful types dodging behind saintly statues.' Hugo looked at his watch. He'd missed the ten o'clock train and there wasn't another express until the early afternoon. 'I'll drive up to town. Tell him, four o'clock.'

Again he put the phone down. Georgia sauntered over. 'All clear so far,' she said, speaking out of the corner of her mouth. 'Is this to do with Emerson and Oliver and the paintings?'

'Yes.'

'Should you be meeting Russian diplomats? Aren't they the enemy?'

Her voice was flippant, but Hugo saw the anxiety in her eyes. 'I trust you and you can trust me. I'm not about to pass over valuable information to the Soviets.'

'They're so interested in statistics, of course I do realise that.'

'Statistics?' For a moment Hugo was lost. 'Ah, because I work at the Hall in the Office of Government Statistics.'

'Exactly. Everyone in Selchester knows what that's about. Pretty poor cover; isn't that what it's called? The phone's about to ring.'

He looked at the silent telephone.

'How do you know?' At that moment, it rang and he lifted the receiver.

'It makes a little click just before it rings,' Georgia said, sliding back to her watch post.

This conversation was even briefer. A few words from Henry, a thank you from Hugo and then he cut the connection.

'Are you really going to London?' Georgia said. 'In the car? Because I will point out that the last time you did that drive your leg nearly dropped off, and you were virtually hopping for a week.'

Hugo knew that was true.

'Ask Uncle Leo to take you. He'll speed all the way and get you there in record time.'

Scene 2

Leo asked no questions, but merely went upstairs to get an overnight bag. 'I assume we won't be driving back this evening, or at
least not all the way.'

Since it was a four-hour drive, he was probably right. Although
Hugo would prefer to come back tonight – there was, after all, a
murderer on the loose, or in the vicinity, even if not at the Castle.
But Gus would be there, and Freya and Mrs Partridge.

Emerson came out as Hugo was putting on his coat. 'I can
guess where you're off to. Remember me to Orlov.' He was jingling
his car keys as he spoke. 'No, I'm not going back to London yet, I've
a call I want to make in the town.'

Georgia and Polly waved Hugo and Leo off and watched the
Talbot Lago disappear out of sight. Polly said, 'He drives awfully
fast for a priest.'

Rupert and Sonia came out on to the steps as Emerson revved
the engine of his Morgan and then drove off in a roar of exhaust.

'What on earth's going on?' Sonia said. 'It sounds like Brands Hatch.'

'Who was that in the Morgan?' Rupert asked.

'A man called Emerson,' Polly said.

'What was he doing here?'

'He came for breakfast,' Polly said.

'And where are Hugo and Leo dashing off to?' Sonia said.

'London,' Georgia said.

'London? Why on earth are they going to London?'

'To see a man called Orlov,' Polly said, the words out of her
mouth before Georgia could stop her.

'I wish to God I could go to London,' Sonia said. 'How come
the police haven't told them they have to stay in Selchester? It's too
bad. Rupert, I want you to drive me into Selchester.'

'In a minute,' Rupert said. 'I have to make a phone call.'

Scene 3

Zherdev? Rupert had seen the man at a reception in the House of Commons, but he'd taken care to keep away from him. Reason told him that Zherdev no more wanted to be identified as Orlov from Berlin than Rupert wanted that old stuff to be dragged up.

Rupert picked up the receiver and told the operator to put him through to the Hall. Then he asked to speak to Roger Bailey.

'Mr Bailey? Rupert Dauntsey here. Yes, the MP. We met in London, you remember? Good. Listen, one of your chaps seems to be up to a spot of mischief, and I feel you ought to know about it.'

At the other end, Roger Bailey seized a pad and wrote down the details. 'A Talbot Lago? That should be easy to trace. And meeting a Russian called Zherdev, from the Embassy? I'll have to inform Sir Bernard. Of course, it may all be above board.'

'Not in my book, it isn't,' Rupert said. 'If your lot don't do something about it, then I'll get on to the appropriate authorities in London.'

'No need to do that. Any contact with a Russian would have to be cleared this end, and it hasn't been. And if he's gone to London, he's AWOL. He hasn't asked for time off nor called in sick. It doesn't look too good for him. Always the same with these chaps who think they know it all. Don't worry, we'll be on to this right away.'

Was there a note of satisfaction in the man's voice? Rupert wondered, as he replaced the receiver and went to find Sonia.

Scene 4

It was when they were on the outskirts of London that Hugo, who'd had his eye on the rear-view mirror, became certain they were being followed.

He said to Leo, 'I'm going to leave you. Pull up at those traffic lights, if you can. Where that van's parked. It'll shield me. Then you drive on. Are you planning to stay at your club?'

'I am.' He slowed down. 'Take care. God bless.'

The van driver had come out of the shop where he was making a delivery and came round to the driver's side of his van. Perfect.

The Talbot Lago came to a halt, two cars in front of it at the lights. Hugo, cursing his stick and leg, slid out as best he could, then ducked down on the other side of the van. The discreet black car, which had been behind them for several miles, stopped a few cars back from Leo. The lights changed, and the Talbot Lago moved smoothly away.

Followed by the black car.

Good. Now Hugo had to find out if, despite the limp, he still had all his old tradecraft. He had three quarters of hour to get to Hampstead. Provided he wasn't being tailed, he could make the rendezvous.

Half an hour later, the Talbot Lago drew up in a street off Piccadilly. The black car moved into position behind it and two men leapt out as Leo locked the car door and began to walk up the steps of a large and imposing building.

The two men waited for a moment and then one of them darted over to Hugo's car. He was back in a flash. 'No one there. He must have got away. We need to get hold of that clerical gent and ask him a few questions.'

His colleague put out a restraining hand. 'We do not. Do you know where we are?'

'Pall Mall.'

'Outside the Athenaeum, that's all. One of those clubs where the great and the good get together. I expect he's a member.'

'So what?'

'We don't have a warrant. We can't take him in. And for God's sake, use your wits. Don't you recognise the person he's speaking to, at the top of the steps?'

'No. Who is he, some other religious geezer?'

'You could say so, since it's the Archbishop of Canterbury.'

They looked at one another. 'Let's find a telephone and report back,' the first man said. 'We've lost our chap, and that's all there is to it.'

Scene 5

Hugo was already seated at a table in the Holly Bush pub in Hampstead when Gregor Orlov came through the door. He was wrapped in a vast coat and had a furry cossack hat on his head. It was some seven years since Hugo had last seen him, and he looked much the same as he had in Berlin. He had a lean face, with amused eyes and a mouth which broke into a familiar triangular smile when he saw Hugo. He lifted a hand in greeting. Hugo bought him a pint of bitter, and Orlov said, 'I've not quite got accustomed to English beer yet, but I dare say I will in time.'

Hugo glanced at the door. 'No minders coming along behind you? Nobody knows you're meeting me?' When Henry had contacted Orlov, he'd made it clear this was to be a private rendezvous.

Orlov's look was mocking. 'Why should I not meet an old friend from the past? I am Colonel Zherdev, Cultural Attaché at the Russian Embassy. I organise for fine musicians from the Soviet Union to come here, and also the ballet, as they are now allowed to perform abroad and I arrange all kinds of what they call cultural exchanges. Writers from here go to give lectures in Moscow and see the wonderful artistic life in the Soviet Union, and we send poets back in return. I'm kept busy; no time for mischief.'

Hugo didn't believe a word of it. Orlov was still MGB, no question about it. It wasn't as bad an appointment as the MGB might have made, for Orlov had a genuine interest in theatre, not surprising given his background, and also a passionate love of music.

'I have come to talk to a citizen of a town called Selchester about a theatrical event you are staging later this year. *Murder in the Cathedral*, with Sir Desmond Winthrop in the leading role. And then, perhaps, it may be presented also in Leningrad, as part of the fine cultural exchanges we foster between our nations.'

How did he know about that? 'I wouldn't have thought Selchester would interest you. It's a small provincial town quite a way from London.'

'On the contrary, Selchester interests me very much. A fine cathedral, as well as other places of interest.'

Such as the Hall, and, no doubt, the Atomic.

'Cultural Attaché, nothing. You're not the kind of leopard to change your spots, Gregor.'

Orlov's eyes widened in a look of perfect innocence. Then he laughed; that familiar, bass laugh. 'No, it is better we aren't seen together but I am perfectly able to get about without my people following me. As for your side, I believe they decided a while ago that I am not up to any what they would call mischief. They tailed me when I first arrived but now they merely check up on me from time to time. At the moment we are in the clear.'

All the same, Hugo looked around. There were a couple of men standing at the bar, but they weren't paying any attention to the two men in the corner. He recognised one of them, an actor, as was his companion, judging by their delightfully spiteful conversation about a fellow thespian who had landed a role at Stratford.

Satisfied, he took a drink of his beer. 'So you're at the embassy now, and all above board as far as we're concerned?'

Orlov drank some of his beer and then flicked the froth at the top with his finger. 'I don't understand the liking the English have for this layer at the top of their beer.'

Hugo said, 'It's called a head.'

Orlov said, 'I pride myself on my English, but why this should be called a head is beyond me. So, my old friend I receive an urgent message for from you by various roundabout means. And you say you must see me at once, and so here I am. What is it about?'

Hugo said, 'It's about something that happened back in 1946 in Berlin. Do you remember when you got hold of those bronzes—'

Orlov put a warning finger on his lips. 'I know nothing about any bronzes.'

'Okay, we'll skip the bronzes. You tipped me off that there was an Army officer who was accepting bribes in kind rather than in money for giving clearance to rich former Nazis.'

Orlov looked into his beer and a sadness seemed to fall over him. He shook his head. 'Nothing happened, nothing came of my warning. You let me down badly there my friend.'

Hugo said, 'I did what I could. But I got slapped down very firmly. The minute they knew that the source of my information was one of your lot, that was it. It was all nonsense, nobody was going to take what I said seriously and a few hours later I was on a plane back to England.'

Orlov nodded. 'I heard that you left Berlin very abruptly. And a little later I heard that you were in Peru. Such a long way from Berlin. So why, after this time do you come to find me? To reminisce about the old days? I don't think so.'

'You wouldn't give me the name of the officer back then, and that's why no one paid attention or did anything about it. If I'd stayed in Berlin, I might have been able to find out who it was.' He went on in a burst of impatience, 'If only I'd had a name, even if they still hadn't believed me, they might have investigated the man.'

Orlov said, 'I wonder. I think he was one of those people who has a lot of protection. There are always such people in any army.'

'Why didn't you give me his name?'

'Come, come, you cannot have forgotten all your tradecraft. No one gives away complete information for nothing. In such circumstances there must always be a quid pro quo.'

Hugo said, 'I wish I'd had something to interest you. Then I would have held back on passing the information along, until I had a name.' He was silent for a moment and then said, 'I suppose you do know who it was? It wasn't that you knew it was someone, but it was a faceless and nameless someone?'

'Oh no, my friend, I knew very well who it was. You see, I'd had face-to-face dealings with him.'

Yes, those bronzes that Orlov didn't want to talk about.

Hugo said, 'That was in the past. Now I want you to tell me who it was.'

'Again you ask for something, and again what do you have for a hard-working cultural attaché in return? Why now, after all this time, are you so anxious to find out who it was. What can you do with such information?'

Hugo drank some more beer, put the mug down and told him about the paintings that had turned up in the Castle attics.

Orlov didn't seem at all surprised. He took another sip of his beer, grimaced and asked the barkeeper for a Scotch. 'I apologise, but this warm beer with its head does not suit my digestion.' The glass of whisky in his hand, he said, 'Selchester Castle. And at that time the late Lord Selchester lived there? He is no longer with us, but there is a new Lord Selchester in possession? An American. I read about it in all the newspapers, very romantic.'

'You will also have read in the papers, that a guest at the castle, one Oliver Seynton, was found dead on Boxing Day. The police have been rather discreet about it. He was electrocuted, but I can tell you – and it must go no further – that it was almost certainly murder. And it seems likely that this murder is something to do with paintings that were hidden in the attics. Paintings that came from Germany in 1946' He gave Orlov a long look. 'Come on, Gregor Gregorovitch, you had no more time for those Nazis than I did. People who should have been hanged for what they did in the war got away scot-free because of some Englishman doing these deals on the side.'

Orlov said, 'What will happen to these paintings?'

'I'm not sure. There's some question about who actually owns them. The late Lord Selchester's daughter claims they're hers.'

'The lovely Lady Sonia. I read about her in the newspapers. A charming woman, by all accounts.'

'Never mind Lady Sonia. What should happen to those pictures is that they be passed over to those people who are trying to trace ownership of such works and return them to the owners. If the owners are still alive. These are well-known paintings and once they are know to still exist, it will be difficult for either the new Earl or Lady Sonia not to hand the pictures over.'

'Ah, so the new American aristocrat is involved in all this too, is he?'

'I don't believe he knows anything about it. The pictures weren't among the items listed as belonging to the last Earl, so it's a bit of a grey area. Lady Sonia is planning a private sale.'

Orlov said, with great good humour, 'I know all about this. It is what in England you call a tax fiddle. That's an ancient and customary practice, why should any human being pay more taxes than they have to? However, in this case I agree with you. Those pictures were stolen and the use to which they were put at the end of the war is something that should not be tolerated. If I tell you the name of the officer will it mean anything to you? Is it likely that he had anything to do with this Oliver Seynton's death?'

Hugo said, 'I believe it does.'

'What do you propose to do with this information?'

'Expose the man.'

'That might not be so easy, as you will understand when I tell you the name. Then he was a major in the British Army of Occupation. Afterwards I heard he had a distinguished war record. Now he is a Conservative MP, a rising man in his party, soon to take up a position as a junior minister. I told you he had protection in Berlin; I think he will still have protection.'

'Out with it, Orlov. Who is he?'

'He was then Major Dauntsey. Now he is Mr Rupert Dauntsey, MP.' He gave Hugo a shrewd look. 'This does not come as a great surprise to you, I do not think?'

No. It didn't.

Orlov finished his whisky and got up. 'I haven't given you his name. I know nothing about it; I have said nothing; there is no way you can call upon me to verify this. It is all in the past, and as far as I am concerned it is finished.' He wrapped his coat around him. 'You will have to find other evidence, and it will have to be copper-bottomed. But believe me, the day I open one of the English newspapers and there it tells me that one Rupert Dauntsey has been arrested on various charges, why then I will have an extra vodka to celebrate and congratulate myself on having responded to your summons, my dear Hawksworth.' He reached down for his fur hat and clapped it on his head. 'Incidentally, that man at the bar talking so convincingly about Stratford is one of your people. He has not heard what we have been saying, you chose a good place to sit behind that glass screen.'

How had he been so mistaken? Losing his skill and his sixth sense; too intent on what Orlov had to say.

'That's your cover blown.'

The Russian shrugged. 'No matter. I've been recalled to Moscow. My superior has given up his position rather suddenly and I am to step into his shoes and sit at his desk.' He clapped Hugo on the shoulder. 'Otherwise, you would have asked me for a meeting in vain. I only hope you do not find yourself in trouble as a result of this encounter. I wonder how they knew we were meeting. He tailed me here, of course. Goodbye, old friend.'

Scene 6

Hugo's tradecraft hadn't deserted him, and he was sure that he'd thrown off the man who'd followed him from Hampstead. But if there was an alert out, they'd have someone watching Paddington. No problem; he'd catch a train at Marylebone and then work his way cross country. It would be a long journey, but he'd be back at the Castle tonight.

At Marylebone Station, he rang Freya. 'I'm coming home by train, can you meet me? Not at Selchester, but at Yarnley.'

That was the next station down the line.

'I'll ask Rupert to come and meet you.'

'No, whatever you do, don't tell Rupert I'm on my way back. And don't ask him to meet me.'

Freya said, after a long silence. 'So it's him? I thought as much, and so did Georgia.'

Hugo's voice was sharp. 'She's all right?'

'She's fine. She's been with Polly all day. Gus is teaching them to play billiards at the moment. I'd be worried for the baize, but that's his lookout now.'

Hugo knew she was striving to sound normal.

'I'll make sure Gus keeps them with him all evening.'

'Georgia shouldn't go to bed in her room.' If he wasn't there, that part of the Castle had nothing but empty rooms. He didn't want her alone there.

'You think she's in danger?'

'Not really. But I think Rupert may have some idea of why I came to London, and I don't want any hostages to fortune.'

'I'll put a camp bed in my tower for Georgia. She'll understand. I'll ask Gus if I can take his car. I'll have to fill him in a bit, but he'll have to know in due course anyway. What time will you be there?'

Chapter Seventeen

Scene 1

Hugo woke early. As soon as he could, he'd telephone Henry and get him to dig around in the registry in London and send Rupert's file up with the courier. He was sure the records would confirm that during his time in Berlin immediately after the war, Rupert had been involved in checking the credentials of Germans who claimed to have no connection with the Nazis. And thus had the opportunity to line his pockets by accepting works of art in exchange for the valued certificates.

Clever to do it that way. Hugo wondered how Rupert would have got the paintings back to England. Not such a problem; he knew from his own time there that planes were coming and going from England all the time. He wouldn't have been the only one shipping illicit stuff out of Germany back to England. A lot of it went on. The authorities knew about it and mostly turned a blind eye. Rupert would have been able to fix it.

But these paintings were different from that kind of everyday smuggling. The way they'd been acquired was despicable and dishonourable. Certainly not the behaviour of an officer and a gentleman. Criminal behaviour that, if it became known, would end any career that Rupert might have in or out of Parliament.

Certainly the stakes were high enough for him to kill for them.

Why would Oliver have connected Rupert with the paintings? Or was Rupert simply afraid that once Oliver had found the Picasso, he would persist until he found out how it had ever got to Selchester Castle?

Who had Oliver made that phone call to on Christmas Day? Did that have anything to do with the paintings?

And then Hugo thought of Saul. He'd been in the Castle that afternoon. Had he come across Oliver? Had he seen or noticed anything?

It was an unreasonable hour to call on anyone, but this couldn't wait. He dressed hurriedly and set off down the hill, wincing as the pain in his calf warned him that his exploits of the previous day had taken a toll on his leg.

He came to the Green and walked across to Nightingale Cottage. Smoke was rising from the chimney, which was a promising sign. He'd half feared that, having discovered that Lord Selchester was dead, Saul might have taken himself off, constable or no constable.

There was no constable on duty. Saul didn't seem unduly surprised by his early visitor. Some of the strain had left his face, but he looked tired.

'Come in. I've a friend staying. He says he knows you.'

Emerson, clad in a huge brocade dressing gown, surged out of the kitchen. 'Morning, Hugo. How did you get on in London? You know Saul, I gather. Cup of tea?'

Hugo sat down, rubbing his calf. 'I didn't see a policeman. Do the police still not want you not to leave?'

'They questioned me again, and I'm still on their list of suspects, but they rather lost interest when I was able to provide an alibi for some other times they were interested in.'

Meaning he hadn't been on the liner, nor in Oxford when there was the hit-and-run attempt.

'They hauled me along to meet some woman who runs the museum, God knows why, and she said I'd not been in the museum. Museum! As if I was here for a spot of local sightseeing.'

'So you can leave?'

'I think so, but I've paid a week's extortionate rent so I thought I might as well stay. I'm staying at a hotel in London; I have nowhere in particular to go. Then Emerson turned up. We were at school together, haven't seen him for years. Well, I haven't seen any of my friends for years. He found out I was here and came to tell me my name had been cleared. Which I already knew, but I was glad to see him.'

Emerson brought in a tray with tea and set it on the table.

'What can I do for you?' Saul said. 'I assume this isn't a casual visit.'

Hugo said, 'No, it's to do with the death at the Castle.'

'Mr Seynton? I suppose they're waiting for the inquest to establish that he was murdered. The police have given some rather vague statements to the newspapers, hinting it might have been an accident. I'm confused; why are they so interested in my swearing vengeance on Lord Selchester, who's alive and well?'

'You didn't know the man who died?'

'No. I didn't know him. But—' He hesitated.

Emerson said, 'Best to come clean, Saul. You can trust Hugo.'

'That's all very well, but if they start casting around for suspects who might have murdered Oliver Seynton, I'd rather not have my name on the list.'

'Tell me about when you were up at the Castle on Christmas Day,' Hugo said.

Saul sighed. 'It's only my word, there's no one to back me up, except perhaps that witchy woman who turned me out in a torrent of indignation.'

Emerson cleared his throat.

'I suppose I may as well tell you. I went in through a stable yard and into what I suppose were the kitchen quarters. I guessed I could go in that way, I'd heard the locals talking about how the back door up at the Castle is always open. You have to understand that I was so angry, I would have climbed through a window or scaled a tower to get in, but in fact there was no problem at all. They need to do something about security at that place,' he added severely. 'I went through to what must be the old part of the Castle. Stone walls, big fireplaces, flagstones underfoot. All very mediaeval.'

'Did you see anyone?'

'Yes. I was standing there looking up at a portrait of the late Lord Selchester – how it pleases me to call him that. Anyway, this chap comes in and stands beside me.'

Hugo held his breath. 'You didn't recognise him?'

Saul looked at him, surprised. 'It was Oliver Seynton. I know that now because I saw his picture in the papers. Then, I didn't know him from Adam. I didn't know anyone at the Castle. The only person I would have recognised would have been Lord Selchester, and unless it was his ghost walking, he wouldn't be there. Anyhow, it turned out Seynton knew who I was. And didn't like me. He was in a state over some picture or other.'

He fell silent.

'And?' Hugo prompted.

'And, we had a bit of an argument, which might have ended up messily for him, only we heard voices.'

'What did you do?'

'I lurked.'

'And what did he do?'

'Went over to the telephone, picked up the receiver and asked for a number. I thought he was calling the police, but he wasn't.'

'You don't happen to remember the number?'

'Flaxman 793'

Emerson's number.

Hugo stared at him. Just like that. 'You have a good memory.'

'I have an extremely good memory.'

'Did you overhear the conversation?'

Saul pursed his lips and his eyes drifted up towards the ceiling as he tried to remember. 'It was a brief call. He listened and then said, "No, no message, I'll ring again tomorrow." Then he put the receiver down and left.'

Hugo said to Emerson, 'Of course, he would have rung you.'

Saul regarded him with wry amusement. 'Don't you want to know about the other chap who came in to make a telephone call?'

'Other chap?'

'Yes. It was as good as a play; as soon the first man exited left, the second man entered right. And before you ask me, no, I don't know who he was because he had his back to me. I didn't see his face. It was a bit odd, really. He picked up the receiver and jiggled the hook to get through to the exchange. Then he said, "Could you get me that number again, please?" And then there was a pause and as soon as the person at the other end answered, he replaced the receiver. Meanwhile, this girl had come in, and she was hovering there for a moment. It was like Piccadilly Circus. She didn't see me, but she buzzed off when she saw the guy on the telephone. Then that woman came in.'

'Mrs Partridge, the housekeeper.'

'All she needed was a broomstick. Anyhow, she asked me what I was doing there and what I wanted. We had a bit of an altercation, and since I had to take her word for it that Lord Selchester wasn't there I took myself off. The whole escapade was stupid. I went on an impulse, having had a couple of whiskies and worked myself into a temper. However much I wanted to have it out with the non-existent Lord Selchester, Christmas Day wasn't the right time to do it.'

It sounded like a frank and full confession, but of course it wasn't.

'Why was Oliver Seynton so hostile towards you?'

'That's my business.'

Emerson stood up. 'I'm going to make breakfast. Time to come clean, Saul. I think what you have to say could help to bring a murderer to justice.'

Saul looked from Emerson to Hugo, who nodded.

'It's not to go any further.'

'It may have to,' Emerson said. 'But you'll have to risk that.'

'And after all,' Saul said bitterly, 'what do I have to lose? I stood up to Selchester and told him, "Publish and be damned" when he threatened to tell all if I didn't play along with him.'

Hugo listened in silence as Saul, without apologies or flourishes, explained just what he'd done. Hugo's own memories of Berlin in those dark days filled in the gaps of Saul's terse narrative.

'You never saw any of the people who owned the things you flew to England?'

'Of course I did. But not the man who arranged for the paintings to be transported. That was a special job, everything had to be crated properly and so on. Valuable, not like the ordinary day-to-day stuff.'

'How did the paintings get to the airfield?'

'They came in an Army lorry. Never driven by the same chap twice. They couldn't care less, just helped me unload and then drove off.'

Hugo sighed. 'That's a pity.'

Saul frowned. 'No, wait a moment. There was one time the driver was different. I couldn't see his uniform, but he was an officer, I'm sure. Didn't say a word and kept his head well down, as if he didn't want me to see his face.'

'Did you?'

'I did, just for a moment, when a light came on.'

'Would you recognise him again?'

'Probably.'

Emerson had been standing at the door, listening to their conversation. He said, 'We'll come up to the Castle later today, Hugo. Sort a few things out.'

Scene 2

As Hugo came out of the front door of Nightingale Cottage, a police car drew up and the sergeant from the police station got out. Had they come to arrest Saul?

They weren't interested in Saul. 'Mr Hawksworth, if you'd be good enough to come with us.'

'What's all this about?' Hugo said.

'Couldn't say, sir. We've just got orders to pick you up and take you to the Hall.'

Scene 3

Suspended. Indefinite leave.

An irascible Sir Bernard, furious at being brought back early from his Christmas holiday, had refused to listen to a word Hugo said. He'd been consorting with a Russian, breaking all the rules laid down by the Service.

'Rules that are there for a purpose, Hawksworth. This will be handed over to Special Branch and our own investigators. Make sure you're available whenever any of them need to speak to you.'

By twelve o'clock, Hugo was back at the Castle. He found Freya in the kitchen with Georgia. 'Hello, what are you doing here?'

'Indefinite leave,' he said. 'Move up, Georgia.' The cat was beside her, and he tickled its chin. 'You too, mog.'

'What does that mean?' Freya said.

'He's lost his job,' Georgia said, alarmed. 'Hugo, will we have to go back to London?'

'I don't know,' Hugo said. The anger he'd felt was dissipating, and he was starting to realise what the implications were. Would Gus mind if he and Georgia stayed on at the Castle for a little longer? There was no point finding somewhere else for them to live, when he might not be working in Selchester anymore.

'Is it because you went to see that Russian?' Freya said.

'It is.' He got up. He'd better ring Henry and warn him to cover his tracks.

Scene 4

Grace Hall was cold and gloomy. Irene was on at the exchange. 'Oh, Mr Hugo, isn't it? Not at the Hall today, I hear, nor likely to be for a while.'

Blast the woman; how had word spread so quickly? He asked for Henry's number.

'I was going to ask you to dig out Rupert Dauntsey's file, Henry, but there's no point now. Yes, the MP. He's a murderer; he killed Oliver Seynton, but I've not a shred of evidence that anyone will listen to.'

After he'd finished the call, he stood for a moment, looking up at the words carved into the stone work. *Deo Gratias*. Leo might take comfort in those words; he didn't.

He wasn't alone. He looked round, and Rupert stepped out of the shadows.

Rupert's voice was soft and mocking. 'Quite the little detective, aren't you. It's a load of nonsense, of course. Why should I kill Oliver? Besides, the police don't even think it's murder anymore.

The inquest will decide that Lord Selchester bungled the wiring. Let him take the blame, I'm in the clear.'

'I know what you were up to in Berlin after the war,' Hugo said. 'Acquiring paintings in exchange for favours granted, and then smuggling them back to England. To sell at knockdown prices to friends like Lord Selchester.'

Rupert said, 'Words, Hawksworth. Mere words. There really is no way that you can prove any of this. I have no apparent motive for killing Oliver.'

Hugo said, 'One of the paintings you sold to Selchester belonged to Oliver's family. His Jewish family.'

'Oh, Oliver was a Jew, was he? I did wonder. Be that as it may, I had nothing to do with Sonia's paintings in the attic. I never set eyes on them before I came here, and you'll never prove otherwise.'

Hugo said nothing. Let Rupert talk himself out.

His voice was more threatening as he said to Hugo: 'You aren't going to be able to prove any of this. And you would be very unwise to suggest to that incompetent policeman that I had anything to do with it. They don't suspect me. As for your fanciful notion of the Special Branch looking into my past, forget it.'

'Do you have them in your pocket?'

'The Special Branch won't go off on any wild-goose chase on your say so. I hope you appreciate just how difficult I can make life for you. I can see to it that your time in the Service ends, and make it very difficult for you to find any kind of a job. It's not simply my influence as an MP, you know. I have a lot of connections who won't want to see me embarrassed by your fatuous allegations. I assure you I have covered my tracks sufficiently well that nobody will be able to link me to those paintings.'

Hugo said, 'A man called Gregor Orlov can.'

Rupert's composure faltered for a moment and then he said smoothly, 'Gregor Orlov? Never heard of him.'

Hugo said, 'Major Orlov, MGB, post-war Berlin. Now at the Russian Embassy, under the name Aleksandr Zherdev. You arranged for him to buy some very special bronzes that belonged to an aristocratic family who wanted you to grant them their certificates.'

Rupert laughed; he sounded relieved. 'Who do you imagine is going to pay the slightest attention to what an MGB officer says?'

That *it* was the devil of it, finding proof that led from Rupert in Berlin and the acquisition of these pictures, to their being in Lord Selchester's attics wasn't going to be easy. Let alone convincing MacLeod that Rupert had murdered Oliver to keep his mouth shut.

Scene 5

Rupert was going through the entrance hall when the front doorbell rang. Hugo opened the door and Emerson came in, followed by Saul.

And by Superintendent MacLeod, who said, 'Just come to have a word with his lordship, if you—'

He didn't get to finish his sentence before Saul pointed at Rupert. 'There he is. That's the man from Berlin.'

Chapter Eighteen

Scene 1

Lady Sonia stormed into Grace Hall, and stood with her hands on her hips, enraged. 'There you are. Would you believe it, Rupert has just simply taken off in his car. Georgia says he'll be heading for London. How the hell am I going to get back to London if I don't have a car? Am I supposed to go by train? Besides, the policeman told us to stay here. I can't think what's got into him.'

Leo, who'd arrived back from London, came into the hall with Georgia. 'It's inconvenient and annoying, but it's better for you – for all of us, possibly – that he doesn't stay in the Castle.'

'What are you talking about?'

'Can we go into the kitchen or somewhere warm?' Georgia said. 'It's cold in here.'

'I will not sit in the kitchen, as though I were a servant.' Sonia stalked off towards the South Drawing Room, where she flung herself on to a sofa, still fuming. 'Why all these mysterious looks? Why has Rupert taken it into his head to drive off at a hundred miles an hour? What is going on here?'

The others looked at one another. Then Leo said, 'There are some things you ought to know about Rupert. Hugo will explain.'

Sonia listened in silence to Hugo's account of the chain of events that had led to Oliver's death, which was interrupted only by Georgia's *sotto voce*, 'I knew it was Rupert.'

Sonia sat up straight. She gave Freya a chilling look that reminded her of Lord Selchester at his most commanding. 'Is this true, Freya?'

'I'm afraid it is.'

'Damn it. That's too much. I can almost understand Rupert killing a man out of temper, in a quarrel or argument or when drunk. That happens. People get wiped out all the time. I didn't mourn for Oliver. I didn't know him but I did know he had blood on his hands.' She paused and exchanged a glance with Freya. 'You know about that, don't you? About Marcus?'

Freya said, 'Yes, but you claimed you knew nothing about Oliver.'

'Never mind what I said. I didn't know it for sure; it was just something my father told me. And I put two and two together. I wonder why the police didn't arrest Dinah for the murder. Oh, you didn't tell them about Oliver's wartime exploits, Freya, did you? I'm surprised you, Hugo, with your infuriating curiosity, didn't find out about it and think Dinah killed Oliver.'

'Unlikely,' Leo said. 'Yes, I know about Marcus, too. Dinah told me. It would need an unbalanced person with an obsession to take that kind of revenge ten years later.'

'It's irrelevant now,' Sonia said. 'Oliver is dead. Rupert should end up with a noose round his neck but he won't. And I won't have those pictures.'

Leo said, 'I don't think Gus will want them.'

'I don't care who wants them. Selchester shouldn't have had them and they must go back to their owners. If any of them are alive.' She saw the surprise on Hugo's face and said vehemently,

'There are some things I draw the line at, you know. If what you've told me about Rupert is true, and I believe you, then that's where I draw the line.'

Hugo was astonished at this moral stance, but he could tell that Freya and Leo weren't.

Later, Hugo told Gus what had happened and he was shocked to the core. 'I never thought that an Englishman in Rupert's position would behave like that. For an Army officer to be so corrupt is truly horrifying. Is there anything I can do to help bring him to justice?'

Hugo shook his head. 'Perhaps I can make some more enquiries, but I suspect that Rupert will get away with it.'

It was a subdued evening. Lady Sonia hardly said a word. Babs and Polly had got the truth out of Georgia, but none of them felt like discussing it.

As she got up from the dinner table, Lady Sonia said, 'Give me the details of that man who traces looted paintings and I'll arrange for them to be delivered to him.' She glanced at Gus. 'If that's acceptable to you.'

Gus said, 'To be honest, I don't think I can sleep easily in this Castle with those paintings up in the attic. They represent such loss and suffering and, yes, evil, as I'm sure you'll agree, Leo.'

'I don't think I can sleep easy in this castle at all,' Polly said. 'It's a horrible place and terrible things happen here.'

'You mustn't think like that Polly,' Freya said. 'It's not the Castle; it's people that make bad things happen. After all, Rupert wasn't connected to the Castle, and nor was Oliver.'

'Maybe not, but people seem to die here.'

Georgia said bracingly, 'Lots did, that's what castles were all about. That was all in the past. It's not really a scary place now.'

Gus said, 'We're not, as a family, happy in the old part of the Castle. So I intend to see what I can do to make Lady Mathilda's wing habitable. I've had a look at it, and it needs quite a bit of work, but I've decided that's where we'll make ourselves at home.'

Polly looked up, eyes shining. 'No old stone walls? No four-poster beds? No ghosts?'

Gus turned to Freya. 'I would be so pleased, Freya, if you would continue to live in the old part of the Castle as you have been. It needs to have people living in it, but I'm too American and not enough yet a Fitzwarin or an Earl of Selchester to feel comfortable. I'll be happier with a more modern place and the amenities that it can have. And it would be better for the girls.'

Then he said to Hugo, 'And I hope that you and Georgia will continue to live here, for as long as is convenient for you and you want to.'

Georgia let out an unrestrained whoop of delight and punched her fist into her other palm. She took a deep breath and said, 'That's jolly good idea. Because they'll have to un-suspend you now it's all coming out about Rupert, won't they, Hugo? And I tell you another good idea, which is that if you're going to live here, then Polly won't want to be away all the time. She should come to the High School with me.'

Babs said, 'That makes sense. I've been talking to Sonia about boarding schools in England and they sound dreadful.'

Sonia raised her eyes heavenwards. 'You'll have to see to it, Gus, that she doesn't acquire some frightful local accent.'

Chapter Nineteen

Saturday, January 19th

'This is the BBC Home Service. Here is the eight o'clock news, read by Frank Phillips.

'It has been reported that Mr Rupert Dauntsey, the Conservative Member of Parliament for Westington, has been found dead in his London house. Foul play is not suspected.'

Mrs Partridge always listened to the morning news on the wireless. As Hugo and Freya came into the kitchen for breakfast she said, 'Mr Rupert is dead.'

Freya and Hugo stared at her.

'Dead?' Hugo said. 'How?'

'He shot himself. They said on the news he was cleaning a gun and blew his brains out. What a shocking accident. Careless; dangerous things, guns, and what did he want with one in his house in London? They're saying all kinds of nice things about him, his war record and service to his country and all that and how it had been thought he might one day be Prime Minister.' She gave a sniff. 'For myself, I don't want to speak ill of the dead, but he wasn't a man I'd ever trust.'

Freya was shocked; too shocked to speak for a moment.

Hugo knew that whatever she'd done in the war, death hadn't been the almost everyday event it had been for him. Yet he, too, was shocked. Rupert might be a ruthless murderer, but they had known him. He was more than a news item to them.

'Was he taking the honourable way out?' Freya said to Hugo. 'Do you think he knew that the police were closing in on him?'

Hugo, instinctively suspicious of accidents with guns said, 'Probably. I saw the Superintendent yesterday. They've had to make sure they have a completely watertight case, given Rupert's position and the kind of friends he has in high places, but MacLeod was quietly confident that he'd be issuing a warrant for his arrest any day.'

'So Rupert decided this was better than the hangman.'

There was a knock at the door. Mr Bunbury with the post. 'Letters for you, Miss Freya, and for you, Mr Hugo, and a parcel for his lordship. Yes, I'll take a quick cuppa, Mrs Partridge, if there's one in the pot.' He mopped his brow. 'This hill doesn't get any easier. Well, that's one for the book, his lordship's guest over Christmas shooting himself like that. It'll be in the *Gazette*, seeing that he stayed at the Castle. If the missing atom scientist doesn't steal all the headlines.'

'Missing scientist?' Freya said.

'One of those boffins from the Atomic hasn't been seen for a couple of days and it looks like he's disappeared for good. They're in a state over there; afraid he's taken himself off to Russia.'

Hugo sighed. Trust Mr Bunbury to have information about something that was supposed to be secret. And if they were in a state at the Atomic, then the telephones would be ringing off the hook up at the Hall. He downed his coffee and stood up.

Mr Bunbury propped himself against the side of the sink, stirring a generous spoonful of sugar into his tea. 'I dare say he's one of those absent-minded boffins and has just wandered off. Why would anyone want to go to Russia? And in the winter, too.'

Acknowledgements

Heartfelt thanks to:

Eloise Aston for amusing and helpful comments.
Anselm Audley for ruthless and excellent editing.
Jean Buchanan for expert advice, plus coffee and cakes.
William Edmondson for electrical knowledge (the shocks are all mine).
Elizabeth Jennings for advice and encouragement.
Nancy Warren for a needle-sharp beta read.
Von Whiteman for listening to authorial agonising.
Andrew Wilkinson for forensic expertise (the mistakes are all mine).

And Emilie, Sana and the team at Thomas & Mercer for their brilliant support and help.

About the Author

Photo: © David Morgan

Elizabeth Edmondson was born in Chile, brought up in Calcutta and educated at Oxford. She is the author of eight novels, including *The Villa in Italy*, *The Villa on the Riviera*, *Voyage of Innocence* and *The Frozen Lake*, which have been translated into several languages. She has a particular fascination for the Cold War era and the mysteries it suggests to her as a novelist; above all she has a desire to enchant and entertain. Elizabeth lives in Oxford, where she writes, rings church bells and enjoys vigorous walks in the University Parks, avoiding lacrosse balls and Quidditch players on their broomsticks.